There was a tall dark stranger standing in Grace North's kitchen

And he was...*chopping an onion?*

Grace stopped short on the threshold of her back door and blinked in disbelief. Twice. At first glance she couldn't place this man. "Uh, hello there," she ventured warily.

He paused in midchop to run a lazy eye over her. An approving smile tugged at the corners of his mouth. "You look wonderful, Gracie."

Ditto, Grace silently noted. He cut a lean and fit figure in worn jeans and faded red T-shirt, exuded strength in a clean-shaven jaw and neatly clipped black hair. Deep sexy voice and twinkling blue eyes ensured the most devastating effect.

Devastating was right. The sudden realization of who he was caused her pulse to jump a mile.

This was *Kyle.* Kyle McRaney. The man who would one day be her husband...

Dear Reader,

This month, Harlequin American Romance delivers your favorite authors and irresistible stories of heart, home and happiness that will surely leave you smiling.

TEXAS SHEIKHS, Harlequin American Romance's scintillating continuity series about a Texas family with royal Arabian blood, continues with *His Shotgun Proposal* by Karen Toller Whittenburg. When Abbie Jones surprised Mac Coleman with the news of her pregnancy, honor demanded he give her his name. But could he give his shotgun bride his heart?

Another wonderful TOTS FOR TEXANS romance from bestselling author Judy Christenberry is in store for you this month with *Struck by the Texas Matchmakers*, in which two children in need of a home and several meddling ladies play matchmakers for a handsome doctor and a beautiful lawyer. Harlequin American Romance's theme promotion, THE WAY WE MET...AND MARRIED, about marriage-of-convenience romances, begins this month with *Bachelor-Auction Bridegroom* by Mollie Molay. And old passions heat up in Leandra Logan's *Family: The Secret Ingredient* when Grace North's first crush, now a single father, returns to town with his precocious little girl and ends up staying under the heroine's roof.

Enjoy this month's offerings and come back next month for more stories guaranteed to touch your heart!

Wishing you happy reading,

Melissa Jeglinski
Associate Senior Editor
Harlequin American Romance

FAMILY: THE SECRET INGREDIENT

Leandra Logan

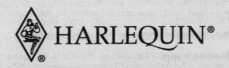

HARLEQUIN®

TORONTO • NEW YORK • LONDON
AMSTERDAM • PARIS • SYDNEY • HAMBURG
STOCKHOLM • ATHENS • TOKYO • MILAN • MADRID
PRAGUE • WARSAW • BUDAPEST • AUCKLAND

ISBN 0-373-16880-2

FAMILY: THE SECRET INGREDIENT

ABOUT THE AUTHOR

Leandra Logan is an award-winning author of thirty novels. Like many of her previous works, *Family: The Secret Ingredient* is set in her home state of Minnesota. She enjoys writing stories with a Midwestern flavor, full of realistic characters of all ages. She presently lives in the historic town of Stillwater with her husband and two children.

Books by Leandra Logan

HARLEQUIN AMERICAN ROMANCE

Don't miss any of our special offers. Write to us at the following address for information on our newest releases.

Harlequin Reader Service
U.S.: 3010 Walden Ave., P.O. Box 1325, Buffalo, NY 14269
Canadian: P.O. Box 609, Fort Erie, Ont. L2A 5X3

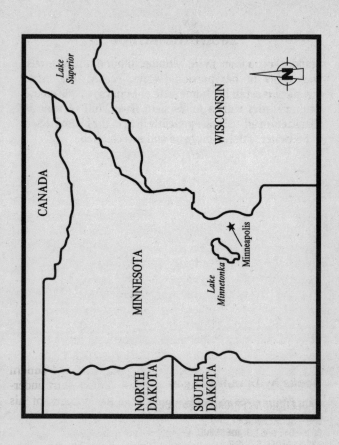

Chapter One

There was a tall dark stranger standing in Grace North's kitchen.

And he was… *Chopping an onion?*

Grace stopped short on the threshold of her back door, shoulder weighted by a huge cloth tote bag, keys digging into her palm. She blinked in disbelief. Twice.

Unexpected company did sometimes show up in her absence, let in by her brother who lived next door. But at first glance she couldn't place this man—or his onion!

"Uh, hello there," she ventured warily.

He paused in midchop to run a lazy eye over her—the pretty flushed features, vivid green eyes, mass of auburn curls and the denim jumper with a tiny pink T-shirt underneath. An approving smile tugged at the corners of his mouth.

"You look wonderful, Gracie."

Ditto, Grace silently noted. Big time ditto. He cut a lean and fit figure in worn jeans and faded red T-shirt, exuded strength in a clean-shaven jaw and neatly clipped black hair. Deep sexy voice and twinkling blue eyes ensured the most devastating effect.

Devastating is right. The sudden realization of who he was caused her pulse to jump a mile.

This was *Kyle*. Kyle McRaney.

Clearly oblivious to his impact, Kyle went back to wielding the wide chopping knife around the wooden paddle, working the thick muscles in his arms, dicing the pungent onion to smithereens. Grace took a deep shuddering breath, sliding her tote bag onto her small drop-leaf table. Not to worry. This impossible scenario was one of those dreams starring her girlhood crush. A regular occurrence over the past seven years since his abrupt departure, whenever she was feeling a bit low or unsure of herself.

So Kyle had returned to ravish her thoughts. Strange, she'd never mentally aged him before, given him a haircut and shave. But it was a fine improvement.

So how would it be this time? Passionate loveplay on the table? The sofa? The bed? She anticipated his touch all over her body. Would her senses be keen enough to smell the onion on his hands? Not in any dream of hers, thank you.

He spoke again, gently chiding. "Wasn't expecting you home so soon."

Her sculpted brows jumped. "Wasn't expecting you at all, Kyle."

"Of course not. This is supposed to be a surprise. I intended to be finished here before you returned." He winked. "But in any case, happy birthday."

Ah, that was it. She was indulging in a birthday gift to herself.

"So how was the dentist? Any cavities?"

"No," she replied dazedly. "It was just a clean and polish."

"Michael assured me I'd have free rein in your kitchen for at least two hours, so I figured you were having major work done."

Grace rubbed her temples at his mention of her brother. Michael was never welcome in these dreams. Not once.

And the residue from the dental paste still clung to her teeth.

She reached down to pinch herself hard. Ouch! It really hurt!

This was no dream. Kyle was really here. Matured to perfection. Better than ever. She blinked, leaning a hip into the table. Amazing what a thread of silver hair and a few grooves around the eyes could do.

"So how old are you today, Gracie?" he asked conversationally. "Twenty or so?"

"Twenty-four," she corrected briskly.

"Really." He grew thoughtful, staring into space. "Why, that's old enough for…"

She smiled thinly. "Let's just say it's old enough."

He tossed his head back, laughing richly.

How easily he slipped into the tease mode of the old days. It was a swift reminder of how things had been left between them. Not being able to discern between true flirtation and masculine jest had landed her in the heartbreak hotel for an extended stay.

Looking back, it seemed highly unlikely that a man fresh out of college would have fallen for a whimsical schoolgirl of seventeen. Being the sister of Kyle's college buddy hadn't helped enhance her womanly image any, either. The guys had shared an apartment near the University of Minnesota campus for four years, but had spent many hours at her parents' suburban Minneapolis home, witnessing her in the throes of teenage angst. She should have known better, no matter how rich her fantasy life.

Common sense suggested a cool head here. Offering proof that she had truly come of age would perhaps finally give her closure on the trouncing she took at his expense.

Still, hope nudged her as she watched his large hands lever the knife through the hill of chopped onion. His ring finger was bare. Could he and Libby have parted ways?

No one had expected the union with Libby Anderson to happen, much less last. A slender, quiet, intense girl, Libby seemed all wrong for the jovial Kyle from the start. Sure, they were dating casually, and she and Kyle worked at her grandparents' downtown bar and grill, Amelia's Bistro, together. But even young Grace was insightful enough to know that the elder Andersons, Andy and Amelia, were working hard to protect their ward Libby from Kyle and all the other males who frequented the college hangout.

Their romance seemed so far off the radar screen that when Kyle had confided to Michael that he intended a surprise proposal, eavesdropper Grace had imagined herself the bride-to-be. She'd played the biggest kind of fool, anticipating a tap at her bedroom window that night, thanking her lucky stars they lived in a one-level home that made elopement ever so convenient.

Michael had been the one to find her at dawn, slumped over in the window seat clutching a handkerchief that would count as something old and something blue. Grace had confided all to him between choked tears, and he had behaved like the best kind of big brother, taking the crisis seriously, rather than making a scene over her incredible naïveté.

It was a mistake they never spoke of again. Kyle and Libby had abruptly moved to Chicago shortly thereafter. Kyle's absence helped buffer the hurt, allowed Grace to move on.

She could barely believe he was back, in her space, tantalizing her in the same old way. But she couldn't allow herself to be so easily lured back into his web. He might still be very married for starters. Maybe he didn't wear his wedding ring when he cooked.

"So, Kyle," she said on a deep breath, "surely you didn't fly in just for my birthday. You and Libby must be here for another occasion…'' It was an awkward play for information, but he didn't look offended, just a bit sober.

"Libby's gone," he said simply. Trying to lift a smile again, he added. "As for me, I'm back in the Twin Cities for good. Yep. Back to stay. Living in the moment. And at this moment, I'm making my special chili just for you."

If this wasn't a dream, it oughta be, she decided. Trying not to allow her weak knees to wobble noticeably, Grace advanced on the narrow alleyway that held her appliances and limited counter space. Sure enough, there was a shiny steel kettle on a front burner, holding a bubbly reddish concoction. Like the onion, the kettle and its contents were new.

"Look good?"

She sniffed appreciatively. "You've managed to overpower any traces of last night's pizza. Though it does seem a little early for lunch. Barely ten."

"It's all in the planning. You'll see."

"But when?"

His controlled expression softened. "Still the demanding princess I see. But Michael wouldn't want me giving everything away."

No, he wouldn't. One thing she could be certain of, however, was that her brother was trying once more to alter her life somehow. As far as Michael was concerned, she lived in a state of chaos, from her in-house clothing design business cluttering every room, to her lack of domestic skills, to her varied tastes in men.

She mulled the minor facts she had. Kyle was a fantastic chef who had, on occasion, worked for pay preparing meals for her folks' lavish parties. He earned cash for college in any number of cooking related jobs. He'd done a bit of everything at Amelia's Bistro, from slapping together sandwiches to bartending.

Still, this catered affair was, today of all days, strange

and unnecessary. Michael knew full well their parents had a formal dinner party planned at the family's Lake Minnetonka home tonight.

"I don't think I'd be stepping on Mike's toes by telling you your kitchen here is a bit of a disgrace," Kyle complained in mock sternness. "Barely enough food to keep a mouse alive. Cheap, mismatched utensils. Outdated stoneware dishes and jelly jar glasses. You have money flowing from your ears. I just don't get it."

Grace laughed in the face of reality. "I am after a more homey feel. When we were kids, we were scared to death of breaking something precious. Nothing in this kitchen is precious."

"You do have wonderful appliances, though." He lifted up the handle of the paddle shaped board and carried it to the stove, using the knife's shiny blade to scrape the onion bits into the kettle. He then hovered over the brew with a wooden spoon, adjusting the burner's flame. "These gas stoves are far superior to electric ones."

"Really? Why?" Grace sidled up to him, placing red manicured fingertips on his arms.

"A true flame makes for quick and even heat."

No lie. She closed her eyes, carrying herself off to an erotic place. The red hot pepper steam was seeping into her pores, making her burn everywhere. Suddenly his broad shoulders seemed the full breadth of the tight alley in which they stood. Time and space were squeezed short.

It took a lot of nerve to raise her gaze to his with cool smoothness. To keep her hand on his arm even as he glanced at it with some surprise. But Grace managed. What she lacked in culinary skills, she made up for in nerve.

A thread of sexual tension pulled tight between them. She could almost feel him wince from the imaginary tug.

"Care to join me for a taste?" he asked flirtatiously.

"All right."

He rooted through the cutlery drawer with a low unexpected whistle, pulling out a tablespoon. He held the curved scoop end flush against her nose, as a magician might doing a spoon trick. "You realize you don't even have eight full place settings?"

"I do so have them," she spouted, swatting the arm she'd just caressed.

"Not a matched set," he persisted.

"See if I care."

"A challenge I just may accept." Cupping one hand on her chin, he used the other to dip the spoon into the chili, guide it to her mouth.

"Blow."

"Huh?"

"Gently," he encouraged. "On the chili. Don't want to burn your tongue."

Trembling with awareness, she allowed him to guide the spoon between her lips. The chili proved thick and satisfying, though a bit spicier than she was accustomed to. A trace line of perspiration quickly formed on her brow.

So much for playing it cool.

He'd set the spoon on the stove top, in no hurry to move his face or hand away from her. "This is a lot of fun," he murmured, "tormenting you all over again."

"You and Michael never did play fair with me," she complained. "The endless teasing about my hair, my clothes..."

"You make us sound awful."

"Precisely!"

He massaged her chin with his roughened palm. "Well, shouldn't hurt to give you a hint. In a way, I'm Michael's birthday present to you."

His tone was unmistakably provocative. If he thought she was still harmless fun, though, he was in for a big surprise himself. She touched his collarbone, skimming a flame-tipped fingernail along his throat. Kissing Kyle full on the mouth, without the old excuse of mistletoe was growing just too tempting. "Well, happy birthday to me," she said huskily. Moving her hand to his neck and she began to pull him down. Their lips brushed in a featherlight fencing.

Then the back screen door slammed.

"Grace, what the hell are you doing to him?"

The pair broke free at the sound of Michael North's boom.

Grace turned slowly to confront her brother saucily. "Once you give a birthday present, you have no control over how it's handled."

Michael broke into a wide attractive grin, which greatly resembled his sister's. They also shared the same sparkling green eyes and reddish brown hair. He was huskier though, and about a foot taller than she. They also parted company in choice of day wear. While Grace dressed the part of the free spirited artist, Michael dressed formally, befitting his position at the family's accounting firm. Today it was a navy gabardine suit.

"He wasn't supposed to tell you anything, brat," Michael complained. "I wanted the pleasure."

"Mike," Kyle broke in urgently, his eyes darting the room. "What about—"

Michael gave a glance out the screen. "Right out here on the stoop."

Kyle sighed in relief.

"What's out on the stoop?" Grace asked coyly.

"Never you mind." Michael kept watch out the door, primed to keep his sister at bay. "We're playing a game."

Grace inhaled in anticipation. She had an idea of what could be out there. The gift she'd asked for!

"So, you give the whole show away?" Michael demanded of his pal.

"Not yet. But she was just about to pry the answers right

out of me. With her wiles. When did Gracie get wiles, Mike?''

Grace tapped her foot on the hardwood floor. ''Fellas, my patience is running thin.''

''You're gonna love this, sis. Kyle's the gift for the girl who has everything.''

Her heart tripped dangerously. ''Meaning?''

''I've hired him to supply you with some sorely needed nutrition, to make sense of this topsy-turvy kitchen.''

''What?'' she asked lethally.

''That's right. Kyle's your personal chef—for three whole months. He came today to give you a sample of his wares.''

''But I'm rarin' to start for real immediately,'' Kyle said. ''It would be best if I came two or three days during the work week. That'll give me time to shop, prep enough meals to see you through.''

Michael knew Grace well enough to read disappointment behind her placid expression. ''You know you eat poorly. Your fridge rarely has more than a bag of apples and assorted yogurts. And who can even speculate as to what lurks in some of your cupboards. Outdated packages full of MSG, saccharine and assorted dyes.''

Kyle was here only because Michael hired him.

Deep inside Grace was mortified, sinking from tempting vamp to an incompetent squirt with much of her personal laundry out to dry.

Doubtless, they'd mulled over her shortcomings in detail. No court in the land would convict her of killing them both—with the thump of a frying pan!

But what had she expected? A burst of passion? Admission of a blunder in choosing Libby over her? She scorned her own romantic foolishness.

''I eat just fine, thanks,'' she asserted frostily, thrusting a finger at the fridge. ''Right now, there happens to be a large carton of Chinese take-away at the ready! Bet you anything!''

Michael raked a hand through his thick hair, regretful. ''That's way too impulsive a bet. You're always too impulsive.''

''Why would I lie about fried rice?''

''Sure, the fried rice *was* there. But I ate it for breakfast, while Kyle got his bearings.''

''You did that to me, on my birthday?'' she asked hollowly.

Michael cringed. ''Sorry.''

''I think you'll enjoy the meals once you get used to them—to me,'' Kyle inserted hesitantly.

Was she to be his new source of income, his new career choice? Last Grace heard, Kyle was managing some fancy restaurant in downtown Chicago. What had happened to that job? To his dream of one day owning his own eatery?

''Is this what you really want to do for a living?'' she couldn't help asking.

''Don't be silly,'' Michael scoffed, embarrassed.

Kyle remained polite. ''It's only a sideline I started up in Chicago—''

''He's got huge plans,'' Michael cut in with cheery faith, again peeking out to the stoop. ''He's back in town at Amelia Anderson's invite. She's opened up her home and is offering him a whack at reopening Amelia's Bistro.''

''How nice.'' Grace sized Kyle up with a pasted smile of confusion. The Andersons had disapproved so strongly of Kyle proposing to their granddaughter that they'd driven the young couple out of state. Even when Andy died, there was no sign of the prodigal couple at the funeral. And now the marriage to Libby was over as well. What would compel the steely Amelia to give Kyle of all people a break?

''That's pretty exciting news,'' she said carefully. ''The

place has been closed for a couple of years now, hasn't it?"

"Since Andy's death," Michael confirmed. "Anyway, Amelia is getting older and needs extra income to preserve her lifestyle, so she's decided to sell out. In a flash of brilliance she realized that Kyle is just the man to resuscitate the place."

"That's pretty flexible of her," Grace noted dubiously.

Kyle was faintly amused. "It does seem like a miracle. And Mike's very kindly stepped in as a silent partner to help me make the down payment," he added gratefully. "A second miracle."

"Michael silent in any capacity is the miracle!"

Suddenly the ping-ping-ping of the back doorbell broke through their laughter.

Michael answered the summons, cracking open the door. "Hey, do I know you?"

"Yeah," a small voice peeped.

"You want to come in?"

"Yeah."

Michael ushered in a small girl with a cream-colored kitten in her arms.

Grace clasped her hands joyfully. "I thought this was your game."

"Just what you ordered, sis. Pure-bred Himalayan long hair. Delivered by the cutest girl in town."

Grace focused on the child. She was a cute one, dressed in a pink short set, with shiny black hair cut below her chin and fringed across her forehead, striking blue eyes, dimpled cheeks. Grace impulsively held her arms out wide. "May I hold the kitten?"

"Tomorrow, honey," she crooned in a patronizing mimic. "Maybe tomorrow."

Grace mouth twitched. The child's imitation of some

adult was quite good. "Did Michael buy the kitten from you, sweetie?"

"No."

"Is this another trick, Michael?"

As Grace glared at her brother, the child scooted by, darting in between Kyle's legs. "My kitty, Daddy. Tell that girl."

Grace's mouth dropped open. "This is your daughter, Kyle?"

"That's right." With open joy he scooped the girl up in the curve of his muscled arm, lines of concern and tenderness grooving his matured face. She cuddled against his chest, nuzzling the kitten's flat face into his throat.

Feelings swelled in Grace, some of which she couldn't immediately identify. But clearly she was upstaged in her own home, on *her* day, by impossible competition.

"This is Grace, Button," Kyle was saying gently. "I told you all about her, remember?"

The child burrowed her face into Kyle's red T-shirt. "No."

"Mike is her brother. You two just went next door to get the kitty from his house."

Button shook her head, keeping her face hidden.

Kyle addressed Grace over his daughter's head. "Sorry, Button has been going through some adjustments. No is a favorite response."

Button raised her face then, lower lip protruded. "Don't talk 'bout me!"

"We won't." Kyle set Button on her pink canvas shoes. "But you must give the kitten to Grace."

"No, Daddy, no." Her black-soled shoes danced on Grace's flooring, leaving some smudges.

"Betsy…" he said more firmly.

"Please?" Grace squatted to the child's level. She finally handed Grace the kitten with an Arctic stare.

"Thank you very much, Betsy, er, Button."

"Button's just a nickname," Kyle explained. "You know, cute as…"

"I see." Grace met Button's gaze again. "I never had a nickname like you."

She placed a hand on her small hip. "*I* never had a kitty."

"It's my birthday today and all I wanted was a kitten."

Button was unimpressed as she continued to stroke the kitten's long pale hair.

"How old are you?"

Button worked with her small wiggly hands, eventually holding up three fingers straight, working to bend a fourth at the knuckle.

"Ah, three."

"And half."

"A nice big girl."

Button thawed a little and began to wander around the kitchen, her eyes dropping covetously to a new litter box and white cushioned basket tucked away near the dishwasher. "Your mommy home?"

Grace straightened up. "My mommy doesn't live here."

"Why?"

"Because she has a nice big house of her own."

"My mommy's in heaven," Button confided in a reverent whisper.

Grace was stopped cold. Kyle said Libby was gone, but she hadn't considered…death. Just selfish things like desertion or abandonment. Things for which Grace could criticize her.

"It was a car accident," Kyle explained in a low tone.

Grace gasped softly. "Oh, no, just like her parents years ago."

"Not exactly. They mercifully died instantly. Libby lingered in a coma for several weeks. There was never much hope. Too much internal damage.''

Generally quick with words, Grace was at a loss. To think she woke up far too jaded to expect any birthday surprise.

Chapter Two

"Here's one to ya, birthday girl."

Michael sidled up close to Grace with a pair of fluted glasses brimming with champagne. He handed one off to her with a flourish and a wink.

"Thanks."

They sipped the quality vintage and scanned the formally dressed guests mingling in their parents' opulent living room that evening.

"I see you slipped a few of your artsy uptown buddies onto the guest list," he teased.

There were a few of Grace's most current friends scattered round. But the majority of the guests were the more established ones: a Minneapolis bank vice president, a prominent St. Paul surgeon, corporate executives from both sides of the Mississippi River, all contemporaries of the elder Norths, included at all North functions. Not wishing to upset her conservative parents, she'd chosen only those likely to blend in, at least to some degree, with the elegant ambiance of the buffet dinner.

Grace and Michael long ago accepted that their parents, Victor and Ingrid, were serious social climbers who would eagerly use any family occasions to enhance social connections. They'd shared their most personal milestones with acquaintances they might not see again for months.

"So, you like my gifts, Gracie?" Michael asked.

"I adore the kitten."

"As for the magic chef?"

"I wasn't going to bring it up now," Grace murmured firmly behind her practiced party smile. "But springing a widowed Kyle on me that way was a dumb stunt."

Michael rolled back on his heels. "I thought it would be fun for the both of you, honestly."

Grace didn't allow his genuine surprise to salve her annoyance. "Not only did you set up that—that situation in my own private space, but you then went on your merry way."

"Merry? I had a lunch date with dad and a very important client we're wooing. Nothing merry about that."

"I was at a complete loss after you walked out, stranded there with—them," she blurted out.

"You, mistress of your own universe, need backup?" Michael regarded her with a keener interest that made her squirm in her tight red beaded dress.

An administrative assistant from their father's accounting firm interrupted them then, anxious to make points with Michael, presently a vice president of North Enterprises.

Michael, a company man at the drop of a coin, turned to address the associate. A chip off the old block, father's ideal offspring, Grace thought wryly. Sometimes his position as favored son entrenched in the family business bothered her, but not at the moment. She welcomed the chance to consider Michael's assured interrogation. It was her own fault, of course. She couldn't resist scolding him for his stunt and now he was curious about her burst of emotion.

She gulped champagne from her fluted glass, trying to once again put her position into perspective by reviewing the events of the morning. Kyle hustling around to get his prized chili into microwavable containers and clean up after himself. Button wheeling around the cluttered and compact town house with Grace's precious gift locked in her small arms: the prized pure-bred Himalayan, which Button insisted upon christening just plain Kitty.

How much should she confide to Michael about the unsettling feelings she was experiencing? Could she even define them to her own satisfaction?

There were solid obstacles to Kyle's invasion. Grace didn't want anyone tampering with her messy life. She'd deliberately set up her fashion design business in her home because she liked the aura of creative chaos and enjoyed mixing business and pleasure in one big jumble of clutter. It was plain to see that Kyle had a frightening sense of orderliness. During his brief visit he'd actually started to rearrange her pathetic kitchen inventory more to his liking, touching everything, silently judging everything with grumbles and mumbles. Surely his tongue hurt from all that tsking.

Who'd have ever guessed at such a turn of events: her first intense crush barging into her creative nest to—to put things away!

Furthermore, Grace was unaccustomed to having children in her home, save for the young actors who came for costume fittings. They were older of course and proud of behaving professionally. Button had proven what was best described as a blissful tornado. Smudging her elegant hardwood flooring, dumping a knapsack full of toys into the center of her living room. She even brought her own music in the form of a battery-operated boom box. Kyle claimed she couldn't nap without the tinny singsongs, but she never did take a nap.

It had taken all of Grace's resolve to endure. After two full hours, she'd finally feigned an appointment and dashed out. Some birthday gift. They'd actually chased her out of her own home! The helpless feeling left her frustrated and uneasy.

"Sorry, Gracie," Michael said. "Pick up where you left off."

Not wanting to appear completely bulldozed by the McRaneys, she went on to relate a condensed version of the afternoon's events, mainly chiding him for not getting her approval for such a setup in advance.

"I probably handled the presentation all wrong," Michael admitted. "I was just so excited to hear from him after so many years. He'd really cut ties, you know. Wanted a fresh start with Libby and I respected that decision. Finally, even the Christmas card exchange fell to the wayside. When he called to confide his new plans to me, I instinctively sprang into action. He suggested I warn you, but I thought, no, why not tease you like the old days. If it's any consolation, he did get into the fun of it. Not many laughs for him this past year. That's about how long Libby's been gone," he added.

"So how long has Kyle been back in the Cities, anyway?"

He gazed up at the high ceiling. "Oh, a couple of weeks—give or take a week."

"Three weeks! How could you possibly lock up your excitement for that length of time?"

He was not the least bit offended. "I come by my self-control genetically. You are the odd one out, the impulsive wild mind."

She folded her arms across her beaded bodice. "Maybe you should know better than to try and tame a wild mind."

"Is that a threat? Hey, you aren't seriously considering giving Kyle the brush-off, are you?"

"I haven't decided what to do—about his services." Her voice wobbled a little, betraying more than she intended.

Michael promptly reevaluated her. "This isn't some kind of payback over that elopement misunderstanding is it? C'mon, he doesn't even know you cared. And you aren't exactly damaged goods who hid in a closet. You've dated a small army of men, probably broken a half-dozen hearts.''

She raised a yielding hand. ''I am steady as a rock concerning him, don't you worry.''

But she wasn't. And she knew she looked more hurt than angry. A dangerous sign with an unfulfilled crush. ''If I stretch it, I can imagine the faded bruise to your ego, but don't try and tell me that you actually have lingering *affection* for Kyle.''

It didn't seem so wrong in her imaginings. Why, she'd been indulging herself for years. But now, in light of Michael's dismay, she felt like a vulnerable teenager again. A waiter passed by with a bottle of champagne and Grace jammed her glass into the vicinity of his scarlet cummerbund for a refill.

Michael paused until the waiter moved on. ''It would be tough for Kyle to discover your secret right now, Grace. His plate is full already.''

''Maybe you should've thought twice before posting him in my home.''

''Okay, I should've considered your feelings. But he needed ready cash for living expenses. And he sure wasn't about to take a handout—from me or anyone else. C'mon, the man wants to cook you some meals, organize your utensils. Just let him.''

''I'll consider it, if you stop trying to second-guess me. I have Kyle firmly in perspective. I'm certainly no fool for him.''

Michael grunted to the contrary. They fell silent then, scanning the guests. ''Hey, look,'' Michael said moments later in a boyish guileless tone, ''Mr. Wonderful is here after all.''

Grace sipped and whirled at the same time, her painted red lips lifting at the corners, her eyes lighting. She faded slightly when centering upon the man standing in the arched doorway with her father. Both were dressed in dark suits, Victor's dark head dipped down to his pale one. Victor had an arm clamped around his shoulders, as if frightened he might somehow escape.

"You look surprised," Michael observed. "Of course you knew I was referring to Dickie Trainor, your *date*."

"He isn't my date for tonight," she was swift to clarify. "Mother invited him and his parents as always, because they're old family friends."

"But admit it, you assumed I meant Kyle."

"Just shut up."

"Gracie. How can you be a natural born North, the way you revel in passion, scheme the impossible? We are a practical people with perfectly useful left brains." He gestured to his glass. "Old painful memories should hold a fizz as long as this champagne."

Actually, Grace had spotted Dickie a full fifteen minutes ago, working the room with her father. Presently they'd paused to chat with Dickie's parents, who were stationed near her mother. Gales of laughter rose as tall slender Ingrid related some story with an elegant flutter of hands and a nod of her blond chignon. Like Victor, Ingrid's touch ultimately landed on Dickie, namely his lapel.

"Mother's stroking him like a collie," Michael observed with a chuckle.

"Wish they wouldn't make such a fuss over Dickie," Grace lamented.

"It's your own fault. A few dates with the guy and they're seeing husband material."

"That's way too premature."

Michael bared his teeth. "Still, you lit the fire."

"Yeah, a forest fire with a tiny matchbook."

Grace sighed in resignation. It started out so casually with Dickie Trainor. She needed an escort for a leukemia fund-raiser at the Meadowlark Country Club. The sensitive artist she was dating at the time didn't meet her parents' club standards as he insisted upon meditating at odd moments in a high-pitched hum and limited his diet to brown rice and chopstick utensils. Henceforth, old reliable Dickie was tapped. A date for the opera followed, as did a basketball game with his law firm friends and a couple of dinners. Dickie was taking the initiative with increasing regularity. Just the same, it was still at the harmless stage.

"Look out, here comes our proud papa with his catch of the year," Michael teased. "Got 'em hooked right under the gills."

Grace smiled as the pair approached.

"This is the end of the line for you, young man," Victor North announced, clapping Dickie on the back.

"Hello, Grace." Dickie Trainor kissed her on the cheek. "Sorry I wasn't here at the start. I was just telling your father, there was a glitch in the trial today. I had to meet with the whole legal team."

"That Freeman case makes the newspaper every day," Michael observed politely. "Must be pretty exciting to be on the defense team of such a high-profile extortion case."

"Well, I'm pretty low on the totem pole at Frazer and Dupont, mostly in the background, doing fact checking in the law library." Despite his protests, Dickie held a certain air of smugness.

"Still, makes our accounting firm look like quite the snore," Victor said, appraising Dickie as he might a humidor of fine Cuban cigars. "Don't you agree, Grace? You're always looking for zip out of us. Dickie must meet your standards for zip."

"Zippidy do dah," she said with forced brightness.

Victor moved away soon thereafter, drawing a hapless Michael along. Dickie plucked an appetizer from a waitress toting a silver tray and devoured it. "Skipped lunch. I'm starving."

"We'll be eating soon," she assured.

He shook his head with wonder as he gazed upon Victor's retreating figure. "Your folks are treating me like royalty these days. Can't say it isn't flattering. I suppose it's because I make a better impression than I used to."

No doubt. Dickie had evolved into a polished attorney, a gorgeous specimen. It was a far cry from his brainy nerd days. Three years older than Grace and two years younger than Michael, he'd never really connected with either of them—or her folks.

The transformation had happened during his stint at Harvard Law School. The country club was abuzz when he returned full of confidence and arrogance, eager to make up for time lost as a nervous wallflower, to use his family's wealth and social standing to his best advantage.

"You look especially beautiful tonight, Grace," he said reverently, his eyes roving her curvy shape, set to advantage in the tight red dress.

"I've pulled a neat trick," she confided. "Mother jumped to the conclusion that this gown is an original Valentino gown, but I made it myself."

He gaped. "You just can't resist bucking the system, can you?"

Generally speaking, Grace felt she was actually being quite cooperative with the North regime. Though her business was a strange venture in contrast with the family accounting firm, she was actually making a go of it, turning a profit. And she was giving the favored Dickie a real chance, wasn't she? It was possible that Dickie's conservatism might add balance to her existence in the long run. And he did seem to enjoy showing her off as his exciting bohemian find, someone a bit different than the left brain type his associates favored.

She would be the first to admit she was still confused about what she truly wanted. That left her exploring her inner self, trying to adjust her priorities without selling out to everything her parents expected.

"So, have you spoken to Heather yet?" Dickie asked, perusing the room eagerly.

"No."

"Well, I have. Just left her and Nate outside. We were trying to set up a tennis date and thought we better clear it with you."

Grace compressed her lips. Dickie was taking too much on for a casual date. Heather was Grace's lifelong best friend and therefore her territory. It was tough enough to accept Nate, Heather's new husband.

"Wouldn't it have been right to consult me first, Dickie?"

He was blindly dismissive. "Oh, Heather mentioned another engagement tonight, so I jumped in. C'mon, let's find them." He took her hand and slowly steered them through the clustered guests. It was protocol to speak to each and every attendee, so Grace pulled rank on Dickie and touched base with as many guests as she could along the way.

Heather and Nate Basset were out on a spacious deck facing Lake Minnetonka, sharing a smooch against the sunset. They made a nice-looking couple, Grace thought, tall, fair, athletically built. Unlike Grace, Heather had not a minute of doubt about her destiny. She made her parents consistently proud with all the right academic achievements in school, gladly worked for her family's hotel, and married a man of similar social standing, a rising star in the real estate game.

Heather sensed their presence and broke free of Nate. "Birthday girl!" she lilted, scooting across the deck in her flouncy silver dress and heels.

"You're just glad we're both twenty-four," Grace teased with a hug.

"It is a long month for me between our birthdays," Heather admitted, "until you catch up."

"It used to be a long month for me," Grace retorted. "When we were kids, you took so much pleasure in being the oldest!"

Nate stepped up to give her a congratulatory handshake. Like Dickie, his hands were thin and manicured. Her thoughts strayed to Kyle's strong, rough, capable hands, doing a variety of tasks around her house. Why, the elbow grease he'd put into buffing away all of Button's shoe scuffs was masterful. But such thoughts were useless distraction, a fantasy leading nowhere. Kyle was far from the reckless mate she'd once imagined. He had burdens, responsibilities.

"What do you think, Grace?" Nate asked. "About duking it out at the club tomorrow?"

"Saturday? Guess that would be fine."

Dickie gave a quick call to the club on his cell phone, then announced, "We've got a court for five."

"Great." Nate glanced at his watch. "Hate to break this off, but we have another stop to make tonight."

Heather leaned into Grace, whispering in her ear. "Hear from Michael there's a new man in town playing with your staples. Sounds kinky. Can't wait for details tomorrow."

Grace felt a tug of loss. Before her marriage, Heather would've called her within hours for details. So this was how they'd be kicking off the start of their twenty-fifth year, Heather cuddling up with Nate, she with her kitten. Grace hadn't felt this empty since…the night of Kyle's elopement.

The buffet dinner proved a lavish feast of salmon, salads and breads, her birthday cake a white tiered monstrosity of near bridal potential.

Over cake she was forced to endure boring remembrances of previous celebrations. Accuracy varied among the storytellers. One vivid account of a pool party drenching was not hers, but Michael's. Another of her tripping headfirst into her own sweet sixteen cake was, unfortunately, her own. Another story followed about a clown gone haywire that was completely unfamiliar. But that's what you got when you invited acquaintances to family affairs, muddled inconsequential memories.

Each year Grace made a silent vow that she would not inflict the same sort of traditions on her own children. Celebrations would be limited to family and close friends. People who gave a damn.

It was close to eleven o'clock when the guests began to drift into the cathedral-style foyer for coats and handbags, salutations and farewells echoing off the marble. Grace was at the door to personally wish everyone a safe ride home.

Soon thereafter only Dickie lingered with the family. Ingrid urged them into the study for a brandy and a look at all the gifts assembled there on a long table. She served the brandy herself, from a small teak bar in the corner of the room.

"To my lovely daughter." Victor stood in the center of the room, lifting his glass in toast. "Many happy returns." Applause rose as Victor bestowed a light kiss on Grace's forehead. A man of stern character and stiff posture, it was all the intimacy Grace ever expected from him, a peck to the forehead, a light palm on the small of her back.

The interaction triggered a vision of Kyle handling his daughter Button at the very difficult moment that afternoon when she was laying claim to Kitty. He'd scooped her up in his arms with warm confidence, getting his way with a loving firmness. It had been nothing short of magic.

Perhaps she wasn't feeling a reawakening of her crush after all. Maybe on some level she was just envious of their father-daughter bond. She recalled thinking that Victor North would have never allowed such impertinence from her even at age three, or encouraged such close contact. And it had stung a little bit to see another father doing the right thing. Yes, she could handle Kyle from that angle, as the kind of father every girl dreams of.

The group sank into soft leather chairs as Grace began to open her gifts. Her parents presented her with a lovely emerald necklace encrusted with diamonds. Dickie gave her a pearl necklace she'd admired while shopping with her mother. Grace was torn between gratitude and suffocation over the precision shopping.

Her friends contributed mostly small humorous gifts. She knew it was awkward for them, wrestling over what to give the rich girl with enough money to open a bank. The rest of the lot were impersonal gifts undoubtedly picked out by secretaries and assistants, gift certificates to shops, a vase, chocolates, a pen set. Some of the things would be routed to the women's shelter downtown.

"So how do you like your brother's contribution?" Ingrid inquired, reaching out to inspect a silk scarf.

"You mean Kyle McRaney?"

Ingrid slipped the scarf over her pale chignon, unusually playful. "Now there's a gift impossible to return!"

Grace swallowed hard, averting Dickie's curious look. "But I am thinking of returning him. If Michael still has the receipt that is."

Dickie perked up immediately. "What's all this, Ingrid?"

"You remember Michael's old college roommate, Kyle McRaney?"

"He's back in town, isn't he? Trying to buy the Andersons' bistro?"

"How do you know that?" Michael asked.

Dickie shrugged elegantly. "Heard it someplace. Lot of buzz downtown, you know. Everyone knows of Amelia's Bistro, and the fact that he is Amelia's grandson-in-law."

"Surprised you remember Kyle," Michael pressed. "Never hung around Amelia's, did you?"

"I was never one of the golden crowd welcomed in there," he said stiffly, his poise making an unusual slip. "Though I did visit on occasion, I found it too dark and loud to study. Also didn't care to be teased about my acne."

"Oh, it's long gone," Ingrid oozed, brushing his chiseled jaw.

"Yes, it cleared up during my sophomore year at the university. Unfortunately by then I was known as Mr. Pock by twisted *Star Trek* fans at Amelia's and every other cool hangout in the Twin Cities. But—never mind. What has Kyle to do with Grace's birthday?"

Victor, always anxious to steer clear of one's frailties past or present, spoke up quickly. "Seems Kyle's a cook of some kind. Michael hired him to make three months' worth of meals for Grace."

"Kyle's a restaurant manager, Father," Michael corrected, "with a business degree similar to my own."

Victor frowned, always annoyed with censure. "Well, he always liked to cook. He is cooking."

Michael was out of practice in building up his old friend in his parents' critical eyes, but fell swiftly back into the groove. "It's been his dream since college to open an eatery and finally he has a chance with the bistro. Amelia's selling it to him."

"Kyle certainly hasn't had it easy," Ingrid mused. "I remember when his father abandoned the family your first year of college. If I'm not mistaken, his mother briefly cleaned house for the Hendersons before fleeing the city too."

"He did strike out with both parents. The old man skipped mainly because he charged up some big gambling debts with local bookies. Subsequently Kyle's mother got tired of being harassed for the same debts and skipped out as well. Luckily Kyle was too young to be harassed. But he did have to make his own way after that. Barely eighteen.''

Victor clamped a cigar between his teeth and lit it. ''Must admit, Kyle always had guts.''

Not a small compliment from Victor. Michael smiled faintly before continuing. ''This personal chef work is only a temporary sideline for extra cash. Kyle started it during Libby's layup in the hospital, when he was forced to quit his job and care for Button. It allowed him flexible hours and time with Button—er ah, Betsy.''

''Button is an odd name,'' Ingrid complained. ''Why do people do that to a child?''

''She's cute as a button, that's all,'' Michael said defensively. ''She's bright and wonderful.''

''What a super gift for you, Grace,'' Dickie interjected, holding his emptied glass steady as Victor promptly refilled it. ''Wholesome food in your kitchen. It gives a hungry man hope, a life preserver for the future.''

Not for the first time, Grace felt he was making too many assumptions, talking way too big for his legal briefs. So did Michael, by the smirk he flashed her. Predictably, her parents sat there glowing.

''Dickie does have a stake in this, of course,'' Ingrid agreed. ''He could benefit from the meals as well. I do worry that you can't entertain properly, Grace.''

Victor glanced at his wife. ''That chopstick phase was particularly odd.''

''I never ate with chopsticks on a regular basis,'' Grace protested. ''You caught Gunther and I at that once. Experimenting…''

Ingrid turned to Dickie, as aghast as if she'd caught them exploring the Kamasutra. ''They were sitting cross-legged on the floor, humming and eating out of wooden bowls.''

"That was Gunther's birthday," Grace announced with a defiant lift of her chin. "Sometimes it's just nice to think of a person's desires on that special day." Her hint went over every head, except for Michael's, who flashed her a maddening grin.

Suddenly, Grace had enough. She forced a yawn, then stifled it. "It's been a wonderful birthday. Thanks to all of you."

"Heading home then?" Ingrid asked.

"Yes. I'll pick up these gifts sometime soon."

"I can drive you," Dickie volunteered.

"That's all right. I have my car. Stay on with Father."

"Yes, indeed, son," Victor concurred. "You haven't even had a cigar yet. And I'd love to hear more about the Freeman case. Anything you're not sworn to secrecy over, anyway."

"So, Grace," Michael intervened guilelessly. "Can we count on you taking Kyle's nutrition makeover?"

We? Grace gritted her teeth. He had a nerve putting her on the spot in front of the folks and Dickie.

"Surely you can't come up with one sensible reason for declining," Ingrid challenged.

Of course she couldn't. Her feelings for Kyle, for her guarded space, wouldn't come close to registering with her impervious socialite mother who put appearances first. There was no choice but to give in.

Feeling it was high time she left, Grace stood up and made her excuses. Scooping up her emeralds and pearls she smiled down sweetly at her brother. "Now, Dad, don't let Michael get away without telling you his exciting news. He is putting big bucks behind Kyle's bistro deal! Isn't that exciting?"

"Is that true son?" Victor's silvered head rose sharply. Glaring at his son, he puffed smoke like a locomotive.

"You actually made a decision that crucial without consulting me?"

Michael whitened. "I am nearly thirty! And when you hand over money to your children, it becomes theirs. Just ask the IRS."

Grace winked at Michael as Victor fell into one of his standardized lectures on wise investment. *And away we go, interfering smarty-pants...*

Chapter Three

Grace took her time navigating through the dark winding roads of the opulent Lake Minnetonka neighborhood, indulging in the guilty pleasure of escape.

She hadn't meant to burn Dickie there at the end by not accepting his ride. But all in all, he was better off with her folks. They'd ply him with smokes and liquor and compliments until his large hungry ego was bloated to the max.

Not as good as sex, but as good as he was bound to get from any of the Norths tonight.

As it was, bed was a place she and Dickie hadn't been together yet. But not for Dickie's efforts. He had begun putting on the subtle pressure to take their relationship to the "stage of consummation." And lovemaking put in such articulate terms didn't do a thing to entice her.

She stared out onto the wide manicured lawns, thick with mature trees. Methods aside, Grace decided she was in no hurry to consummate their relationship. It seemed a bad sign for any lasting union. But passion wasn't predictable, couldn't be measured like the temperature on a thermometer. Perhaps a relationship that was slow heating up wouldn't burn out so fast. Who knew?

At last she turned off into her Edina town house development, passing small neat yards fronting beige, blue and white duplex structures. She didn't always roll by the front of the attached structure she shared with her brother; it depended upon which entrance she used to the community. As it happened, she was doing so tonight. And to her surprise, there was a familiar black Jeep parked at her front curb—with a security car alongside, its roof aglow with flashing lights.

Grace pulled up in the rear and alighted to the street. On highs heels she clattered up between the vehicles to join the security man standing there. She recognized him immediately as one of three uniformed men who patrolled the community round the clock.

"Ben! Hello!"

"Evening, Miss North." He tipped the brim of his gray hat to her.

She pulled the shawl covering her bared shoulders tighter against the evening chill. "Trap a dangerous invader on my property?"

"Seems harmless enough."

"Harmless?" she gasped in doubt.

"Well, he knows you were in Minnetonka. And knows it's your birthday. Has the cake to prove it."

A peek into the Jeep revealed Kyle, looking very glad to see her.

Without a doubt, she could become addicted to that look.

She shuffled her heels like a little girl in tennis shoes. "You came all the way back here to bring me a cake?"

He rubbed his chin. "Yeah."

"Gee."

"I never expected to run into you," he admitted. "Michael gave me a spare key to your place, so I just expected to be in and out in a flash."

"Well, come in now," she urged.

Ben cleared his throat. "I suggest you park round back, son. In Miss North's driveway."

"Yes," Grace agreed more firmly. "Follow me round back."

"THANK GOD YOU CAME along when you did!" Kyle had eased the truck up close to the open garage door and was moving to join her in the garage.

"It's not that serious. Ben would've called me at my parents' place and you would've been cleared."

"That would've been a little embarrassing for me," he admitted, ducking into the garage. "I haven't even seen your parents since my return. Hardly a great way to reconnect, collared like some vagrant."

She flashed a sympathetic smile, then jabbed the remote to lower the garage door and beckoned him to the service door connected to the house.

She led him through the mudroom to the kitchen. Palming the wall, she flipped the switch controlling the overhead fixture.

"Aren't you afraid of waking your kitten?"

Grace gestured to the empty basket beside the dishwasher. "She has decided my space is far superior to her own. Found my bed and just stretched out flat."

Kyle had a sudden and vivid image of doing much the same. Startled by the idea, he avoided her eyes. Instead he concentrated on the cake keeper on the table. He whisked off the lid to reveal a homemade two-layer chocolate confection. It was slightly uneven and held a birthday salutation etched in white icing, which was signed off with a *K* and a very squiggly *B*.

Grace gasped, placing a hand at the sweetheart neckline of her dress, on the soft skin of her rising breasts. "It's absolutely beautiful!"

"Yes. Absolutely." Kyle's eyes centered not upon the cake, but her breasts, imagining his own hand checking out her heartbeat. Heaven help him, she was a sex goddess in that dress.

For the first time in his life, Kyle envied a bed-hogging kitten.

She peeled off her shawl and moved closer to the table, yet unaware of her sensual impact. "I haven't had a wonderful homemade cake since camp. I can't believe you went to the trouble. That you did this for me."

Clearly, the gesture meant something special to her. To think he actually had some impact on this pampered, beguiling princess. Seemed impossible.

"Button helped," he erupted. "No big deal." In fact, the cake was sort of an afterthought that deserved little attention, just an impulsive gesture to seal their deal. Moreover, he'd thought it a good exercise for Button to do something kind for someone she didn't particularly like yet. He could only imagine the monster cake she just bit into at her official party.

Arms folded over her chest, Grace was presently giving him the once-over. Lost in her, he'd forgotten about his own sorry state of dress. Allowing Button to run the eggbeater had left his decent shirt and slacks speckled with cake batter. Having little clean laundry he'd thrown on a faded gray T-shirt and some very sorry blue jeans with fabric so thin, they left little to the imagination.

There as a strange light in her green eyes now, suggesting hunger, delight, desire.

It was one thing for a male deprived of intimacy for a full year to feel lustful in these circumstances, but Grace… Surely she wouldn't use her imagination on him this way, would she?

Dammit, this was little Gracie, the lanky tagalong. And he was unsure of her thoughts!

It was a struggle to trigger lucid conversation, but he managed. "So how was the big party?"

She shrugged, sinking into a chair at the table. "Probably as you remember. Routine."

Kyle did remember, having helped with the catering on occasion. Never before had he ever been concerned over whether or not she had a date, though. The relief that she'd proven to be alone out on the street tonight had been overwhelming. For no good reason, he was very glad indeed.

She was staring up at him in curious amusement. "All in all, Kyle, you'll find you haven't missed much around here."

Kyle sank into a chair beside her. Setting his elbow on the table he propped up his chin and stared her down. "For starters, I missed watching you grow up."

She shot him a pained look. "I wasn't exactly a baby when you left."

"Guess not," he slowly relented. "But I was graduating college and you were still too young to vote. There must be some events worth a report."

She deadpanned him. "I am voting now."

He laughed richly. "Still quick with the wit. But seriously, fill me in."

"What do you want to know?"

"Anything that will help me get my balance round here, help me belong again."

SHE SIGHED CONTENTEDLY. "Well, Michael and I have shared this duplex since my senior year at St. Catherine's. I have a degree in theater arts, but my first love is fashion design. Did a lot of work for the plays there, discovered I was more comfortable offstage creating the costumes."

"Far away from the North accounting empire."

"Oh, yes. That's exclusively Michael's forte."

"Wondered which way he would fall. When we were roommates, he seemed more interested in juggling girls' phone numbers than any other kind of numbers."

"He works way too hard now. You'll be good for him, Kyle. Maybe you can rediscover his playful side."

"What do you do for fun these days? Still pal around with Heather Crain?"

"Definitely. Though she's Heather Basset now. Married a very nice guy from our old crowd, a real estate agent."

"That scrawny blonde with the blue eye shadow and in-line skates is married?" He wiped some imaginary sweat from his brow. "Look out!"

She huffed in frustration. "You always end up impossible, Kyle."

"Okay, I'll back off. Just one last thing. All the instances that I've thought of you over the years, believed you were perfectly happy, breaking boys' hearts, was I on the right track?"

He'd thought of her over the years? The news made her melt into the hard wooden chair. "You were close. But I'm still sorting things out."

"Guess a fair amount of confusion goes with the territory." He sobered, raking a hand through his jet hair. "I too am still sorting."

Her face crinkled tenderly. "I'm so sorry about Libby."

"Yeah."

"It must be hard, raising Button on your own."

"Amelia will be helpful."

"How old is she now?"

"Late sixties, I think."

"Wow."

He shook a finger at her. "Gotta warn you, she wouldn't care for your doubtful look. Button's given her a new lease on life. She is a challenge Amelia intends to conquer."

Grace conjured up a picture of the tall, broad-shouldered woman with deep lines around her eyes, her hair in a long salt and pepper ponytail. "She did seem like the invincible kind," she heartily assured.

"Perfectly said."

"Would I be prying too much if I asked you how you ever connected with Amelia again? It must have been terribly hard."

"The initial call with the news of Libby's death, the existence of a secret great-granddaughter was very difficult." He paused, wincing. "Amelia was stunned, then harsh over our defection—as was her right. But amazingly she showed up in Chicago for the funeral. After that, her visits became a regular thing. Eventually I must've passed some kind of benchmark, for she made me a proposition— move in with her, reopen the bistro and try to make a go of it." He marveled over the memory. "She put it in such a way as to make it sound like a favor to her, a second chance at family. I'm not the smartest man around, but I did see a hell of a deal there for all three of us."

She patted his hand. "A terrible twist of fate for you, losing Libby."

"Maybe I could've averted the disaster. Looking back, there are things I'd have done differently. But hey, no one can turn back the clock."

He clapped his hands together then, as if to break the mood. "Hey, this is way offtrack. Part of my reason for coming is to firm up our deal, decide my weekly hours. You dashed out so fast today, we never settled things."

"Well, demands of the job." She bit her lip self-consciously. Bailing out in a panic was kind of embarrassing now.

"I would prefer to come Mondays, Wednesdays and Fridays, from nine to whatever," he said, unaware of her discomfort. "Probably work sometime after the noon hour, depending on the meal prep. I promise not to be too big a pest," he added jokingly.

"Hah! You've already rearranged my kitchen."

He was disgustingly gleeful. "For your own good, trust me."

She smacked the table hard. "You think I'm going to fall for that old line all over again? You and Michael always had me running in circles, washing your car, running your errands—to learn!"

"This time you will benefit, princess, I swear."

She smiled lamely as he waved a white paper napkin in truce. "Somehow, I doubt it."

"For the record," he went on huskily, "if you don't know it yet, Grace, I am so thrilled to have this job. I need to make the money somehow, and a sweet distraction like you is an unusual bonus."

"Glad to help," she said haltingly. "Anything I can..." Her mouth went dry as cotton.

His blue eyes brightened. "Anything?"

Her heart tripped alarmingly. "What have you in mind?"

"I wasn't going to impose this soon, but if you know something about wallpaper..."

"What about wallpaper, Kyle?"

"The bistro needs some and I am a dunce when it comes to decorating."

"Oh." She was sinking in quicksand, pure and simple. "Well, I guess I could help with that."

"Busy tomorrow?"

"I can spare some time," she stumbled.

"Super. You're the best." He shifted in his chair. "Suppose I should be going. Unless you'd like to share this cake first."

"I'd love to," she retorted, "if I could find my knife set."

"It might have been a knife set once, Gracie. Now, it's a pile of ragged steel blades with dried wooden handles." He eyed her knowingly. "You aren't supposed to put them in the dishwasher."

"Oh, never mind." With a crooked grin she dragged a manicured finger into the thick fudgy frosting.

He was aghast. "Hey, you didn't learn that at home."

"Did it at summer camp. Have you ever tried it?"

He opened his mouth to protest, only to find her finger full of frosting smack dab on his lower lip. With artist's flair she began to frost his mouth. "There now. No cleanup."

Kyle snagged her wrist, aghast. "You did that to the boys at camp?"

"Never you mind." With a squeal she tried to wrench from his firm grasp. Shaking with laughter they stood up and began to tangle for control. In their struggle Kyle pulled her against his chest. Then the laughter died off.

This was her chance. To steal the kiss that had eluded her over and over, as recent as today when Michael stormed in here. Tired of fretting over her every move, she stood on tiptoe to lock lips.

Clasping a hand to her head, meshing the frosting between their lips, Kyle savored the taste of Grace. Her lips were so warm and soft. He was tempted to plunge his tongue into her mouth, until he remembered who she was, where their relationship belonged.

"God, Grace." With a heaving breath, he let her go. He searched her face in a shell-shocked way. "That was…"

Her mouth curved naughtily. "Much better than camp."

"I was going to label it an accident."

As much pride as she had, she couldn't let that go unchallenged. "I'd rather you consider it a nice experiment."

He sighed indulgently. "Fair enough. It's something I wanted to try too, since the moment I saw you."

"Now you sound apologetic!"

He lifted his brows, perplexed. "You're taking a great little kiss and beating it to death."

"Oh, you—you—kitchen cop!"

He broke into spontaneous laughter. "Is that supposed to be an insult?"

"Yes. Now find my knives and cut that cake!"

Tension broken, they began moving about the kitchen like a couple, dodging one another with a twist, a turn and a laugh. Kyle produced a knife and two forks while Grace opened the refrigerator. "I don't believe it. You brought me a carton of milk!"

He'd brought it earlier with all the other groceries. How scary that she hadn't even noticed. As Michael intimated, her meal schedule must be a disaster. "Can't have chocolate cake without milk," was all he dared to say.

Twirling round she grabbed two plates and mismatched glasses from the cupboard. The tall one was plastic, bearing the likeness of Michael Jordan, the stout glass bore a picture of Wilma Flintstone. She filled them with milk and brought them to the table.

"Take your pick."

Kyle sank the knife into the cake with practiced strokes and eased layered slices on two plates. "My heart is with Wilma, but I am thirsty. Guess I'll go for Jordan."

They settled in cozily at the small round table.

His mouth curved warmly. He reached out and touched some of the smaller auburn curls at her temple. "Never expected to celebrate the tail end of your birthday this way."

"Mmm..." The feel of Kyle's roughened fingertips on her face was exquisite. She leaned into his hand as her new kitten might.

But this couldn't be the beginning of something. Kyle was here because Michael had hired him to nurture her. He was widowed a year, full of secrets and troubles, with a small girl to raise.

She shouldn't dare to hope for anything.

But neither should he be running the pad of his thumb

down her jawline with that dreamy expression. "So, I'll call you first thing tomorrow."

"Really?" she sighed.

"Sure. About the wallpaper."

"Oh. Right. Whatever you want. Whatever you say."

"That doesn't sound like the Gracie I know."

She sighed in resignation. As if he knew her at all.

IT WAS NEARLY ONE O'CLOCK in the morning when Kyle rolled down Amelia Anderson's sedate Golden Valley street of modest homes and aged trees. Reaching her Cape Cod home, he expertly pulled into her narrow driveway. He'd swung into this drive so many times during college, when Libby was alive and living here with her grandparents, that dodging the plank fencing against the neighbor's property and parallel hedge siding Amelia's yard had become a practiced art.

Kyle parked and shut off the engine, his thoughts turning to his late wife, who had felt trapped here as child under Amelia's suffocating tutelage. How gladly he'd played the hero, coming to rescue her by night, arranging their elopement, whisking her off to a new independent life in Chicago.

Since then, he'd come to feel more like a thief than a hero. How naive he'd been—they'd both been—to consider only their feelings in the equation. There were many factors over the years that caused him to reflect, all the lonely holidays, the lack of any new long-term relationships. Many of the friends they'd made eventually moved on or had extended families of their own to focus on. Unlike his own dysfunctional parents who'd basically ignored him, Libby's grandparents—if a bit possessive—had at least wanted her in the bosom of their family.

He emerged from the Jeep, happy enough with the state of the union. Dashing across the shadowed lawn he noted that light streamed through the bay window from the living room. Perhaps Amelia had fallen asleep in her chair again, television droning, a knitting project for Button askew in her lap.

He unlocked the front door and stepped over the threshold into the small living room. The scene was partially as he expected. Amelia was in her recliner all right, her long gray hair loose round her shoulders, dressed in her long terry cloth robe, feet up, skein of pale yellow yarn in her lap. But she proved wide-awake, knitting needles clicking madly upon half a dainty mitten. Kyle often teased her about knitting in July, guessing Button's size six months into the colder weather, but Amelia assured him she knew these things.

"You've been gone a good long while." She regarded him over the tops of her reading glasses. Her lips puckered in disapproval. Kyle sighed, hanging his zip sweatshirt in the small hallway closet. He knew she was trying to be less controlling, but it was an ongoing effort. Old habits were tough to break.

"Grace showed up before I could leave." He moved closer, hovering over Amelia's chair. "So we ate some cake and firmed up plans." *And then she kissed me, with the gusto of a barroom floozy and the sweetness of a prom queen. I felt dismay, shock and complete helplessness for a matter of about sixty seconds.*

He could feel a blush rising from his neck. Hopefully, his suntan would disguise it a bit. Avoiding her survey he stretched his arms over his head and glanced around. To his alarm, there lay Button, dressed in her frilly cotton nightie, curled up in the window seat. "What the..." He stalked across the room.

"I would have carried her to her room myself..."

"You know better, Amelia." He gave the old woman a worried backward glance.

"I do know the limitations of this old body. Did what I could under the circumstances, though. Covered her with a blanket, rested her head on a sofa pillow."

Kyle scooped up the child in his muscled arms with ease and strode back to sit in the chair adjoining Amelia's. "Why can't she go to bed like other people?" he asked, perplexed.

Amelia shook her head. "She's inconsistent on that score, it's true."

He sensed her hesitancy. "But?"

"Well, Kyle, you said you'd be back in an hour. She believed you. Decided to keep watch for your car."

"Oh." He gulped, reaching down to push black silken hair from Button's cherub face. "Daddy is too blame, isn't he?" With a sleepy moan Button twisted in his lap, sucking harder on her thumb.

"You are her everything," Amelia chided. "And small children interpret things quite literally."

He rubbed his mouth, sheepish. "Seems I slipped up."

"Mothers have better radar for such things than fathers," she granted. "You can't hope to get every move right."

Kyle sensed some disapproval in her voice that suggested he could've done better, but he kept on smiling.

"So, tell me, was the cake a success?" she asked in a kinder tone.

"Yes." Kyle cuddled Button against his chest, sniffing her hair, which smelled faintly floral. "Grace appreciated it very much."

Amelia adjusted her needles thoughtfully. "I remember the girl quite clearly, tagging along after you at the bistro. Bubbly, pretty. Curly reddish brown hair. Full of cheer and questions. Seemed crazy about you."

She did? Kyle's heavy black brows jumped.

Amelia didn't acknowledge his reaction, if she noticed. "I never had much contact with the parents though. They came into the bistro a few times to get their son, Michael, gift certificates or to pick up the girl. Struck me as the cold fish type.''

"They are restrained," Kyle admitted. He was deliberately careful in his wording. Victor and Ingrid had never treated him badly, but he had a sense that he didn't quite make their grade. It was a vague feeling that didn't warrant his resentment. Resentment took energy and he'd learned to reserve it only for extreme cases.

Her forehead furrowed as she inspected her stitching. "Don't get me wrong about the Norths. I'm sure they're decent. But you'd best keep in mind that the rich are different. Many of them have never felt the raw panic of facing mounting bills. It sets people apart, the yearning for more."

The advice never stopped flowing. But he did have some recourse here, which he used gently. "We can be grateful to Michael for funding my payment to you," he said. "He'll be a good partner, as he's far more interested in his father's accounting firm and won't be bossing us around. And working for Grace will allow me more time with Button and some extra cash. Just so you know, we're set up for Mondays, Wednesdays and Fridays."

Amelia stuffed her knitting in the canvas bag beside her chair and released the footrest on her chair. "I generally do have activities to fill some of those days. How will you manage? Perhaps I should cancel—"

"You shouldn't," he said adamantly, touched by her distress. "Our general deal is that you watch Button evenings and weekends, while I'm busy at the bistro. The weekdays are all yours, to follow your own schedule, no matter what."

"I don't expect that, and you shouldn't guarantee it."

He chuckled, gazing upon the bundle in his arms. "Guess you're right."

Button stirred in his arms then. Focusing on Kyle, she threw her arms around him. "You come back."

"I always come back, honey."

She pressed her soft little nose against his. "No heaven, Daddy."

"Now, Button," Amelia reasoned succinctly, "your father is not going to heaven any day soon. He was delivering a cake. You know that."

Kyle squeezed her tight, exchanging a concerned look with Amelia. Button had been so insecure since Libby's death, afraid she'd lose him to heaven too. "You did a good job on the cake, baby. Grace loved it."

She set her chin stubbornly. "How's Kitty?"

"Kitty was sound asleep, just like you should be."

"My kitty," she whispered fiercely.

"No, Button. You can visit Kitty, but she belongs to Grace."

With pouty lips she crashed against Kyle's shoulder and fell back asleep. He expelled a lung full of air. "That went well."

Amelia regarded him sympathetically. "Lighten up. Isn't your fault you got dealt this bad deck. Most fathers can slip away a few hours and not be concerned that their three-year-old will write them off as dead. It's no one's fault. We're just left with…a situation. One we can surely handle."

Kyle tried to appear convinced.

Chapter Four

Michael North was backing his dark green Porsche out of the garage the following morning, when Grace's adjoining garage door began to rise. Quite an unusual sight so early on a Saturday. Unable to resist confronting her, he braked on their mutual driveway and shut off his engine.

He ambled into the garage to discover her standing by the driver's door of her silver BMW. Dressed in aqua capris and a matching striped cropped top, a tote bag and melon work smock in her arms, she definitely had plans.

"So it is you."

Startled, she asked, "Who else?"

"I don't know, thought maybe the opener mechanism short-circuited."

"Ha-ha."

He chuckled. "Admit it, you normally don't see the a.m. side of Saturday very often."

"Oh. Well, I have several errands to take care of. Need an early start."

"Kyle on your list?"

"Huh?"

"I saw his Jeep parked here last night."

Grace moved closer to the open door blinking sheepishly in the sunshine. "You saw that?"

"I did. After all your whining about him at the party, you turn right around and throw out the welcome mat."

She smiled dreamily. "Had an unexpected change of heart. He brought me the nicest cake! Made it himself..."

"Like you deserved it, telling Dad about my investing in the bistro."

"I might regret that little admission. But you gave me such a hard time yesterday. Back with Kyle and you're a team, playing the same old tricks, treating me like a kid."

He had the grace to look guilty. "Sorry."

"And Father was bound to find out soon enough." She patted the shoulder of his suit jacket. "Just don't let him bully you out of the deal."

"Don't worry. I'm hyped about the project. It's so different from the sedate work at the firm. I am looking forward to the change."

"I like the way you've decided to buck the North system a bit, chasing a separate dream without Father's stamp of preapproval."

Her ruthless assessment irritated him. "You only hope I'll take some of the heat off your stunts."

"Of course!" She glanced at her watch. "Now I really—"

"What can you possibly be doing for Kyle? He need a baby-sitter?"

"No!" She looked a bit terrified. "Button can barely stand me."

"Oh, you gotta give her a chance. She was shy with me at first, but it got better. Now we're buddies."

"No, I'm working in safer territory. Kyle needs wallpaper advice, so I've agreed to bring some sample books round to the bistro."

"Is he stripping paper today?" Michael demanded in surprise.

She reared. "Sounded like it."

Michael slammed a fist into his palm. "Damn, he's proud. He knows I want to help him with those jobs, yet he keeps me in the dark."

"I imagine he wants to make it look its best, to impress you."

"But I don't need—"

Grace's cell phone rang in her tote. "Hang on here." She dug around for the slim folded instrument. "Hello, Dickie. I was going to call you. Yes, I'm still on for tennis, but don't come for me early. I'm off to pick out some wallpaper for the bistro and need time. Yes, things are moving along. Michael?" She eyed her brother. "We're talking right now. My opinion? About what?" As she listened, Michael began to wave his arms in protest. "I'm a bit surprised, Dickie— I'll discuss it with him. See you about four."

She disconnected the line and dropped the phone back in her tote bag. "Dickie wants to be an investor in Amelia's Bistro?"

Michael made a boyish face of discontent. "Said so last night after you dropped the bomb about my investing."

"Seems strange."

"It did until I thought it through. The odd kid out makes good as an adult and now wants to show off, be a part of what he missed."

"Oh. Suppose that does make sense. His voice did a crack a little when we were discussing the past after my party. People really called him Mr. Pock? Can't remember that myself."

"I remember. But aside from the family get-togethers, I had little to do with him. Mostly because he was younger than my friends."

"And older than mine."

"In any case, I was not responsible for any name-calling."

"Of course not. We never watched *Star Trek* in the first place, so wouldn't have quite understood the name."

"Bottom line, Gracie, he's not welcome in this venture. I'd tell anyone the same. Kyle is battling with his pride as it is, accepting iron Amelia's assistance. He wants to accomplish something for himself. The last thing he's trolling for is another investor of any kind."

"Too many cooks spoil the broth?"

"Something like that."

"Shouldn't be a problem to just tell Dickie no."

"Really? Haven't you noticed he is getting pushier and pushier, niggling his way into our family from all angles? It's so bad, I've been taking a back seat whenever that guy's around."

Suddenly it occurred to Grace that as the only son, maybe Michael felt threatened by Victor and Ingrid's interest in another male.

"How much do you like this guy anyway?" he asked guardedly.

"I don't know yet. But in Dickie's defense, it isn't his fault the folks are chasing him."

"Well, I hope you're not dating him just to please the folks."

She hesitated. "That bonus has been nice, after all the men they have disapproved of."

"Fine. Just be careful."

First advice on her crush on Kyle, now this lecture about the dangers of Dickie. Grace wasn't about to take any of it to heart. After all, Michael was pushing thirty, still single— and in her private estimation, lonely. Despite his autocratic hand with her, however, she hated to see him blue.

"Hey, it just occurs to me that Father must have been really torn, approving of Dickie's every move, but disapproving of any investment in Kyle's venture. That must've have been a fun struggle of hypocrisy to watch."

Michael grinned widely now. "That was the only comic moment of the night. Dickie's wild interest in the bistro took Father completely off guard. He never really did recover, just did some gruff mumbling and then bailed to make some suspect phone call. I think he went off to scream into a pillow."

"See, every cloud has a silver lining." She cuffed his chin. "Now I have to get moving."

Michael gave his watch a startled glance. "Me, too, if I'm going to drop by the bistro first. Seems the perfect chance to barge in on the nuts and bolts of things."

"Won't Father be expecting you at the office pronto?"

"He's not even going himself today." With that he stalked to his car.

"I'll meet you at the bistro, with wallpaper samples." Grace watched him roar off, feeling smug. This new rebel side to him was a very good sign indeed.

"MIKE?" KYLE WAS startled as a slice of bright morning sunshine illuminated a figure in the doorway of Amelia's Bistro. "Is that you?"

"Only me."

Michael North let go of the heavy steel door and it slid shut with a thump. There was a cool hollow feeling to the place now, nothing like the Andersons' glory days of the eighties and nineties.

Had he jumped the gun, agreeing to invest in this place sight unseen? No, he wouldn't have done it differently. He had faith in Kyle and this had always been a sound building, a good location in reference to downtown Minneapolis and the University of Minnesota campus.

Faith. It was probably the most precious and most lacking commodity in Kyle's checkered life. If Michael could change that with money, he'd gladly do so. But he did want entrée to the behind-the-scenes action.

Michael leveled a finger at the ladder and professional steamer near the kitchen door. "Grace tells me you're stripping paper today…"

"Yeah, hoped to get things in the works before I exposed you to the nitty-gritty."

"That's unnecessary. I'm in. We have a deal."

The men closed the space between them. Michael's heels echoed sharply on the cracked tile flooring, Kyle's were more of a rubber-soled slap. Their shoes represented their general level of dress. Kyle was no frills in a gray sweat suit and athletic shoes. Michael was casual but smart in his khaki slacks and green plaid shirt and loafers.

"Nostalgic trip, isn't it?"

"Oh, yeah." Michael shoved his hands in his pockets and took in the scenery. The wooden L-shaped bar, the booths lining the walls, the round tables and bamboo chairs scattered about. There were a few familiar prints hanging on the red-flocked wallpaper and an old gold clock about to strike noon. "Lots of fine memories here."

Kyle followed his old friend's fond gaze, and wondered if they were sharing some of the same flashbacks. "It was the perfect hangout. The close friendships, all the laughs you could handle."

"Not to mention the food! Especially Andy Anderson's huge roast beef sandwiches with the special sauce, those fried appetizers Amelia whipped up herself. And there were the imported beers Andy kept discovering, putting on special for a whole month. The college kids must've made a lot of his business back then. They brought their homework here and their card games. Watched basketball and football on the TV over the bar."

They stared up at the empty shelf that once held Andy's old nineteen-inch television. "I used to kid him about being his headhunter on campus. Giving me an extra commission above my salary."

"You did end up with his greatest asset," Michael blurted out. Watching Kyle's face fall, he said, "Sorry. It must be painful to talk about Libby, especially here, where it all began."

"It's okay." Kyle rubbed his temple, his smile only faintly strained. "Old Andy was a pretty good guy, all right. But he sure liked me a lot better when I was only his ace bartender and chef, not a rival for Libby's heart."

Michael hesitated. "Are those hard feelings what kept you from showing up for Andy's funeral?"

"Hell, no! We didn't know about his death," Kyle quickly assured. "An old friend's letter caught up with Libby too late. We'd moved a lot over the years and mail had a way of getting lost. Anyway, it was two months afterward. It was Libby's call on what to do. She assured me she sent Amelia a nice sympathy card, explaining that we hadn't known, but we were very sorry, in spite of our differences." Kyle shifted his stance, averting his friend's steady gaze. "But now I doubt she ever sent a thing. I've tried to fish to Amelia, but so far, have come up empty."

"I remember Libby as a headstrong girl."

"To a fault." Then, feeling a rush of compassion for his late wife, Kyle added, "Deep inside she was confused, loving and resenting the Andersons all at once."

"Must've been hard for the Andersons, too," Michael mused, "thrust back into parenting after their son died. I don't think it was all that personal to you, Kyle. Libby was pretty young yet and it was probably impossible for them to imagine her leaving the nest."

Kyle laughed shortly. "Having Button has introduced me to many of their protective feelings."

"I suppose so." Michael smiled awkwardly. "That's one area in which I am helpless."

"Too bad Libby didn't live to see how Amelia's mellowed. It takes effort, but she is so patient with Button and me, believe it or not."

"It has to be awkward though, with your history," Michael wagered.

"At times. But hey, a drowning man doesn't inspect his life preserver for a brand label. If it floats, it's valuable. This new life with Amelia floats."

Michael sensed a defensiveness in Kyle's message. He stared down at his loafers, gleaming against the dull flooring. "I'm probably not handling this very well. I don't mean to pry into your affairs. Go ahead and tell me to butt out if you want."

"Forget about it." Kyle clapped him on the back. "You've been wonderful. Picked up right where we left off. Not every guy would do that, after the way I bailed out."

"Not every guy pushing thirty is still a bachelor with time on his hands," Michael pointed out honestly. "Your friendship is a big deal to me, too. The older I get, the tougher it is to find good friends." He sighed. "Just believe that I want to be here for you. Like it used to be. And with time, you'll see more opportunities to charge up old friendships. Lots of the guys are still around. They've fallen into routines, lost hair, added a few pounds. But they're still *the guys,* at least when their wives let them out."

"With that attitude, no wonder you're still single!"

Wincing, Michael shifted the subject. "So, you think you can reopen in early August?"

"*We* should be able to do that," he promptly corrected. "As I told you, there isn't anything that needs a major overhaul. Aside from some plumbing problems in the kitchen, the main weakness is the decor. The restaurant business is so trendy, competitive. This place needed to change with the times and it hasn't."

"It had fallen out of favor in general—before Andy's

death," Michael admitted. "It's considered a bit too old world for the college kids, too dark and stuffy for business lunches."

Kyle brightened up. "Once we fix it up, it'll appeal to everyone. But mainly our peers, who are on their way, have a little money to spend and want some elegance for it."

Michael beamed. "Perfect."

Kyle picked up a clipboard off the bar. "Amelia and I have been here a few times, brainstorming. I've made notes." He showed them to Michael.

"Toss rickety bamboo stuff," Michael read, running a finger down the list. "Replace flooring. Sand down bar, apply lighter varnish. Polish brass bar rail. Brighten up lighting." He looked up. "Gee I hope you aren't planning to light this place too much."

"I intend to make that possible, but dimmer switches will provide the necessary control."

"Good idea." His finger slid to the end of the list. "So today we strip."

"We?" Kyle set the clipboard back on the bar and moved around to switch on every light.

Michael rubbed his hands together. "Remember the improvements we made on our old apartment. It'll be just like old times if I stick around and help."

Kyle assessed him doubtfully. "In those fancy clothes?"

"Hey, you make fancy sound sissy."

He grinned in affirmation.

"I have some sweats in my gym bag. Out in the car."

"For squash?"

"Maybe. But this is bound to be as fun. I so seldom get the chance to use my hands for more than pushing a pencil, hammering a keyboard."

Kyle shrugged. "Well, then, let's have some fun."

The steamer worked best with an extra man, Kyle quickly came to realize. It had a flat broad surface that spewed moist heat to loosen the dry paste beneath the wall-paper and had to be run slowly over the surface of the paper, sometimes more than once. They took turns standing on a stepladder with the clumsy machine, while the other stood underneath with a chisel to coax the peeling seams back, catch the gooey paper as it fell.

With every strip of paper removed, they admired their prowess.

"Have you any idea what you want on the walls next?" Michael asked.

"I did tour some of the places in Chicago before leaving, so I have an idea of what works. Grace will be invaluable with a final decision, though."

"She'll expect to take over," Michael choked out in warning from under the tented paper. He smiled wanly as Kyle lifted it off his head. "She's still petulant to a fault."

Kyle deliberately broke clear of his pal, folding the paper, dropping it into the nearby garage bin. He was secretly busy digesting the new and surprising layers to the cute bratty kid he remembered. More layers to their relationship, too. She'd been openly knocked over by his simple cake offering, truly thankful and overwhelmed. He'd returned the sentiment at the sight of her in that sexy red beaded dress. The lusty ideas that had tumbled through his brain at the sight of her in it.

Then there'd been the kiss. A playful birthday peck that had gone much deeper into a velvet chocolate ecstasy. He'd totally lost himself in the moment. Now he was doing it in a flashback. And it was still good.

Dammit! Kyle grimaced and tried to shoo the visions off. But they were stuck, as if pasted to his brain with wallpaper paste.

Logic suggested he was probably just lingering over a very harmless flirtation. After all, she was the first woman he'd encountered here upon his return. And he hadn't been with a woman since Libby, aside from the occasional dinner date back in Chicago.

The whole thing was as random as a lightning strike. He'd been in the right place at the right time, perhaps looking for an electrical charge.

This rationale calmed him. Gesturing to the row of stainless steel bar stools with his gooey chisel, he addressed Michael easily. "Can't argue that Grace is spunky. How many times did she sit on the end stool popping off to Amelia over the trials of algebra, or the war between Coke and Pepsi soft drinks?"

"She still likes Pepsi best. "

"Of course!" Sharing a chuckle, they got back to work, Michael at the steamer, Kyle edging his chisel along the next seam. "Girls like her know what they like. Stay loyal. Stick to it."

GRACE BARRELED THROUGH the door soon thereafter, laden with two heavy wallpaper sample books, a melon-colored work smock open over her aqua capris and cropped top.

"Speaking of spunky!" Kyle teased.

"If you're going to tease me again, I'm leaving!" she trilled.

"No, no, simmer down." Promptly ignoring his assistant, Kyle left his post at the ladder, just as a second strip of paper in a row fell on Michael's head.

By the time Michael peeled himself free and descended the rungs, Kyle and Grace were in conversation at the bar, having effectively dismissed him.

Kyle was leaning into her, whispering in her auburn curls. "Don't even think of bailing out. I'm locking you in here until we find a pattern."

She slid onto a bar stool, then glanced back at her brother as he made a snorting sound. "You should see yourself, full of paste and red fuzz—like a clown."

"So is Kyle!" he argued.

"Guess he wears it better somehow. Your face is just a little fuller at the cheeks."

Kyle laughed out loud. "This is just like old times! Even your bickering." The siblings stared at the jubilant bistro owner. "Forgive me guys, it's just so good to be home again. Should've never left."

Grace could feel her brother weighing her delighted expression. He had to think she was imagining life differently, if Kyle had discovered her first rather than Libby, stayed put here in the Twin Cities. In truth, she was doing just that. It was only a game, she thought defensively. Even if they'd stayed, they would've probably married and produced Button.

Button. Possessive of Kyle, ruling his emotions with her broad range of temperament. Daddy's girl a hundred percent.

Grace hadn't even considered children as yet. And Button, with her belligerent attitude, didn't cast a warm Gerber baby glow over her heart, give her maternal instincts the slightest tug. The idea that Grace might be a bit afraid of the child was something she refused to face.

Grace looked around the room, wondering if Button was going to leap out at her, make some kind of scene over her arrival. Seeing no trace of the child, she asked Kyle about her.

"Button?" His handsome face lit up a hundred watts. "She'd only be in the way on a project like this. Amelia has her. Cares for her as much as possible, in fact."

"Oh, she does." Grace's face lit up too, as she envisioned the sturdy woman managing Button's day-to-day care. Apparently the child wouldn't be tearing around her place as much as she feared.

Kyle would be concentrating on her alone. Even now, he

had a hand resting on her shoulder with a comforting familiarity. What on earth would it be like?

"Grace, you've been staring at the cow pattern for five minutes," Kyle said with some confusion. "You aren't considering that…"

"No way," she scoffed. "I glanced at the books in the store, tagged some wonderful options with Post-it notes." Flipping through the book open before her, she showed off some possibilities. They were all lighter hues, with faint patterns, like pinstripes, sea grass, diamonds.

"These stripes are nice," Kyle declared. "What do you think Mike?"

Michael leaned into the bar, putting a hand on the book. "I like this textured eggshell one. The tough matte finish should be easy to wipe down."

After intense discussion the threesome decided upon that particular pattern.

"We'll just do some measuring," Grace said, "figure out how many rolls you'll need. Then I'll stop back at the shop and place the order."

Kyle beamed. "You're a wonder."

"You'd be a bigger wonder if you'd help us strip the rest of these walls first," Michael suggested.

She held up her manicured hands, twinkling with magenta polish and gemstone rings. "With these nails?"

Kyle grabbed her wiggly fingers, as intrigued as a child with an unfamiliar toy. "Are these things for real?"

"The stones are," Michael cracked.

"I believe he means the nails." Grace felt butterflies in her stomach as he slid a thumbpad over her shiny fingertips. "They're partly real, enhanced with acrylic."

"You do them yourself?"

"Sometimes."

"Don't believe it," Michael scoffed. "Some little Frenchman named Chev comes to her place every week."

"I repair them," she said haughtily. The men laughed indulgently, causing Grace to repeat her threat to leave them in the lurch with no measurements.

Kyle sobered instantly. "We are sorry if we offended you, Gracie. We need you. We want you. We love you."

Of course he didn't mean the latter endearment. But they were words she'd longed to hear for such a long time. Her butterflies multiplied—by threes.

Digging her tape measure out her smock pocket, she began to make some estimates, dodging gooey strips of paper that somehow kept falling in her direction as the guys continued their work. To make the job more festive, Kyle cranked up the jukebox. Soon they were singing along out of key with all the old tunes. They didn't notice they had company until the music stopped.

Everyone whirled toward the jukebox. There stood a tall middle-aged man dressed in linen slacks and an open oxford shirt. His face was long and narrow, his hair a salt-and-pepper crest. His expression stern as he assessed the pasty red-flocked trio.

They gawked in return. For a moment it was like traveling back to a day long ago, for the man bore a startling resemblance to Andy Anderson, former owner of the bistro.

"Jerome?" Kyle queried.

"Yes, Kyle. Don't pretend you aren't expecting me."

Chapter Five

Kyle continued to stare mutely at Jerome Anderson. He wasn't expecting him. And wasn't sure why he looked so angry. "Mike, Grace, this is Amelia's nephew by marriage. Andy's brother Frank's son."

Michael was quick on the uptake, extending a dignified hand despite his scruffy appearance. "I'm Michael North. Don't think we've ever met."

"That's because I've lived on the west coast for years," he said curtly, keeping his hands clasped behind his back. "It's only recently, upon hearing from my relatives that Amelia intends to sell this bistro, that I have come back."

"What has that to do with you, Jerome?" Kyle wondered. "When Andy died, his property passed to Amelia, simple enough."

The older man bristled. "It isn't simple at all! My father, Frank, and Andy were equal partners in this place."

"At one time they were—"

"That agreement has hardly expired!"

Kyle struggled to keep his tone even. "It's my understanding that Andy bought him out, back in the late seventies."

"Well, if that's the case, I'd like to see some proof of sale."

"Have you spoken to Amelia about this?" Grace asked.

Jerome gave Kyle a strange smile. "She insists Andy paid Dad off. Still, she has no paper to substantiate it."

"What does Frank have to say about it?" Michael asked.

"Nothing, as a stroke has incapacitated him. He's in a nursing home up north near our relatives."

"Surely some of these relatives recall the events," Grace spouted.

Jerome remained unflappable. "Hardly. They live three hundred miles from the Twin Cities. It was only after Dad's stroke that they were updated on his affairs."

Grace opened her mouth to argue such a flimsy claim, but Michael sent her a hush-up look.

"Having Dad's power of attorney," Jerome continued, "I've been through his papers and can find no indication of a buyout."

Kyle's temper began to show. "Andy always spoke highly of Frank. I doubt your father would like this trick."

"Everybody round here knew Andy owned the place himself," Michael cut in reasonably. "Frank even came in from time to time, just to see how Andy was getting along."

Jerome still gave the appearance of calm, though his padded jaw tightened a bit. "Perhaps. But knowing Dad, his big heart and scattered brain for business most likely failed him. At best, he probably made some verbal agreement with Andy, gave Andy his share for a few hundred dollars."

"Andy was an honest man!"

"A shrewd businessman, if memory serves. Face it, Kyle, without proof in writing, you are sunk."

"What do you want from me, Jerome?" Kyle asked.

"I—am not sure yet. There is sentimental value here to consider." He closed his eyes and shook his head, as if warding off some emotion. "I may accept a buyout offer, or perhaps offer you one. I may even decide to just help you run the place. I don't know. Yet.''

"That's ridiculous! This is my dream. What's keeping me together—'' Kyle broke off, a flash of vulnerability chasing through his eyes. "Be warned that I have no intention of halting my work here,'' he said more evenly.

Jerome glowed with triumph. "Go ahead and fix it up if you like. Just keep in mind that it's still part of Frank's estate.'' With that he turned on his heel and left.

Muttering an oath of despair under his breath, Kyle sank onto a bar stool, burying his face in his hands.

Grace moved in to place a comforting hand on his shoulder. "This can't be hopeless.''

"Oh, yes it can. Seems no matter how a guy tries, there's no escaping past trouble.'' Kyle rubbed his mouth and set his fists on the bar. He quickly fell into a deep funk, immersed in his own private misery, as if replaying an awful movie in his mind.

Grace spoke up encouragingly, breaking the silence. "Surely there are papers someplace to back up the sale.''

"There was such a paper. Saw it myself once. Andy kept it in the office safe in back.''

"I suppose it was taken in the robbery,'' Michael inserted with new realization.

"Yes,'' Kyle said matter-of-factly. "Along with three grand in cash, some rings and a coin collection—mint Kennedy half dollars.''

Grace gasped. "There was a robbery here?''

Kyle nodded. "You were just a kid, so we didn't tell you.''

"Thought it might upset you,'' Michael added.

Grace marveled over the turn of events. Ultimately, a glaring issue stood out in her mind. "Funny that Amelia didn't caution you about Jerome's claim in advance,'' she said, "something so important.''

Kyle looked at her piteously. "She probably didn't see it as a huge problem for me."

"This missing agreement not a problem!"

"Gracie," Kyle said softly, "Amelia believes I pulled off the robbery."

"Oh." She glanced helplessly at Michael. No wonder he didn't tell her anything at the time, considering how crazy she was for Kyle. It would've been extremely upsetting to handle at seventeen.

Kyle sighed. "By not warning me, letting me face Jerome, Amelia was probably hoping I would produce the paper to appease him and effectively put an end to his claim."

Grace was stunned. "Hardly seems in Amelia's bulldog character to avoid confronting you on the issue. She was always so forthright."

"When she invited me back home, she made it clear we both had suffered enough, that we would do better with a clean slate. Appears she's trying especially hard to stick to the bargain."

"Well, it's high time she face the fact that you weren't the thief in the first place!" Michael paced around, shaking his head. "Even though I bet she wishes more than ever that you've had the agreement all along."

"Oh, the whole accusation was made on a wish in the first place," he ground out. "Figured if she could blacken my reputation in Libby's eyes, I'd be gone. Like father, like son, she said. I was bound to grow up a no-good gambler just like my father, probably stole from them to pay off Dad's debts so he'd come back home." He pounded the bar. "What a crock!"

"By then Libby had her heart set on you anyway," Michael comforted. "She didn't believe you a thief."

"No, she didn't. And sadly, it was Amelia's accusation that spurred Libby into action. After that, she was insistent that we elope and start over in Chicago. We were on the fence about what do with our future until that ugly scene happened." Kyle sighed. "Even now, it's so hard to think about, being accused that way by people I wanted so much to impress. At least the police detective investigating the case had more faith in me than the Andersons. He tried to tell them there was no proof of my guilt, that it could've been any employee or patron who knew the layout of the office."

"It was mostly Andy's own fault," Michael recalled. "He left the wall safe unlocked to see to a sink overflow in the kitchen."

"Gone ten minutes and the box was picked clean."

"Is there any way to still figure out who the thief is?" Grace wondered. "Maybe get that agreement back?"

Kyle smiled wanly. "The Andersons and the police did a pretty thorough investigation at the time, spoke to everyone on the premises."

"The police must still have a list of those questioned."

"Probably, but we can't go around drilling those people. They'd get the law after *us!*"

"But if someone just wanted the valuables, why not hand over the agreement now?"

"If he or she kept it," Kyle said doubtfully. "Dammit, I can't believe this mess is back to haunt me. It was as unfair then as it is now!"

Michael slapped Kyle on the back. "We will work this out somehow."

"I don't see how. I could never share partnership with Jerome."

"Well, if you ask me, Jerome's whole claim is plainly a way to extort money from you," Grace asserted. "I don't think for a minute he really cares about running this place."

"Gracie," Michael chided. "You don't know that for sure."

"Why would he want a share in it? He lives three hundred miles away, far from the action here. And he didn't even try to stop you from remodeling, a weird oversight. All in all, he struck me as a cheater looking for a payoff." She took a deep breath. "Now don't look so glum. At the very worst it'll mean we write the bastard a check. I mean, I will write it myself," she amended.

Kyle reddened. Logically, he agreed with her theory. He also knew that the offer from Michael wouldn't have stung half as much. But the idea that this young pampered woman-child could solve his problems with a flourish of pen bruised his ego big time. "Excuse me, princess," he said sharply, "but some things can't be settled with the North checkbook!"

"But in this case—"

"Butt out, Gracie," Michael agreed, smiling at a grateful Kyle. "Kyle's first order of business is to speak to Amelia, hash out possibilities about the robbery with her."

Kyle's frown now included both siblings. "Forget I said I enjoy your bickering. Grace, Jerome will not get a nickel from me without a fight. As for confronting Amelia, Mike, have you any idea how much emotion Amelia and I are suppressing over the past? Words put wrong could blow up like TNT. No, our reunion is simply too new to be put under so much pressure. If a talk backfired, Button and I would be on the outs, with no home, no hope of having the bistro. And Button would feel abandoned by another female."

"My idea is the better of the two," Grace insisted.

"No way," Michael argued.

"Forget about it!" Kyle squared his shoulders as the pair backed down. It was a rare feat, but he'd managed to effectively shut down both the Norths at the same time. There was little satisfaction for him though. He was too worried about Jerome. What if he did want a piece of the action here? What if he hoped to take over the place completely and shut him out?

IT WAS NEARLY FOUR o'clock when Grace arrived home. As she swung her car into the driveway, she caught sight of Dickie Trainor's sleek black Jaguar sports car on the street. He was seated on the back stoop like an abandoned boy, twirling his tennis racket. She rolled to a stop, offering him a feeble wave.

"Finally!" he exclaimed.

"Told you I'd be cutting it close." She brushed by him to slip her key in the lock. With a wince at her disheveled appearance, Dickie gave her a wide berth. They burst into the small kitchen, Grace unloading her shoulder bag on a chair.

"I'll shower quickly."

"Have you time? Heather and Nate will be waiting."

She posed coquettishly in the doorway, wrinkling her red-flocked nose. "Sure you want to argue?"

"Guess I don't."

Good. She'd suffered enough argument for one day.

When Grace returned in her crisp white tennis outfit, Dickie was eating a huge slice of her chocolate birthday cake.

"This is superb." He tapped a fork on the plate.

"Hey, easy on that stuff."

"Why?"

"Because it's mine."

"Where did it come from?"

"Kyle McRaney, personal chef."

Dickie savored his last bite of fudge frosting. "He offers the full treatment, doesn't he?"

Grace's thoughts shot back to the previous night. The intimacy she'd felt, alone with Kyle in the house in the middle of the quiet night, left her fulfilled, hungry, agitated.

Her thoughts then ricocheted to the events of today, which unfortunately, left her feeling just plain agitated.

"You're keeping this guy, aren't you?" Dickie asked eagerly.

"Excuse me?"

"This Kyle character. I can count on him being around?"

As uncomfortable as she felt with the aged and more complex Kyle, she certainly hoped so.

THE PRESTIGIOUS Meadowlark Country Club was nestled in an older section of Edina, several miles from Grace's town home. Built in the sixties like many of the area's homes, it was graced with nice-size trees and acres of flawless lawn.

Grace's parents were long-respected members. She and Michael considered it their own posh playground since their toddler days, frolicking in the pool, on the courts, in the restaurants among the privileged class. It was here that Grace first met Heather and Nate.

As Dickie turned his Jag sports car over to a valet at the club entrance, they discussed the newlyweds. "Heather and Nate fought constantly as children," she confided with a laugh. She walked through the glass door he was holding open for her. "When they got older they discovered exactly why they put so much energy into their bickering. It was a romantic static."

"I vaguely remember taking golf lessons with Nate here at the club," Dickie confided. "But nothing clicked with him at your party."

"We were all a year or two apart, which made a difference back then," Grace reasoned. "And you used to go by your more formal first name. Then there are the changes in your, uh, appearance."

"Yes, yes," he cut in. "I only bring it up because I'd rather not get into the connection."

Grace understood. Dickie was sensitive about the past, had gone to such trouble to reinvent himself. Had Nate been cruel at one time? Called him Mr. Pock? These thoughts led her back to his phone call of the morning, his fishing about investing in Kyle's bistro. Hopefully he would forget about it for the time being. She didn't care to discuss the murky developments with Jerome Anderson, felt she had no right to.

They checked in at the front desk. The uniformed man told them that the Bassets were already out on the courts. As they strolled through the clubhouse with rackets swinging at their sides, people eagerly acknowledged Grace and Dickie, some commenting on last night's party. Grace realized that she enjoyed the admiring glances women were giving the handsome blonde at her side. He was only a few inches taller than her five-foot-four-inch frame, but he moved with an elegance and confidence.

There were advantages to dating within her own social group. And surely, passion would—could—evolve from comfort. Right?

They were scheduled to play on the outdoor courts. As they stepped back outside they immediately spotted the Bassets, dressed in matching cream outfits with navy pin-stripe, whacking a ball back and forth across the nets with good-natured taunts.

"Hey, honeymooners!"

The newlyweds responded to Grace's shout, abandoning play. They trotted across the court with huffs of laughter.

"No fair practicing in advance," Grace chided.

"We're still trying to work off that meal at your folks last night," Nate claimed, rubbing his washboard stomach. "Great party by the way."

The men shook hands and exchanged pleasantries.

"So, who's teaming up with whom?" Heather asked cheerily. "Boys against girls?"

Nate winked at Dickie. "You any good?"

Dickie's smile tightened slightly. "Very good."

Heather touched Dickie's wiry arm. "Nate just hates losing at anything."

"Good thing I'm such a winner myself," Dickie murmured, leading the others onto the court.

They played two hot sets, a win on each side. The men broke the tie on the third set. Which led Heather to some comical pouting.

Afterward, they settled into one of the smaller bars for some drinks. The women took a quick break into one of the plush powder rooms. Alone in the spacious mirrored room, they dug into their small clutch purses for hairbrushes and makeup.

Heather removed the barrette at her neck and shook her pale hair loose around her shoulders. "Gee I can't remember the last time I saw Dickie Trainor, before your party last night, I mean. His looks have sure improved."

"No kidding!"

"Just how serious is this romance?"

"We've had a half dozen or so dates," Grace said mildly.

"Really? Why didn't you say something?"

"You've been busy, hon, with the newlywed game."

"Guess we have drifted apart." Heather sighed. "You feeling bad?"

"A little," she admitted.

"Nate and I are falling into a routine now, so I'll be more available. In fact, if you'd like to lunch Tuesday, I'm free."

"Great. So, what do you think of me with Dickie?"

Heather met her smile in the mirror. "His image overhaul is a plus, but he seems a little conservative for you. A lot like the boys your parents dug up in high school."

"I know." Grace sighed, carefully applying lipstick.

"Guess you could say I'm exploring every conceivable option. And it's partly your fault. Your successful marriage has gotten me questioning my own goals. Where am I going? Should I marry? If so, what kind of man is the right kind?"

"You really want to settle down?" Heather asked excitedly.

Grace's heart skipped a beat of panic. "Eventually."

"But not with Mr. Pock!"

"Even you know about that name?"

"Didn't you?"

"Don't remember it. But it reminds me, Dickie doesn't want the past brought up, wants to be judged as is."

"Okay. But you have to know, this trip into the white-collar territory is highly unlikely to work out."

"You did some experimenting yourself during breakups from Nate over the years, yet you came back to the conservative side, will live very much as we were raised."

"Do you think Dickie has real potential?"

"Not necessarily. We aren't even dating exclusively. Though I have enjoyed my parents' approval for a change. They've backed off about my design business, given up parading men by me here at the club. And wait till you see the emerald necklace they gave me last night."

"What did Dickie give you?"

"Some very lovely pearls."

"That's a semiserious sign."

Her forehead puckered in doubt. "Might seem so. But he hasn't shown any territorial signs as yet. He's not the least bit jealous of Kyle invading my house."

Heather regarded her slyly. "So how did the Ultimate Crush hold up with time?"

Grace opened her compact blusher, dabbing color on to her already flaming cheeks. "You mean the childish one-way crush that went nowhere?"

"That's a pretty cold description. For a husband hunter exploring all her options."

"The man is carrying several extra years of bad road on him, with a spitfire three-year-old to raise. He's transformed from a reckless heartthrob from the wrong side of the tracks to a tamed parent living with his former grandmother-in-law."

Heather sighed. "Beyond all that, he's also on the poor side."

Grace frowned. "I'd say struggling."

"Rougher than ever around the edges, too, no doubt."

"You could say he's ruggedly handsome," Grace amended.

"But can you imagine him slipping in here to play tennis?"

"Well. With the right clothing, maybe."

Heather tsked in regret. "He probably has no cuff links, though."

Grace's green eyes narrowed. "You're needling me on purpose."

Heather flashed flawless white teeth. "Just suggesting that, on a gut level, he's an option after all."

THEY JOINED THE MEN BACK in the bar to discover they'd already ordered cocktails and a platter of stuffed mushrooms. To Grace's amazement, they were discussing Kyle.

"Grace could use him full-time," Dickie was saying. "The wonders he does with food. Thank God she decided to take up him up on his services." He turned to Grace as she sat beside him. "So, did you speak to Kyle about my investing in the bistro?"

Grace munched delicately on a mushroom. "Not yet," she said, trying to be diplomatic in the face of the curious Bassets.

Nate surprised Grace by speaking up. "Believe me, Dickie, that's a deal you want to steer clear of."

"What do you know about it, darling?" Heather prompted.

Nate sipped his Manhattan, intent on impressing his bride. "As coincidence would have it, I am very familiar with the bistro property. The son of one of the original owners dropped by our agency a while back."

"What did he want of Landlock Realty?" Grace demanded.

Nate didn't seem to notice Grace wasn't as cooing as his wife. "Made some initial inquiries," he replied importantly, "about resale value, perhaps listing with us if the time comes."

Grace pinched the stem of her daiquiri glass. Maybe she was wrong about Jerome Anderson's intentions after all. Maybe he didn't just want a settlement, but felt he'd be best served in a sell-off. Letting Kyle go ahead and redecorate would only boost resale value and keep Kyle occupied while Jerome was angling the way to get the most out of the place.

Nate rambled on, giving no one's privacy a care in the world, laying out the story of brothers Andy and Frank, the unsolved robbery and missing sales agreement. "Everything stems on convincing old Amelia Anderson to do what's best for everyone," he said in conclusion.

"But Amelia is trying to do what's best for herself and Kyle," Grace asserted.

Nate balked. "Even if Kyle pulled the theft?"

"But he didn't!"

"It was certainly an inside job."

Grace knew she was getting shrill, so she made an effort to tone down. "If Kyle pulled the robbery, he could presumably produce the missing agreement. He would have known its value from the start, he wouldn't have disposed of it.''

Nate paused, clearly stumped. ''Hadn't considered that logic.''

So cocky, Grace goaded silently. So anxious to make a big score.

''Or consider this,'' Nate countered. ''Kyle did steal the safe's contents, but cannot produce the agreement because it was never a part of the booty—never existed outside an aging woman's mind.''

Grace was annoyed to note that even Dickie was nodding on the theory. ''All in all, I wouldn't count on getting this sale,'' Grace cautioned Nate with a hard gleam in her eye.

''Never can tell.'' Nate said nothing more, draining his drink.

Heather broke the stiff spell of silence to follow with a query to Dickie. ''What's the attorney's opinion on all this?''

''They could land in court, I suppose,'' he replied glumly. ''Maybe I shouldn't try to invest. I don't know.''

Grace sighed, wondering if there were two more self-centered men on the planet than the pair seated at this table. And if this was the sort of company she wanted for the rest of her life.

Chapter Six

Grace was awakened Monday morning by the ringing of her doorbell. Half-blind without her contact lenses she grabbed her glasses from the nightstand, jammed them on her face and pitter-pattered on bare feet to the front door. She peered through the side window to find Kyle standing on her stoop.

She opened the door a crack, cringing in the sunshine. "Hi."

"Hi yourself. I didn't get you out of bed, did I?"

"Well. Gee." She smothered a yawn and raked her mussed curls.

He pushed the door between them open. "Get with it, sleepyhead. It's Monday. Nine o'clock in the morning. Time to get cooking. If you still want me, that is."

His sexy baritone made her knees weak. She leaned against the door frame for support. "A deal's a deal, I guess."

He braced his arm against the outside of the door frame, tipping closer. "This isn't exactly a brass band welcome."

She rubbed her forehead groggily. "I'm never excited before coffee."

"If it's about Saturday's run-in—"

"Meant no harm offering you the money." She glanced

down at her painted toes. "Saw the chance to be really helpful and took it."

"It's such a wonderful bonus, Gracie, you caring so much."

"Have you thought about yesterday's new message? You did get it?"

"I got it." He rolled his eyes. "Leave it to you to go for the dramatic telegram."

"Seemed a fast, concise way to give you the scoop about Jerome visiting Nate Basset at Landlock Realty."

"I appreciate your concern. But at this point, it doesn't change anything. I already distrust Jerome, figure he's up to no good. But unless a bolt of inspiration comes my way, I will probably have to reach some kind of compromise with him."

"So you didn't break down and speak to Amelia about Jerome's interference?"

"No," he said firmly.

"But she has a right to know—"

"At some point! No offense, Grace, but you're trying too hard again."

"Okay, okay."

"I'm hired to take care of you, remember?"

"Oh, yeah…" She gazed up at him with dreamy eyes.

"Right." He tapped her nose. "For starters, you shouldn't answer the door in a skimpy outfit like that."

"Well, uh…" She gaped at him through askew glasses, realizing he'd been wearing this same expression the other night while inspecting her in the red beaded dress. This body scan didn't match his present businesslike tone—unless he was a sultan collecting new members for his harem.

"This is a perfectly modest nightshirt," she finally retorted. "Like you've seen me in before."

"Sure. In the old days. When you were—well—a skinny kid," he fired off in a sputter.

Kyle off balance? Grace gaped at him, pushing her glasses up her nose to get the full view. He pushed the door open wider to step in. Grace leaned away to give him berth only to feel someone plow into her thigh. A miniature linebacker in a tiny pink sweater, yellow T-shirt and blue jeans, her black hair fastened in pigtails that stuck straight out over her ears.

"Oh!"

Button tipped a moon-shaped face upward, full of wonder. "Don't you 'member me?"

Grace nodded with a wry smile. "Of course I do." She closed the door behind them, standing in the entryway with a hand on her hip. "I thought you stayed with your Grandma Amelia, that's all."

"She's a great-grandma." Button pushed a small finger to her lips, unsure. "Or great, great. What, Daddy?"

"One great will do it," Kyle assured his daughter. He bent over to take off Button's pink cardigan. She made it difficult, turning in a circle, her left arm curled around a tote bag of belongings.

"Button," he beseeched, "please give me your sweater."

She giggled, spinning faster, tiny shoes dancing wildly.

Kyle paused, staring into space. "Gee, I wonder where the kitten is?"

"Kitty." Instantly distracted, Button froze, allowing Kyle to take the cardigan. "Where is Kitty?" she asked no one in particular, looking around with huge, curious eyes.

Grace yawned, raking a hand through her hair. "I don't know for sure."

Now she looked at Grace, with open disapproval. "That's bad. Poor Kitty."

Grace held her ground. "I haven't given the kitten a name yet."

"I do it," Button said matter-of-factly. "Kitty."

"We'll see."

Button wandered closer to Grace. She fingered the ruffled hem of her short floral sleep shirt, exposing the matching panties underneath. "Is that underwear in 'dere?"

"Uh, no." She brushed Button's fingers aside, glancing at Kyle. "I think I'd better go get dressed."

He winked. "Good idea."

Button glared at her retreating figure. "*That girl's* all messy, Daddy."

Kyle agreed that Grace was disheveled in the harsh light of day. Sleepy, disoriented, cranky, were fair assessments too. But lord help him, she did it up sexily, filled out her nightshirt so thoroughly. And she knew. The tease knew.

Without doubt, she was programmed to turn a man on, from the top of her tinted auburn curls to the tips of her painted toenails. Seemed unbelievable no man had as yet swept her off her feet. But just no man would do, either. It would have to be someone masterful, and mentally quick to handle her strong, vibrant personality. Like himself, maybe?

Not at all. Kyle had no room in his life for a new romance. His relationship with Libby still haunted him. Her abrupt passing left him with doubts and questions about his capabilities in general. And there was Button to consider. And Amelia. Kyle owed her a lot, and struggled with the tensions their long separation caused. Reconciling with her would take time.

More than anything, Kyle needed a sense of peace in his existence. Gracie was no tonic for that. It would be like holding a live sparkler in his hand: mighty exciting but bound to leave a lasting burn.

Mike's wages were generous, but hardly seemed enough now. Not when one was calculating in hazard pay.

Feeling trapped in a hazard zone herself, Grace had bolted for her bedroom, shutting the paneled door firmly behind her. Pressing her back into the wood panels, she placed a shaky hand on her racing heart. How could she possibly survive this invasion? By keeping it objective, professional?

Tell that to Kyle! With all his troubles, he'd wasted no time noting her state of undress. And then there was the Button factor, casing the situation with insightful eyes and a spunky attitude. She'd been naive to assume Amelia would be taking total charge of the girl as a rule.

In any case, she was wide-awake now. Launching into the room she tore off her nightie, intending to take her usual morning bath. Then, dressed only in her panties, she halted halfway to her master suite bath. There was no way she could enjoy a relaxing soak, wondering what they were doing in her house. No, she would have to shift her bath to evenings.

Already, the concessions to her precious routine began.

She moved to her dresser for underthings, then into the closet for an outfit. The closet was a room in itself, nearly as large as the town home's spare bedroom. The rods running on the longer parallel walls were jammed with clothing for every conceivable occasion. The rear wall was a honeycomb of drawers and shelves, housing a host of accessories from belts to hose, to jewelry, to shoes counting in the hundreds. To the back of the door was fastened a full-length mirror.

Unlike the rest of her cluttered creative environment, Grace held her personal belongings in the highest order of esteem. Once a month Heather came over, and splitting a bottle of chardonnay between them, they tidied up this closet, categorizing everything first by season, then color, weeding out tired things, marveling over additions. Then it was on to the master bath to realign her makeup, nail polish and toiletries, which were stored in a huge cupboard originally designed for linens.

The question of what to wear today shouldn't be a hassle, she chided herself, thumbing through the left rod of casual garments. It was a workday, with clients calling for costume fittings. On these occasions she generally wore sweatpants and a white T-shirt, topped by a multipocket smock holding measuring tape, pins and other tools of the trade.

The effect was so baggy though. So teenybopper.

Not a welcome vision with Kyle on hand, who, whether he knew it or not, reflected her passage into womanhood with open masculine appreciation.

No matter that he seemed to be pulling back from his flashes of desire. His eyes were a reliable indicator, glittering—then shuttering behind thick dark lashes, only to reopen with a dull finish. Grace suspected he might not be in touch with his own responses; in fact he probably would deny all if cornered.

Perhaps a harmless flirtation could be enjoyed under the circumstances. They were two adults, trapped in a situation for several weeks. And the chance that Kyle McRaney might feel an itch for her even for a little while, was the ultimate girlhood dream come true.

She eventually decided she would wear some yellow slacks and a peach top under her smock today. True, the stiff cotton pants would pinch a little in places if she had to bend and squat too much, but the sacrifice would have to be made. It was necessary. This was *Kyle*.

Grace found Kyle and Button in her kitchen, fussing over her new kitten, nestled in her basket by the basement door. Kyle snapped to full height upon her return. Button knelt closer to the basket, laying a possessive hand on the pet's creamy hair, making cooing sounds.

Kyle took Grace's elbow and guided her near the sink. He hovered over her, speaking in low tones. ''Is it a problem, Button being here?''

"I wasn't expecting her, that's all," she repeated, this time more evenly. "Will she always be along?"

Kyle's smile shadowed patience, and perhaps a hint of regret. "A lot of the time, I guess."

"What will she do with her time, Kyle?"

In an old unconscious gesture of comfort, he reached out and pushed a stray pincurl off Grace's forehead. "Aw, she's got a bag full of toys and games. And there is Kitty."

"I need space and peace to work," she asserted. "The whole upstairs is my studio. Clients move in and out of here on a schedule...."

Her mind scattered as she inhaled his Aspen aftershave. His gaze was so earnest, so steady, so repressed. Still, had she ever seen eyes so blue? His bright colored work shirt was pale in comparison.

"Amelia helps, it's true," he said quietly. "But I am trying hard to work with Amelia on her terms. She has her clubs and meetings and habits."

Suddenly, the stress point shifted from Grace's house to Amelia's. Grace had vivid memories of the powerful woman who ran the bistro and could understand why one might want to tiptoe a bit around her. "I think I do understand that," she admitted.

"I guarantee Button will be good—as good as the average three-year-old."

Grace smiled lamely, having no idea how comforting a guarantee that might be.

"Hey, we can't hear," Button piped up. She plopped onto her small bottom with Kitty landing in her lap. "You gotta talk louder."

Kyle laughed, and to her own surprise, so did Grace.

"Is it all right, Gracie?" Kyle murmured. "Both of us as a package deal?"

"Have I ever denied you anything?"

Kyle stared hard at her. He'd never asked for anything, had he?

She noted and understood his confusion. He had no way of knowing how completely she'd given her heart to him.

"I have my hours planned for today," he reported. "I'm going to cook up a roast and bake some sourdough bread for sandwiches. Both were specialties of mine back in Chicago."

"Can't wait," she lilted.

"But first you need breakfast. Sit down and I'll get you some toast."

"And coffee."

"And fresh juice," he negotiated.

There was a rap on the back storm door a short while later and a middle-aged woman peered through the screen.

"Ah, Mitzi." Grace motioned her inside.

A plump robust blonde of about fifty bounced inside. She had in tow three youngsters, two girls and a boy aged eight through ten. "Good morning, Grace!" she proclaimed in a musical lilt. "Hope we're not too early."

Grace assured Mitzi they were right on time. "Mitzi, Tony, Rachel and Kristin, this is my friend, Kyle, and his daughter, Betsy."

"Button," the child corrected. She appraised the children with keen interest. "You come to play with me?"

"Isn't she a darling?" Mitzi boomed, bending over to tug at one of Button's squat pigtails. "I wish we could, Miss Button, but Grace is sewing costumes for us." Mitzi straightened and addressed Kyle with an approving smile. "These youngsters are in my summer acting class at the community center and we are putting on a rendition of Cinderella." She raised her puffed hands for effect. "Actually, it's called *Cinderella, the Musical*. Lots of singing and dancing. It will be spectacular."

"We got that storybook," Button piped up. She tugged

on Kyle's T-shirt. "When's the singin'? Don't 'member no singin', Daddy."

Kyle cleared his throat. "Can't say people ask for my singing, Button. Luckily," he intimated to the actors, "there are different ways to tell a story."

The kids laughed. Kyle good-naturedly went back to preparing her breakfast.

Grace checked the many pockets of her work smock. Finding her tape measure she looped it around her neck. "Well, guess we better get busy. You all know the way." With Grace in the lead they moved into the living room and single file up the open staircase flanking the far wall.

Her work studio took up the entire second story of the town house. Unlike her brother next door, who kept the developer's original floor plan intact, Grace had carpenters construct a large double door opening between the two bedrooms for fluidity, add skylights for optimum use of the sun, and install plain floor tile for practical cleanup. As for the color scheme, she'd rejected the usual beige tones for bright red flooring and blue curtains, and spent days painting colorful murals on the bare white walls, everything from scenes of frolicking children, to floral bursts, to models in high fashion.

These alterations were criticized by her parents, who thought this "designer phase" did not warrant such an elaborate setting, and that the "resale value" would be diminished beyond belief. But Grace waved them off like pesky flies. She intended to live here indefinitely.

Mitzi's presence was always overwhelming and she chattered a mile a minute as they flooded into the studio. The kids were always well behaved during these fittings and today was no different. They took care to step gingerly round her works-in-progress on dressing dummies, dual ironing boards, the tables piled high with scissors, yard stick and plastic boxes, the sewing machines on stands, and the bolts of fabric propped everywhere. Without direction, the kids gathered round the closet housing their costumes, thumbing through hangers sheathed in plastic. Kristin was to play Cinderella, Rachel, a stepsister and Tony, Prince Charming.

Grace consulted her notebook for this project. Without lifting her eyes from the page she pointed in the general direction of the decorative screens on the far side of the room. "Kristin, you'll be first with the ball gown. Back to the screens for a costume change. Tony, Rachel, this fitting will take the longest. If you like, go downstairs for a drink or sit on a beanbag, or—" She paused as they began to giggle.

Suddenly Grace noted a guest bobbing in and out of the tangle of legs. She snatched the pencil out from behind her ear and aimed it at Button. "Hey, little one."

The kids, recognizing the no-nonsense note in Grace's voice, backed away from the child. Button stood stiff, hands on hips. "Whatyouwant?"

Grace's mouth twitched. "I want to know what you're doing up here?"

She affected a helpless shrug. "You said come."

Grace shook her auburn curls. "I meant the bigger kids."

Button's lower lip protruded. "Pwease."

The kids spoke up on Button's behalf. Grace listened patiently to their promises to watch over her.

"Will you sit quietly on a chair?"

"In the corner?" she peeped in worry.

Grace wondered if that was a punishment cooked up by Amelia. "No," she said, gesturing to a small love seat. "Right over there—with Mitzi, maybe?"

Mitzi, presently inspecting a partially constructed vest on one of the sewing machines, looked startled by Grace's proposal. She was in the habit of pacing the room during fittings, leading the children in renditions from the upcoming musical. Ultimately being a trouper who prided herself on handling any child, she plunked down on the love seat and held her fleshy arms wide. "Very well. Come here, chicken."

KYLE WAS JUST FINISHING up Grace's breakfast when he realized Button was gone. Seemed odd, as she clung to him during nearly every waking minute. Feeling a rush of guilt and panic he dashed around the main floor, whispering her name. "Button? Button. Button!" he hissed desperately.

He didn't mean to pry, but he had to search every place. If a child wanted to hide, this would be the ideal layout for it. Grace's living room was full of low, wide leather chairs, tables holding fragile vases and assorted knickknacks, stacked high with magazines. There was a sitting room of sorts with a television, bookcases, risqué statues that passed for art.

He paused at her closed bedroom door. No man's land, he wagered. Unless a man were to be invited. He sighed. What an idea... He shook off such notions. He had a search to conduct.

Nothing could have prepared him for the feminine paradise beyond that door. Sateen and linen of cream and mint. Champagne-colored carpeting. A huge queen-size bed of ruffles and pillows. A giant television built into a wall unit. It was a lush master suite fit for the lush ruler of a small country. Grace might be bucking her parents' rigid class system to some degree, but she certainly was enjoying all the comforts of wealth. There seemed no comfort she'd denied herself. This place as a whole was best described as decadent disarray.

Throughout the eye-popping tour, there was no sign of his daughter.

It seemed likely that Button had crashed into Grace's work space. It was with trepidation that he climbed the staircase, gripping the wrought iron rail with a huge tight hand. It was so obvious that Grace was uneasy with Button. Though this disappointed him, he knew Button wasn't being as charming to Grace as she could be. A tight fit for all of them.

Kyle stopped dead at the top of the stairs. There were two doors. One led to a bathroom. The other proved to be a portal to a wonderland. Keeping out of sight, he glanced into the bright colorful workroom, jammed with stuff, alive with creative energy. There sat Button beside Mitzi. She seemed completely welcome, a rhinestone crown atop her head, watching the proceedings with uncharacteristic serenity.

The proceedings. Kyle found himself with a particularly advantageous view. Grace hovering over a girl dressed in a jade gown of some shimmery fabric, taking a hem measurement between the fabric and floor. She moved with the grace of a dancer. No wonder, after all those years of lessons he and Michael had delivered her to.

Grace had been such a part of their lives back then, serene and full of wonder. But she was a child no longer, with those full breasts spilling out of her knit top and curved hips on display in those tight pants.

Kyle felt a tightness below the belt. How tempted he was to hold Grace close, skim his hands over her curves.

Mitzi abruptly burst into song then, making him jump. It was an original tune, he guessed, meant for Cinderella. The girl in the ball gown joined in, lamenting her desolate existence. Seemed out of place in this luxurious nest.

He wondered about Grace's charmed existence in general. The girl with so much, that she was presented a chef for her birthday. Surely life had to be challenging for her on some levels, ones that dashing off a check couldn't cure.

Below the surface, there had to be more than layers of design wear and gallons of nail polish. A reckless part of him was sorely tempted to peel off her fancy layers and find out.

Chapter Seven

Kyle was sure he caught a glimpse of Amelia at the front window when he and Button returned to her cozy Cape Cod style house at sunset. He moved to the back seat of the car to unhook Button from her seat, with the wry thought that Amelia never ceased to be anxious when Button was away.

"Piggler pwease, Daddy," Button chirped, crawling over the car seat to grab hold of him.

He sighed as her soft arms curled round his neck, locking him up tight. How Kyle loved these clutches, to be called Daddy. Under the circumstances, there was no way he'd deny his girl a simple piggyback ride. Unfortunately such play unnerved Amelia. It was only expected that she would harbor some fears, having first lost her son, Libby's father, then Libby to accidental death.

But they couldn't stop taking every conceivable risk, could they? With a burst of joy Kyle trotted across the lawn with his whooping daughter on his broad shoulders.

"We're home, Amelia!" he called out extra cheerfully, upon bursting into an empty living room. He discovered Amelia at the kitchen table clipping store coupons. Bless her, she was pretending she hadn't been hovering at the window. A shadow of distress did flicker in her eyes as she raised them to Button's high perch. However, she kept silent.

"Passengers off," he announced. Hoisting Button over his head, he set her tennis shoes gently on the linoleum.

"There's my girl." Amelia exhaled with relief, shifted on her chair, straightened her housedress at her lap, and opened her rail arms to Button. The child was still a bit shy around her at times, but she was intrigued to have a grandmother of her own and was making an effort.

She leaned against Amelia's frail form. "Hi, Grammy."

Amelia stroked the jet bangs hanging across Button's small forehead. "Tell Grammy about your day."

Button's eyes shined. "I played with Kitty. And saw Cinderella."

Amelia gasped in wonder. "You did?"

"*That girl* made Cinderella a pretty dress."

Amelia tsked. "You must mean Grace. Address her by name."

Button went on in a high-pitched babble, describing her day. Kyle dropped in a line or two to fill out the adventure.

"That's all fine and well." She tapped a crooked finger to Button's nose. "But did you have a nap?"

"Nobody did that, Grammy."

"Then we'll have an early beddy bye, won't we?"

Button grew thoughtful. Hooking a finger in her mouth, she looked up at Kyle. "Where's my Cinderella book? I want it for beddy bye."

"Gee, honey." Kyle raked his raven hair, stumped. Things were weeded out with every move they made. Especially this last move. He stuck to the basics. All of Button's favorite things. But books had seemed replaceable. He'd given the worn beat-up stack to their last landlady.

"Don't you got my books, Daddy?"

"No, I—"

"Oh, Daddy!" Button cried out at ear-piercing level, and stomped her foot, barely missing Amelia's slippers.

"We can get a new one. Soon..."

"In the meantime, we can go to the library," Amelia proposed.

"Now," Button fumed. "I hafta know that story."

"They lived happily ever after," Kyle suggested faintly.

"I don't think she had a mommy. And she had bad sisters. So sad."

Amelia's gray brows drew together as she voiced practicalities. "You will have to wait. The library is closed by now."

"No!" Button twisted away from Amelia, tearing around the kitchen with a head of steam. To save them all from a collision, Kyle grabbed her under the armpits the next time she charged by, lifting her off the floor.

She dangled in midair, kicking her tennis shoes. "Bad-bad-bad."

"Hey, simmer down." Kyle's tone was beseeching. But it was tough to get stern when he felt so guilty about the books. Button had so many things taken away from her already—Libby, familiar surroundings, playmates. Damn, he should've kept those books. A mother would have realized their importance. Though he could never completely *mother* her himself, he so badly wanted to be the ultimate parent who sensed things in time to avoid mishaps.

Amelia was getting openly agitated with Button's performance, her withered hands shaking. "Do you want to sit in the corner?"

"I never do that," Button sassed back. Still, she did settle down a bit, going slack in Kyle's grip.

Kyle set Button back on her feet, marveling that Amelia had any clout. Despite her gruff delivery, she had yet to follow through on one threat of punishment. How tough these parenting moments were! He and Amelia both seemed like bunglers in the hands of this tiny operator.

"Perhaps together we can tell the story from memory," Amelia proposed.

Kyle was stunned. "You've got to be kidding!"

"Do calm down," Amelia fretted. "The baby's tired, is all."

"Call *that girl,* Daddy. She knows that story."

Kyle leaned a hip into the counter, folded his arms across his chest, and stared up at the old kitchen light fixture. He was fairly certain that Grace had had enough of them for one day. Button had been a bit of a nuisance, stirring up the bigger kids, asking some of Grace's unusual drop-ins personal questions about their haircuts, earrings in odd places, offbeat clothing—and those were just the men.

"I like the library idea best myself," he said.

"Oh, give her a call," Amelia encouraged much to his surprise. "Grace is a nice young woman. She'll understand."

"I guess so." He touched the large phone on the counter near the bread box, skimming the keypad with his fingertips.

Kyle wasn't sure what the mannerly Amelia would make of it, but he wouldn't bother to pretend *not* to know Grace's phone number. He already knew it, her address, an approximation of her vital statistics, and other various trivia collected during his innocent search of her room. White Diamonds perfume was a favorite, as was peppermint toothpaste.

"I do the talkin'," Button proclaimed spunkily.

"Good practice for you," Amelia said with pride. "Bring the phone over here, Kyle. Don't worry, the cord's plenty long."

He sat at the table, placing the black console before him.

Button crawled onto the last vacant chair, rising to her knees.

"Grammy calls the medicine man on the speaker," Button told him.

"I called the pharmacy for my medications," Amelia translated.

Kyle punched in the number. The line opened on the second ring.

"Hello? Gwace?"

"This is her mother," a crisp voice announced. "And you are?"

"Button," she said wispily.

"What? Who?"

"This is Kyle McRaney," he inserted. "Button is my daughter. She wanted to ask Grace about something."

"Oh. *Betsy.* I'm sorry, but Grace is busy at the moment. We're going out tonight. To a pops concert at the Ordway. Perhaps I can help you."

"About Cinderella," Button began.

"Cinderella?" she asked in disbelief.

Button nervously put a finger to her lip. "How'd that story go? About the mommy? About the sisters?"

Ingrid made an exasperated sound. "I'm not sure I recall exactly. She had a fairy godmother, a mean stepmother. She went to the ball and the prince fell for her."

"Fell down?"

"No, child, no." She paused. "Grace does know these things. Better than most, I imagine. Better than she should. Still, we are busy now. Perhaps she can tell you another time."

Button's eyes fell to the table. "Oh."

"Goodbye, then." A dial tone buzzed in final rejection.

Kyle buried his face in his hands as Button dashed out of the room.

"Lighten up, Grace. Once and for all, I didn't do anything wrong."

"As you say, Mother." Grace sat up stiffly in the back seat of her parents' Cadillac luxury car an hour later, staring out the side window as they rolled through the dark streets of downtown St. Paul.

Ingrid kept shifting from the windshield to the back seat, clearly agitated by her daughter's disapproval. "You are deliberately blowing this way out of proportion."

"All I said was that I would've handled Button's call differently."

"You mean I should have done so, don't you?"

She sank her teeth into her neatly painted lip, stifling the obvious. "At least I should've called them back."

"We would've been late."

"A little, maybe—"

"And you were frazzled not an hour after they left," Ingrid pointed out. "You told me so in no uncertain terms."

Grace sighed in regret. She had blown off some steam about Button as she prepared for their evening out, so this was partly her fault. Her mother took everything literally and thought she was only echoing Grace's discontent. But there had been some light moments during the day too, ones she hadn't had a chance to confide to her mother. Button had been so enthralled by Grace's world that she had dropped her guard a fraction to reveal a very charming sweetness. She was so taken by the child actors, so proud of her Cinderella book. Grace wondered what happened to the book, why she'd called about the story. Most of all, she wondered how Button had taken Ingrid's brush-off. She was so…small.

"This issue doesn't deserve this level of attention," Ingrid rattled on. "Kyle McRaney, though very nice, is little more than domestic help. The child is along due to your goodwill. You are entangled enough.''

Black and white. Cut and dried. The rich are different. Grace smiled grimly in the dark tense quiet. It was just this kind of narrow scope that had kept Ingrid from noticing Grace's teenage crush on Kyle. Or, more currently, from even questioning whether Grace was truly serious about Dickie Trainor. Ingrid saw what she pleased, period.

It was Grace's father at the wheel who finally broke the tense silence. ''Tonight's orchestra is supposed to be superb,'' Victor said as he braked for a red light on Robert Street.

''What wonderful seats we have,'' Ingrid enthused. ''Your father bought a block of them in order to include employees of the firm. Won't it be nice to see them?''

''Many of them were at my birthday party,'' Grace objected.

''The rank and file weren't at your party,'' Victor said. ''It's vital that we appear in public as a family on occasion, reinforce that North Enterprises will carry on to your generation.''

Ingrid patted her golden chignon. ''Do try and play the game. Michael does. Look how well things are going for him.''

''On the subject,'' Victor said, ''have you given any more consideration to making a real showing at the firm?''

''Been a while since you've suggested that, Dad.''

''I haven't given up on you yet, dear.''

''But my business isn't failing as you predicted. It's going well.''

''Still believe your creative lean could be funneled into something at the firm.''

A smile twitched her mouth. ''Like what, Dad?''

''I don't know. Yet.'' Despite his exuberance, he looked baffled.

"Maybe we'll just have to settle for a son-in-law and some grandchildren," Ingrid said with anticipation. "There's nothing wrong with being a good wife and mother, either. Pursuing charitable causes, supporting your husband."

They were playing the marriage card, too? Grace wished she'd taken more herbal supplements to bolster her defenses. "I hope to someday mix family and work," she said carefully. "Believe I'll be good at it."

"Does Dickie approve of your business?" Ingrid turned round to ask.

Grace balked at her mother's unusual coyness. "I have no idea. I never ask my dates questions like that."

She inhaled sharply. "Dickie's merely a *date* in your mind?"

"Yes, Mother. We're not exclusive."

Her parents sighed in harmony.

There was a fair-size crowd milling round the Ordway lobby. Grace and her parents joined the formally dressed concert goers, greeting people as they looked for their small party. The elder Norths were a familiar couple around the Twin Cities and Grace always felt some pride as people made a point of singling them out. Someday she hoped to be singled out first and foremost for her own accomplishments in fashion design.

They soon discovered the North entourage, lingering near a sweeping staircase. Grace sized up the group: brother Michael, two men from the firm and their wives.

Michael approached, giving her the once-over. "Looks like you survived your day with the McRaneys."

"Was there doubt?"

He leaned a shoulder into the pillar, a twinkle in his eye. "No offense, but I was driving down the street this morning and spotted him dragging Button up the front walk."

"For your information, Button had a lot of fun."

"Whew!" He wiped his forehead.

Put out, Grace looked away.

"Hey, you want her to like you."

His superior smile made her steam. "I feel responsible for her while she is under my roof. How's that?"

"Not bad," he said more gently, "considering how you cherish your privacy." They shared companionable silence, nodding at acquaintances. "Can I get you anything?"

"Dickie," she murmured with some surprise.

"I'm not that talented," he teased.

"No, I mean he's here, with a very good-looking girl." Michael's interest flared upon that news. "Where?"

Grace didn't move her hands, but described the proper direction. "Two pillars over on the right by the windows."

There stood Dickie in a neat black suit, standing beside a young woman with waist-length brown hair, dressed in a royal blue dress with a flared skirt and scooped back. Michael whistled softly. "She is a looker. No more than twenty-two, I'd say."

"Imagine, a girl younger than me out on a date," she mocked. "Where is her overprotective brother?"

Michael surveyed her curiously. "You don't seem too broken up."

"Not at all. In fact, it gives me a little welcome breathing room."

"Well, the folks are stewing," he reported with some glee.

Grace smiled too. "If Father had a lasso, it would be looping Dickie as we speak."

"And if Mother had a whip," Michael added, "it would be cracking the marble floor at his feet. Hee-haw!"

Grace nailed her parents with a frown. "No wonder they dragged me along, probably knew Dickie was attending. If only they'd back off."

"Spoilsport," Michael groused. "This is getting good."

"Huh?" Grace turned back to Dickie. To her surprise, his companion was heading their way, appearing anxious.

"Grace North?"

"Yes." Grace returned the girl's unsure smile and handshake. "This is my brother, Michael." Michael shook her hand with an admiring once-over.

"Would you mind if I spoke to Grace for a minute? Alone?"

Michael was disappointed, but wandered off.

"My name is Haley Evers." Haley turned slightly so she could catch a glance of Dickie. He was just noticing her desertion. Her smile froze, she spoke rapidly. "I work for Frazer and Dupont with Di—Mr. Trainor."

"You don't owe me any explanation," Grace said kindly. "I don't know what you've heard about Dickie and me, but it's fine if he's brought you here."

"He has, but—"

Dickie caught up with them then, sliding his arm around the waist of each female. "Didn't know you'd be here tonight, Grace."

"It's an accounting firm thing," she said with merry misery. "Dad insisted."

"We're here for a law firm thing. Aren't we, Haley? So, do you two know each other?"

"Haley just wanted to introduce herself," Grace hastened to explain.

Dickie's expression was courtroom inscrutable. "Did she?"

Haley spoke brightly. "Grace designed a Mardi Gras outfit for my sister last year and I wanted to tell her that it won a nice prize in New Orleans."

"Who is your sister?" Grace asked.

"Tiffany Evers. Remember?"

"Oh, yes, the Harlequin costume. How nice to hear about the award!"

Dickie relaxed. "Tiffany is the one who moved to New Orleans then?"

"That's right." Haley managed to worm out of Dickie's grip. "By the way, sir, would you mind if I caught a ride home with some of the girls from the typing pool? They're going out for drinks after the concert."

Dickie beamed at her proudly. "Certainly not. Have fun."

Haley escaped then, leaving Grace with a lingering sense of uncertainty over what the woman truly wanted. Seemed silly to trouble herself, though. Dickie was in a position high enough to make young ladies at his firm a bit uneasy with his very presence.

The elder Norths invited all their guests to a postconcert dinner at Kincaid's, but Grace declined, feeling she'd supported the family unity enough. She would've bummed a ride home with Michael if not for Dickie's staying power. He insisted upon giving her a lift home.

As they sat parked in her town house driveway talking, Grace felt perhaps he was trying to overcompensate for the Haley incident. More than ever, Grace was sure they'd been on a date.

"Let me come in," he coaxed softly against her ear. "I won't stay a long time. Just for a little nibble on your ear and maybe some food from your magic chef's latest dish."

Grace laughed softly. Playfully pushing him back in his bucket seat, she attempted to read his glazed look. Instinct told her he intended to try and take their intimacy to a higher level, something she was unprepared for. She begged off as kindly as possible. "It's a weeknight, Dickie. We both have to work tomorrow." She began to reach around the seat for her handbag. He rested a hand over the passenger side headrest.

"Grace?"

"Yes?" she asked distractedly.

"About Haley…"

"Seems very nice."

"But her behavior usually isn't so odd."

"Does it seem odd that she would praise my work?"

"No. But she isn't normally so tense around me."

Grace stiffened, sensing that he wanted to know if he'd missed something. Though not in the habit of answering to anyone, she hated to see the woman questioned this way later on. "I suppose employees frequently are nervous when out with their superiors. I'm glad she spoke up about the Harlequin costume," she said lightly. "Made my day."

He reached over to stroke her cheek. "Let me make your night."

She'd never thought much about how soft his fingertips were. But having Kyle's rougher hands on her face twice now brought the difference in sensation to her attention. Dickie's touch was pleasant enough, but Kyle managed to cause…static. Their kisses fared about the same in comparison.

"Something the matter?" he asked.

Her expression had undoubtedly fallen, but she couldn't help that. "No, I'm just tired. If you don't mind, I'm going to say good-night."

She raised a quick objection as Dickie made motions to exit the driver's side. "Don't bother to see me to the door."

"But I should. Always do."

"No need." In a fluid motion she exited the car. With a flutter of fingers she passed through his headlight beams reflecting on her garage door, and vanished into her town home's shadowy backyard.

On a night like this it was Grace's habit to lie in her huge luxurious bed, drift off to sleep while reviewing the evening's highs. The pops concert had been heavenly music, and there were several dresses on other concert goers, ranging from poetic to tragic, that she couldn't wait to discuss with Heather at lunch tomorrow.

Still, no matter how hard she tried, Grace couldn't calm down. She tossed and turned between her soft cotton sheets, trying to shake off her feeling of discontent. She hashed through the deal with Haley and Dickie, concluding the situation had ended peacefully enough to close the books on it.

So what was haunting her?

For that answer she had to scroll down further into her day. There she discovered Button's small cherub face stalled in her thoughts. The piteous image stalled, making Grace face a disturbing question: Had Button managed to fall asleep after Ingrid's brush-off?

Darn Ingrid! She'd created this mess without a care or remorse—when a few facts about Cinderella would've settled it. Grace knew firsthand how hurtful her mother's abruptness could be, and in a way it forged a strange kinship between Grace and Button.

Grace cuddled up on her side as a small girl might, stroking Kitty, who had come to enjoy sleeping near her pillows. Michael's taunt about needing Button's approval haunted her. Was it true? Could a child hold an adult hostage that way? Certainly not a wise, clear-thinking person like Grace!

Still, Grace had to set right this wrong. It wasn't a weakness in her, but merely a question of fairness, to a friend's daughter.

What course of action was best?

They'd be back on Wednesday, of course, for Kyle's regular working hours. That wasn't so far away, it was already into the early hours of Tuesday.

But to Button it would no doubt seem a lifetime.

She should act tomorrow. But there was a luncheon date set up with Heather to consider, the kind of date so rare now. Still, there was no alternative. Button had to come first. Then lunch.

That settled, Grace stretched, deposited a dozing Kitty up near the headboard and flipped onto her back. She was soon fast asleep.

Chapter Eight

"Take a right turn here, Grace," Heather directed with a swing of her long tanned arm. "This is Berry Street."

Grace braked, hit the turn signal and guided her silver convertible neatly round the corner. She glanced at her passenger, studiously reading her scribbled directions from a scrap of paper. "Nice of you to take this detour to Golden Valley before our lunch."

"No problem, just adjusted our reservation." Heather's arm swung the other way. "Ashford Lane is coming up. Left turn."

Grace scanned the quiet tree-lined street. "This is getting familiar. I only dropped by the Andersons a couple of times with Michael, but the house is a Cape Cod, on the right hand side, I think."

"I remember you saying Amelia was up on her own roof once," Heather recalled. "That really happen?"

A vivid memory of the scene came into focus. "You know, it did. She was rescuing a neighbor boy's ball. I remember fidgeting on the grass with excitement, shading my eyes with a hand as she climbed a giant metal ladder like a big stocky handyman, hoisting herself over the gutter and onto the shingles. She snatched that ball and flung it through the air with such force that it ended up in a backyard across the street!"

"Guess it's no mystery where Button gets her spunk," Heather declared.

Grace stiffened with apprehension. So concerned about Kyle and Button's reaction to Ingrid's brush-off, she hadn't considered how Amelia would take it. What if Amelia wanted to fling her off the roof, with a gleeful Kyle and Button standing on the grass this time, shielding their eyes from the sun?

"I can't help wondering if this is a good idea after all," she said.

Heather adjusted her sunglasses with a philosophical air. "Well, you certainly wouldn't want to get in the habit of spoiling your mother by cleaning up her small disasters. I can say that as your best friend and the daughter of a similar mother," she inserted hastily. "But your instincts to take action here seem right to me, too."

"But I could make it worse somehow. I have absolutely no connection with Button yet, and am too inexperienced to fix that."

"You and Button are probably in the same sad mood, though. Common ground to start with."

"True."

Heather reached over and squeezed her arm. "Girls rule!"

She couldn't recall in recent memory ever feeling this vulnerable. In fact, it had been a good long while since she moped in her window seat waiting for Kyle to whisk her off for a wedding. That vision was still her most potent Achilles' heel. She gripped the steering wheel harder. "Maybe I'll drive on by, after all. Speak to them tomorrow. They'll be at my place tomorrow."

"Oops, too late. This is a dead end street. Look up there to the right, Grace. That's either Kyle standing on the sidewalk, or just your average neighborhood bronzed god."

Grace was riveted to the sight. Bare-chested, Kyle was

hacking away at the front hedge. Major muscle groups were working overtime beneath tight tanned skin sheened in perspiration. Faded jeans rode low on lean hips. A hint of white elastic peeped up over his belt as he stretched over the hedge to deliver even hacks with his clippers.

Sensual excitement steeped Grace's voice. "I had no idea all that was happening underneath his clothes. In my house."

"Mmm, if that man is carrying several years of bad road on him—as you suggested back at the club—he wears it extremely well."

Grace could think of no adequate comeback for the blatant truth.

Heather whistled softly. "I love Nate to pieces, but he doesn't look like that with his shirt off." She glanced at Grace. "Have some naughty thoughts for the two of us, will you?"

"Get serious."

"At least tell me if you've considered my advice to give him a chance. You are two adults. You are on the lookout for husband material. He's broken in as a husband."

"Gee," she drolled, "that sounds naughty."

Heather was merrily calm. "If there were no sparks flying, you wouldn't be all hot and bothered right now."

"There are sparks," Grace admitted. "But he isn't exactly giving in, either," she pointed out defensively. "I'm sure he's way too preoccupied to even consider a relationship. Even if I...well, wanted a shot."

"Briefs versus boxers," Heather mused appreciatively as she continued to ogle him. "Yes, I would have anticipated that. Even without that hint of proof just above the belt—"

"Heather!"

"I'm merely trying to jump-start your fantasy for you."

Grace's spurt of laughter peeled from the open car. "As if it's all for me—you awful liar!"

Heather tossed her mane of thick blond hair. "I take offense. I'm a mighty good liar."

Kyle noticed Grace's convertible the moment it hit the end of Amelia's elm-lined street. Standing on the sidewalk at the old woman's unkempt hedge gave him a clear view of everything happening on the quiet street.

His heart gave an involuntary lurch. What did she want? Was she so annoyed with Button's phone call that she'd come to complain? It was nothing Ingrid hadn't managed to efficiently field herself in a practiced lady-of-the-manor tone.

The car was moving along slowly, as if scanning addresses. He knew exactly when she'd homed in on him behind her trendy sunglasses. He felt a vague stir in his belly, a bit like a life-size lawn ornament. Not a bad feeling, really, he realized. Kept himself in shape. Never had been uncomfortable with the female once-over, when he was aware of it, anyway. Naturally, sexual chemistry had diminished from his life since Libby's passing. Women might have sent him signals during the subsequent months, but he'd had his antenna shut off.

But Grace was changing all that. Her vitality was a sharp reminder that he was a vital male.

The car pulled up to the curb, Kyle got a good look inside and sucked in a greedy breath.

A pair of wild and wind-tossed babes best described the pair. Grace's shiny auburn curls, Heather's buttery mane, reflected the brilliant sunshine in points of light. Both were dressed in tiny pastel tank tops that outlined their high plump breasts. A surreptitious glance into the car revealed short white shorts on endless length of leg.

It was a scene right out of a MTV video.

Freedom was a word that sprang to his mind. Those adolescent summers when it was the job, the beach and the girls. If only he could steal back to those days, just for a single day. *With a grown-up Grace right beside him.*

Kyle forced such an impossible fantasy right out of his mind. Instead he concentrated on the effect they were having on the neighborhood. A flashy BMW convertible had to be a rare sight in this predominantly senior neighborhood. Lace curtains were twitching on a few front windows. Old Mr. Carlisle halted his daily stroll to inspect a sagging lilac bush just across the way. And Mr. Winkler, presently next door marching round his grass with a weed killer wand, nearly injected his foot with a needle full of poison.

With forced calm, Kyle spoke up. "Hey, ladies."

"Hey, yourself," Heather crooned, her face alive with mischief.

"How are you Grace?" he asked on a cracked note.

"Fine," she said softly. Their gaze locked with uncertainty. This was going to be every bit as tough as she'd anticipated. With her luck Amelia would swoop out into the yard with a rolling pin. "I ah… Are you alone?"

He wiped his forehead with the back of his hand. "Amelia's got bridge on Tuesdays. Has her time pretty well organized. Button and I are trying not to tamper with that."

"That's nice," Heather said brightly.

Grace winced as Heather gave her hip a nudge. Ever so reluctantly she opened the driver's door, stepped onto the street and moved round the front of the car. Even Heather's dark-lensed stare wasn't enough to will her off the road, however. She halted in the shade of a large elm.

"Button's inside getting me a glass of lemonade," he blurted out.

"She can do that by herself?" Heather marveled.

"Yeah. She's pretty capable."

"So I hear. Grace has been singing her praises."

Kyle's flinch of disbelief hurt Grace. She hadn't been

mean to Button, her mother had. This opening seemed as good as any to bring up that fact.

"Kyle, as you've probably guessed, I came to apologize for Ingrid's behavior on the phone last night."

Kyle balked. Second-guess Gracie North? Not in a million years! Trying to recover, he said, "There's no need."

"Of course there is," she scoffed gently. "You should see your expression."

He moved over to join her in the street, jabbing the clippers into the lawn. "Okay. Ingrid did upset Button."

"I am so very sorry," she gushed, emotion charging her words. "Button already dislikes me, then to have this happen..."

"Button doesn't dislike you. She's just trying to adjust to having you in our lives." He rubbed the back of his neck, looking rather sheepish. "Doesn't like to share me with anyone."

"Who can blame her?" Grace blurted out. Blushing hotly, she added, "I mean, you are her everything."

"I am teaching her how to share, though. Don't want a pampered princess on my hands."

She ripped the glasses off her face to confront him with emerald chips. "Hey, what does it mean when you call *me* a princess?"

His mouth twitched suspiciously. "It's just an observation. Up to interpretation."

"Well, look out for princess power!" She reacted with a swing to his bare chest. Flesh connected with a sound smack, startling them both. Grace couldn't resist moving her palm over his smooth moist skin covered with deliciously crisp hair. His heart was thudding crazily beneath her touch.

Their eyes locked for a brief knowing moment. She snatched her hand back in a nervous gesture.

"I do happen to like being pampered on occasion," she announced. "But today, I'm in a sharing mood."

Was she? Kyle folded his arms, rested his shoulder against the trunk of the tree, assessing her. Despite Grace's privileged existence, she had an enduring innocence. It occurred to him that she still wanted to be liked—presently by him of all people. Nervous, even awkward, under his scrutiny, she seemed to have no idea how truly beautiful she'd grown up to be.

She patted her tote bag with the hand still tingling from the feel of his skin. "I brought Button a book, about Cinderella."

"No way!"

Grace gasped. "Every time I speak you look like you've been zapped with a stun gun!"

As he fumbled for a comeback, his daughter diverted their attention.

"Hey, Daddy!" Button eased through the screen door, balancing a paper cup full of yellow liquid in her hands.

"Careful, Button. Take the steps slowly."

"Com-i-ing." Once she hit the grass, she broke into a run, holding a hand over the top of the glass which bounced wildly with every footfall.

"Lemonade." Button handed him the glass and licked her hand. "Mmm, good."

"Thanks, honey." Kyle downed the liquid in just three gulps.

Button tipped her face up to study Grace like a bug on the wall. "What's *that girl* doing here?"

"Grace came to see you. She feels bad about what her mommy said."

Button sidestepped the couple and moved to the convertible. She extended a finger at Heather. "Are you the mommy?"

Heather gasped, a trifle put out. "No way, shrimp. I'm Grace's age. Exactly."

Kyle leaned over Button, gesturing to the women. "This is Heather, Button. She and Grace are twenty-four."

Button put her hands on her hips with a gasp. "Her mommy's older than *that?*"

"Let's change the subject," Kyle said, handing Button his empty cup. "How about we serve some lemonade to everyone?"

She screwed up her round face in fake concern. "Sorry, we don't got 'nough."

"Oh, yes we do. It's nice to share, remember?" Hesitantly, Kyle turned to Grace. "Want to come inside?"

"We'd love to," Heather inserted smartly, swinging open the passenger door.

Kyle tugged his clippers out of the dirt and led them to the house. Setting the sharp tool near the stoop, he ushered them through the front door and into the living room.

"I'll just wash my hands," Kyle said, making for the hallway. "Be right back."

Grace and Heather strolled round the gold carpeting. The house was quiet and cool. Old dark furniture dominated the small space, a rocker, rust velvet sofa set, a plaid chair, an end table and coffee table.

It was very much like Grace remembered. Though there was a new photo collage on the plaster wall. She sidled up for a closer look. Young energetic versions of the Andersons at work and play smiled back at her. There were many of Libby at different stages of her life as well: a childish beanpole on a two-wheeler, a fixture in the high school choir, two prom pictures with different boys. There were even a few college snaps, a campus rally, graduation. Though Kyle was in Libby's life by then, his presence was nowhere to be seen. Understandable, as those were the days when Kyle had been an outlaw to the Andersons. Grace marveled at his strength, the way he was facing the past and present all at once in this house, somehow managing to put past slights into perspective and reap the best of things.

"Mementos from the bistro's office," Kyle murmured in her ear suddenly. He had moved up close to discover Grace in a pensive state, inhaling light fragrant cologne.

Grace glanced back at him then to discover he'd slipped into a light plaid shirt. It was cotton and ironed rather clumsily. Professional assessment aside, she found the effect endearing. "I suppose Amelia misses the old days," she ventured.

"That's an understatement."

The huskiness in his voice squeezed her heart. Suddenly his tight spot—losing Libby prematurely, faced with the Andersons' past, a place he had never been welcome—seemed overwhelmingly real and close to her.

Why, even if Amelia wished she could add him to the memory collage, she presumably would have no old photo to do so.

Rocked with emotion over his troubles, his unwitting rejection, Grace moved a few paces away from the memories and lifted a gilded frame from an end table. "This likeness of Button is nice. Looks recent."

Kyle cleared his throat. "Yes. Professional photo studio. Last week."

She nodded in approval. "Ah, a new memory base for you."

"Yeah, so it is."

She tsked in mild reproof. "You should be in the picture with her."

He shrugged, self-conscious. "Next time, maybe."

Heather tapped him on the arm. "Hey, I bet you're real photogenic."

Kyle laughed. Women. Teasing *him*. After all these years, it was just as much fun.

Feeling Button suddenly clamped to his middle, Kyle ruffled her shiny black hair. "Let's have that lemonade."

They trailed through the dining room into the kitchen. Kyle reached into a painted white cupboard for some tall plastic cups.

"Olive green appliances," Heather marveled, touching the stove like a prized museum piece. "Do they still run efficiently?"

Kyle felt a bit defensive. "Why wouldn't they?"

"They have to be thirty years old!"

"Twenty-five," he corrected evenly. "I know because I just repaired the fridge."

Heather winked. "You are the handyman, aren't you?"

Button was busy at the table, kneeling on a chair, splashing lemonade into glasses from a small plastic jug. "My daddy can do everything."

"I believe it." Heather playfully snatched a glass out of the lemony puddle.

Button gasped. "Don't drippy on Great Grammy's floor."

Kyle stepped up to swab the table with a sponge. Grace discovered a napkin holder and passed out napkins. Silently, they sipped their drinks.

"You made this from scratch, didn't you?" Grace noted.

He raised his palms and wiggled his fingers. "With these."

Visions of his strong hands curled around lemons made Grace a little light-headed. Leaning back against the counter, she imagined those hands clamping her breasts, giving a gentle squeeze to her flesh, running down the length of her naked body.

It took a good deal of willpower to dismiss that powerful image. She had to focus on her mission. She reached for her tote bag and produced a large elaborate picture book. "Button, this is for you."

Button screamed gleefully and slid off the chair. Dancing on her toes, she asked, "For me?"

Grace nodded, handing over the book. Button took it in her small hands. Scanning the cover, her mouth widened to an *O*.

Kyle surveyed Grace, clutching her tote, looking exceptionally pleased with herself. Whether she knew it or not, Button's approval meant something to her. Didn't take long for a child to get under one's skin. He felt some pride and joy that his daughter could have this kind of impact on the charming princess Grace.

"Shall we read it?" Grace asked.

"I save it for beddy-bye," Button declared. "For Great Grammy."

"Oh." Grace forced a smile.

Kyle was sorry to see Grace's hurt, but he was delighted that Button would be so insightful concerning Amelia. If she hadn't said something, he would have had to himself. "Why don't you put it on your nightstand, honey?" he suggested.

"Okay, Daddy."

"I'd like to see your room, Button," Heather announced excitedly.

"Why?"

"For fun!"

Catching her father's encouraging nod, Button beckoned at Heather. They exited the room, their voice's echoing in the hallway.

"Gracie, I'm sorry about that...." Kyle gestured helplessly. "It's just that Amelia reads to Button every night some old battered book of nursery rhymes. It's a bond they share."

"I'm totally fine with it. Really."

She wasn't of course. Grace always got her own way. Oddly, she seemed embarrassed now. An unfair result. He shoved his hands in the pockets of his jeans, selecting what he hoped were the right words. "It was great of you to come over this way. After all, we'll be back at your place tomorrow. Your apology and gift could've waited till then."

"I doubt Button has much of a concept for time. One night without Cinderella seemed the limit."

"That is so true. You got it just right."

She hugged her tote closer, intensely relieved. "Was no trouble at all. It's a book from my collection. I have all kinds, use them for reference when I'm designing."

He assessed her curiously. "You are serious about your business, aren't you?"

"Naturally! Is that a surprise?"

"Thought it might be a hobby. It's not as though you need to work."

"I wouldn't be satisfied not working at all," she shot back. "I am doing the work I love. Though, must admit it seems more like play to me. But don't get me wrong. It's very successful! I'm making my way quite nicely." She broke off, feeling like a babbling fool.

"Well, congratulations." He knocked his cup against hers and drank some lemonade. "So, you do a lot of small plays like this one with Mitzi?"

"A few a year."

"I'm surprised that they're profitable," he mused half to himself.

"I donate my services to community projects like that one," she said defensively. "Sometimes time and effort are far more important than money, you know."

"*I* know."

"But?"

He faltered, feeling trapped. "You do seem addicted to a life of stuff."

Her artfully shaped brows narrowed. He had complained that her kitchen was a barren wasteland. "Like what kind of stuff?"

"Well, shoes, dresses, movie screen, television—"

She gasped. "How do you know that?"

Curse his big mouth, his superior take on a sensible lifestyle. He was trapped now. "I was searching for Button yesterday," he faltered.

"In my room?"

"Everyplace. I panicked." He shook a finger at her. "And you took her upstairs, don't forget. Without a word to me."

"She followed us, Kyle! Snuck upstairs." She paced back and forth. "I can't believe you went into my room— into my closet!"

"Button likes closets, so I thought maybe she—" He broke off awkwardly.

She was absolutely steaming. He had crossed the line of privacy, inspected her most personal possessions without permission. "You are the limit!"

"It was only a matter of seconds. I dashed in and out."

She rolled her eyes. "Not with the inventory you took."

He waved in surrender. "Okay, I couldn't help gawking for a minute."

"My personal space is not a sideshow!"

"No, it's more like a Broadway show—with all the props."

"Your snooping is not funny. And not fair."

"How can I make it up to you?"

"You can't!"

He thought for a moment, mouth quirking slyly. "Tell you what, I'll show you my bedroom in return."

"Excuse me?" She started, jerking her auburn head back like a skittish thoroughbred.

Kyle reared in mock amazement. "Wouldn't that even things up?"

Grace was stunned. He was using humor to brush this off? Bedroom humor? How quickly he could make her feel like an awkward adolescent again. How easily he diminished the bonding she'd been working for.

She leveled him with a gaze that would have electrocuted a lesser man. "Thanks for the tempting invitation. Another time, maybe." She marched to the hallway. "Heather!"

"Grace," he called after her. "You can't be mad."

"Oh, yes I can. Heather! We're leaving."

Heather's blond mane swung forward as she peered out the far doorway. "Come take a look at Button's bedroom first," she urged.

"Well, it's always nice to be *invited*," she said with a hint of sarcasm.

The room proved to be about the size of Grace's walk-in closet. Button was standing in the center, expectantly. She clapped her small hands together. In tour guide demeanor she strolled by her low dresser, touching a brush, comb, piggy bank and her new book. Then she passed on by a laundry basket full of plastic toys to a closet holding several tiny outfits and stacked boxes. "My mommy's stuff is in the boxes," she announced proudly. "Stuff for big girls."

Still in a jovial mood, Button bounced onto the futon against the back wall. "This is really a bed," she squeaked. "Folds out flat." She shook her head, shiny black hair swinging. "No jumping. Ever never. And this is my kitty lamp." She leaned over her nightstand. Small fingers reached under the shade adorned with kittens and clicked the single bulb on and off. "See?"

"Very nice," Grace enthused.

"I think Kitty would like to live here," Button suggested coyly.

Kyle appeared in the doorway suddenly, looking a bit pressurized, Grace thought with some satisfaction. "Now, honey, you know that Grace's kitty belongs with her. And," he quickly added, "Grandma has an allergy to pet hair."

"Pet dander," Button supplied in succinct explanation, puffing hard enough to lift her bangs.

"She doesn't understand about allergies yet," Kyle explained to no one in particular.

"We all have lots to learn," Grace couldn't resist retorting. She wondered if Kyle would respond, but he said nothing, just leaned against the doorjamb with a tight look. "Well, we'll be going. Enjoy the book, Button."

"Thank you," she piped up.

With chin high Grace wheeled for the doorway, which Kyle stumbled to vacate.

Chapter Nine

"So, Michael, what do you think?"

Michael paced across Grace's upstairs studio with a frantic glance to his watch. "I said the thread match was good enough. Just sew, Gracie!"

Grace, seated in a comfortable chair under a tree lamp, her brother's dress shirt in her lap, sent him a glare. "I am not talking about stitching this ripped cuff. I'm talking about my run-in with Kyle."

"Please," he beseeched, "I have a date with a real sweetheart tonight. It's our first. I don't want to be late."

"I'm doing the best I can. Now tell me, did I overreact this afternoon?"

"Of course you did. Over an eyebrow wiggle and a little bedroom humor." Clearly, he disapproved.

She pinched the button to the cuff with force, darting a threaded needle in and out of the torn seam. "It's just that a woman doesn't like any man snooping in her bedroom without permission."

"I'll remember that. If I ever have a date of my own."

"Now if he's invited, that's a different situation...."

"I'll remember that, too."

She didn't even notice his patronizing tone. "He shouldn't have mocked my complaint."

"Grace, he was probably sorry and hoped to joke his way out of it."

"Maybe," she relented pensively. "Sometimes men blurt out the worst thing when they're uncomfortable."

He glared as her fingers stilled. "Don't slow down now."

She picked up the pace, though still thoughtful. "Wonder if I should call. Apologize."

"Give the guy some breathing space. He's got so much to concentrate on. I found out today the plumbing work isn't going as well as planned. The city inspector had unexpected complaints...." He trailed off in disgust. "You aren't Kyle's only concern."

She rocked back in her chair. "He isn't my only concern, either!"

"You act like he is."

"What if I don't call and he decides not to come back? You wouldn't like that, would you?"

"He'll come. He took payment in full. He's stuck."

"Stuck!"

"Yeah, stuck."

She rocked forward and held up his shirt by the collar, as one might grip a hostage by the neck. "I could sew up your armpits with a few quick stitches."

He jumped to his feet, his confidence shaken. "No, Gracie, don't even think it. That shirt is a custom number from London, means more to me than a bottle of '83 Cabernet Sauvignon."

"Then don't be so impossible."

Noting that the kitten was winding in and out of his legs for attention, Michael picked her up and began stroking her creamy long hair. "You got a name for her yet?"

"It may as well be Kitty, officially," Grace mumbled.

His eyes twinkled. "Button's doing all right. She's

named your kitten, has you dashing over to Amelia's to make up for Mother's snub.''

"We're surviving in the same orbit, I guess." She shook her curly auburn head. "I only hope Mother will be more patient with her own grandchildren—if and when the time comes."

"They say even the frostiest people melt for their own grandchildren."

"We'll just see." Grace reached for the tiny scissors in the supply box beside her and snipped thread around the button. "There you are. Good as new."

"Thanks."

"I like to get you out of a pinch when I can."

"Same here." Michael sobered. "In return I'll give you some advice, simmer down about Kyle."

"But I'm not—"

"You are! Whatever you intended to deny, you are doing it, feeling it, or anticipating it." He smiled wanly in the face of her glower. "It's only my opinion, but I figure Kyle will always see you as the cute little tagalong. If you'd accept this fact, you wouldn't get so—so overheated."

Grace sniffed. He was right about one thing. It was only his opinion. There was something building between Kyle and herself. Something...hot. She bristled as she realized he was trying to read her mind, determine whether his advice had any impact. "Oh, take your shirt and go!"

"Sure. But, uh…" he trailed off with a charming smile.

"Is there anything else, brother? A pint of blood? A pedicure?"

He nuzzled the kitten. "Could you…you know…iron it for me?"

She rose from her chair, waving the shirt like a menacing banner. "If you don't find a wife pretty soon…"

"You'll find one for me?" he finished hopefully.

"Better. Next birthday, I'll hire *you* a keeper, too."

BACK IN AMELIA'S Golden Valley home, Kyle was thinking of Grace. Amelia's rhythmic reading and Button's chirps had drawn him from a kitchen table cluttered with paperwork to Button's bedroom, where he'd paused to spy on great-grandmother and child. He'd intended to join them, but then thought better of it. Plainly, he would be disturbing a "girls only" moment.

The picture of them seated together on the upright futon engrossed in Cinderella's escapades brought a lump to Kyle's throat. Amelia had the book and half of an awestruck Button draped over her lap, and was patiently reading text and fielding questions with flushed excitement.

What a precious moment in time.

All because of Grace, who'd dropped everything to deliver the perfect gift. Marvelous, sensitive, impetuous Grace.

Or so she'd been until this afternoon's visit was nearly over. An up-to-the-minute forecast would better describe her as a restive, annoyed, impossible Grace.

Kyle rested a shoulder against the door frame in the hallway, rubbing at the worry creases in his forehead. How could he have so carelessly offered to show her his bedroom? Because that's where he wanted her most?

Without doubt, the very concept of an adult Grace crowding his space was proving disconcerting to his system. Like it or not, the sexual tension had been there since the moment she'd discovered him in her kitchen. Their eyes had locked and wham!

The way she'd watched him chop that onion. No onion in memory ever had it so good.

How naive of him to expect her to remain frozen in time, the same gangly teen full of crazy ideas and sass.

Well, in any case, she was no longer the least bit gangly.

Kyle had been working hard not to agonize over Libby as much, not to review their marriage, count up the mistakes and letdowns he felt responsible for. It was over. She was gone.

As he thought of Grace as a partner, he couldn't help but draw comparisons to his late wife, however. It had to be a natural step for any widower looking into his future.

Amazingly, he could not strike a single chord they shared. Libby was never bubbly, never off guard, never exuberant. She existed on an even keel with rare flashes of mood swing. For the average male who had trouble digesting the dramatic, this wasn't necessarily bad.

Grace, on the other hand, was not one for bottling things inside. She would bust open with champagne cork force if she ever tried such a thing. This, too, wasn't necessarily bad. Just different. And Button had these kinds of tendencies. He had better get used to them.

"Hey, Daddy!"

"Hi." Self-conscious, Kyle sidled into the room. "Didn't want to disturb you two."

"You can 'sturb us."

"What did the plumber say about the inspector's complaints regarding the bistro?" Amelia asked.

"Mainly, that his bill was going to be a whole lot more."

"You do think you are capable of undertaking this project, don't you? You are new to this sort of responsibility."

But he wasn't. Years in restaurant management prepared him very well for this step. Gazing into her pale doubtful eyes, he felt like a young reject all over again.

To think he had been reconsidering Grace's advice about confronting Amelia about Jerome Anderson's allegations, had hoped to try it tonight. Under Amelia's puckered frown, however, he dismissed the notion. No telling how negative she might become.

Grace's suggestion to have a look at the police report would be a decent start, though. Maybe the thief had hung on to that agreement. Unlikely, but possible. How he wished to discuss it with her! But he'd acted like a fool, teasing her mercilessly with bedroom humor. She did tend to steam over things for hours. If he called now, she just might fire his ass on the spot.

Button's chirp ultimately broke into his thoughts. "Come see my book, Daddy."

He sank down onto the futon, wedging Button between Amelia and himself. Allowing Amelia's flawed assessment of him to spoil moments like this would be wasteful, a repeat of the same old mistakes. Running a long arm along the steel frame of the seat, he concentrated on the lush illustrated pages. On one side Cinderella was dressed in a tattered dress, on the other she wore a dazzling gown.

Button moved a finger over the pages. "See, first she's messy, then she's pretty."

"A real improvement," he agreed.

"This book is certainly worth a lot of money," Amelia noted. She gazed at Kyle over Button's head, apparently clueless that she had even offended him. "You don't think it's a loan, do you?"

"Definitely not," Kyle hastily assured. "It's a gift."

Amelia relaxed. "How nice of Grace. How very nice."

At the mention of Grace, Button's chin lifted. "Wonder what Kitty's doing? Let's call Kitty on the phone."

Kyle groaned. "No way."

Button balled her small hands. "Want to!"

"You'll see Grace and her kitten tomorrow," Amelia consoled.

"And those kids," Button persisted, tapping her dad's arm.

"The kids there for the costumes? I doubt they'll be there, Button."

"Sure they will. They like me."

He sighed. "Maybe Grace can better explain things." If she lets us back inside, that is.

GRACE GREETED FATHER AND daughter Wednesday morning with a wide-open door. "Come on in."

Kyle managed a guarded smile as he ushered Button inside. Grace actually seemed all right. Cheery even. Balancing two grocery bags in his arms, he said, "I know we're late. There was a long line at the store."

"I wanted candy," Button reported indignantly. "Still want candy."

Grace led the way to the kitchen, speaking airily. "Next time buy her a candy bar and put it on my tab."

Kyle shoved the bags onto a countertop, quick to retort. "It isn't the money. Button has plenty of sweets as it is. If I bought the candy this early, she'd nag me for it all morning long."

Her mouth gaped open as the simplistic logic set in. "Oh. We wouldn't have dared nag, so that angle didn't occur to me."

"I want Button to express herself honestly, but only to a point. When I can outfox her on these little things, I do."

Grace lowered her brown lashes solemnly. "Understood."

Kyle couldn't help feeling the discussion had a family feel to it, the kind he missed out on being a widower. But this was princess Grace, young sexy cyclone, pampered beyond belief, who at one time couldn't see beyond her own immediate needs. He shook his head to clear the feeling.

Placing a hand on the edge of the sink, he stared at the ceiling. "Look, Grace, I want to apologize for spoiling your apology yesterday. I felt funny in your bedroom and knew on some level that it was an invasion. It was stupid to try and tease my way out of it."

"I'm sorry, too," she mumbled. "Button can get away pretty easily I'm sure. You would have to search for her, of course."

"Won't happen again. I've told her she must stay put—

here or in the living room. She has her own toys to play with."

"Truce then?"

"Absolutely."

Grace couldn't help but note how relieved he was. Because he cared for her? Or because as Michael said, he was *stuck,* having been paid in full. Probably was a combination of both reasons. Feeling they weren't doing half-bad, she moved back to the living room. Button had dumped her knapsack of toys on the carpet and was crawling around, spreading out plastic dishes on her patchwork quilt.

"A tea party?" Grace asked.

The shiny black head bobbed. "For the kiddies."

"For Kitty," Grace clarified.

"No, those kids. When they coming?"

"They don't come every day," she said evenly.

Button stared up with a pushed-out lip. "Why?"

"Well, because they have other things to do. And so do I."

"I want them."

"They won't be back until I've worked on their costumes."

"Hurry up."

"I will do my best." Grace moved briskly to a chair where a lightweight linen blazer and her work tote lay.

"Pwomise?"

Grace shrugged. "Well, sure."

"Going someplace?" Kyle asked.

She began to rifle through her tote, checking its contents. "Yes, I have an appointment in St. Paul—North Oaks to be exact. A mother-of-the-bride dress."

"You refer to your clients by their orders?"

"Frequently." She eased into the white jacket, which Kyle noted matched her square neck sheath dress. The effect was nothing short of stunning.

Grace was startled to feel his gaze burning straight through her. "Anything the matter? Spot on my dress?"

"Uh, no," he fumbled. *You're gorgeous. Perfect. Too damn irresistible.*

"You sure I look okay?"

"That outfit just doesn't seem like your usual work clothes," he said lamely.

She glanced in the foyer mirror, using fingers to fluff her hair into puffy curls. "You're right. This is a preliminary meeting, which is different. I dress up in one of my own creations to sell myself."

"What's this first meeting entail?"

"I will make some dress sketches in my pad, discuss different options for sleeves and collars and other details. Once that is settled, I will suggest fabrics which suit the chosen style best. I take notes on everything, then come back here and figure out how much the job will cost me, when I can deliver. Then I call the client with an estimate. When I'm lucky we seal the deal with a down payment. Then I go out and buy—"

"Diamonds?"

Her eyes narrowed. "Usually just some ice cream."

"Ice cream?" Button piped up. "I like that."

Grace smiled upon Button, behaving good as gold on her quilt. "Then we shall have some. Today."

"After lunch," Kyle suggested. "If you plan to be here for lunch."

"I should be. For now, though, I really have to go." Slipping into some red heels, she moved for the kitchen. "By the way, Button, don't touch any of my glass things on the tables—or use them for your party."

"Don't worry," she said blithely. "Dere ugly."

Kyle sighed apologetically. "Out of the mouths of babes." To his delight, Grace was laughing as she whisked out the back door.

Kyle set up Button's cassette player with one of her favorite nursery song tapes then retreated to the kitchen. He couldn't help humming a tune of his own as he set about preparing his beef burgundy. All seemed mended. Grace had offered them a clean slate. He could barely believe it. She'd been so angry yesterday.

What a roller coaster ride she was. And to his own amazement, he was responding to her every dip and curve with uncharacteristic emotion. He'd shut himself down so completely after Libby. It was unreal that tagalong Grace possessed the power to dig under his skin.

Today, in this moment in time, life was easy and glorious.

Kyle was not surprised later on when the doorbell rang.

He was already a quick study on fielding artist types and delivery people on Grace's doorstep. With swift movements he wiped his hands on a towel at the sink, gave his simmering pot a stir with a wooden spoon, then moved to the back door.

To his surprise the caller was a businessman. He stared at Kyle hovering behind the screen. "Hello. I'm looking for Grace."

"She isn't in. Care to leave a message?"

"I'm Dickie Trainor." Kyle was taken aback as the slender, slighter blonde opened the door to step inside. "Kyle McRaney, isn't it?"

"Yes."

Distracted by the flame under the burner, Dickie moved over to the stove. "What's cooking today?"

"Beef burgundy over rice."

Clasping his slender white hands reverently, Dickie turned to Kyle. "This service you provide is an absolute godsend."

"You think so?"

"Know so. Grace is a horror in the kitchen. Not only

can't she cook, she can't even stock up on food properly."
Dickie cracked open the oven door and took a deep whiff
of the simmering casserole dish. "This looks absolutely
delicious. I can smell the fresh-ground peppercorns.
Mmm."

"Thank you."

Dickie was too self-absorbed to sense Kyle's wariness.
"Surely Grace has mentioned me."

"No, can't say she has."

Dickie was thrown for a moment. "But I thought... Are
you sure?"

"Positive. Though your last name sounds familiar. We
know each other in the old days?"

"Uh, not really." Dickie was thrown for a moment, but
recovered. "No, I thought perhaps Grace had discussed my
offer to you."

Button dashed into the room then, her boom box in her
arms. "I need a wind-up, Daddy!" She halted at the sight
of Dickie Trainor.

"Button, this is Mr. Trainor. A friend of Grace's." Button's withering look made Trainor blanch a little. Kyle was
half ashamed—of his own glee. Seemed the hotshot wasn't
an instant hit with all females. "You don't need another
rewind yet," he told his daughter. "We'll just turn the tape
over and play the other side." He took the boom box in
hand and made the adjustment.

Dickie Trainor regarded her as one might an ant. "I've
heard of you."

Button extended her lower lip. "Don't know 'bout you."

"Here you go, honey," Kyle said.

With a sniff and a whirl, Button retreated with her boom
box.

"She's touchy."

Kyle smiled thinly. "She's only three."

"Don't know much about children, I'm afraid. Now about my offer, McRaney—"

"I'm not taking any more chef work," Kyle said bluntly.

"No, no, I want to buy in on your bistro deal."

Kyle was shocked. "That would be impossible."

"It might seem so, with your current hassle over ownership. But—"

"What do you know about my business?"

Obviously sensing menace, Dickie worked the knot of his tie. "Only what Grace and Nate Basset told me. We were at the club, playing doubles you see…"

Kyle's mind clicked into gear. Dickie Trainor had been at hand when Nate spilled his guts about Jerome Anderson nosing around at the real estate office? He burned as he imagined Nate and Heather, Grace and Trainor discussing his affairs. "You another real estate agent?"

"No, an attorney at law. The Norths can vouch for me. My family has been friends of the Norths for over thirty years."

"Oh."

"I barely know Nate Basset, if that's bothering you."

Kyle only cared how well Dickie knew Grace. Quite well apparently.

Dickie wandered back to the stove, a covetous eye on the kettle full of rice. "I hoped to lunch with Grace. She expected back soon?"

"Really couldn't say."

"She would want me to help myself."

The possibility existed. Trainor gave every indication that he had a place round here above Kyle's hired help status. Kyle probably had no right to turn him out with his head stuffed in his fancy shirt and his shoelaces tied together. No, that would be too rude. Kyle cleared his throat, straining to disguise his temper. "Feel free to have some lunch."

As Kyle feared, Dickie knew the kitchen layout. Without hesitation he reached into the drawer that had once held Grace's utensils. He was dumbfounded to discover some neatly folded dish towels instead.

"Try the drawer underneath the cupboard holding the plates," Kyle instructed.

"Interesting placement, I guess."

"It makes better sense, having the utensils near the stove and the dishes."

"I'm not sure I agree." Dickie went about the task of getting a plate and scooping it high with rice and beef burgundy. "Still, you are the expert."

Dickie's excitement over the meal was lost on Kyle, who was feeling sharply put-out by his mere existence. Grace hadn't uttered a word about a boyfriend, or even a tennis partner. On top of which Kyle had come to think of this kitchen as his territory, set up the way he liked it, beyond alternation.

But all these complaints paled in the face of one concern, that Dickie Trainor, attorney at law, was welcome in that precious bedroom of hers.

He squeezed his eyes shut against an image of Grace in Trainor's wiry arms. Damn, it was none of his business. And this lack of self-control was not like him. But he was being sorely tested.

Dickie had seated himself at the table and was eating. "Mmm. This is every bit as good as Grace's birthday cake. You are the king of kings!"

Grace had shared her cake with *him?* After that intimate time they'd shared over the same cake?

Kyle felt as though he'd been slapped.

It took some rigorous pot scrubbing, cleaning and knife sharpening, but Kyle managed to work some of his anger through. Who'd have guessed he'd ever be this wound-up over Grace? Why, if he were looking for a new relation-

ship, she would be…*his first and only choice*. But the very
idea of encouraging her would cause a lot of trouble. For
starters, her parents would be distraught. And upsetting another set of guardians was unthinkable.

Besides, Grace could do better than a broken-down widower with a child. But Dickie Trainor was no match for
her either! he decided with a flare of temper.

So what was worse? Trying for Grace, or watching this
ding dong do it? He'd have to think that through very carefully.

It was another trying thirty minutes before Grace appeared at her own back door. "Oh! Dickie!"

"Hi, Grace." Dickie jumped up from his seat at the table
and tried to aim for a kiss. Grace made sure he got a lip
full of cheek.

Grace was breathless, disconcerted. "I wasn't expecting
you."

"Came in surprise. Ended up having a little lunch. To
the strains of…" Richard glanced at Kyle for verification.

"Sesame Street Live," he replied.

"Grace is more of a Sheryl Crow fan."

Kyle affected mock interest. "Is she?"

Both men stared at her for some kind of ruling. Grace
knew without a doubt that Dickie was the odd man out
here. Their relationship hadn't reached the impromptu visit
stage—especially to this degree. Dickie was making himself too at home, intruding in Kyle's routine. Only she had
the right to do that.

"I am very busy today, Dickie," she said. "You
should've called ahead."

Kyle couldn't help beaming in triumph. Dickie appeared
unfazed. "No matter, I've finished eating."

"Sit down, Gracie," Kyle suggested. "We'll eat now."

"All right." Finding Dickie standing straight in her path

to the table, she felt compelled to invite him for a last cup of coffee. "And what about Button?" she asked Kyle.

"She had cheese and crackers an hour ago. Fell asleep on her quilt in the living room."

"Then perhaps we could turn off that infernal noise," Dickie fussed.

"It helps her sleep."

Grace didn't care much for the high-pitched singsong either. "Perhaps we could turn it down just a bit," she suggested lightly.

"Sure. No problem." Kyle strode out of the kitchen. His subsequent gasp brought Grace—and Dickie—scurrying along.

The quilt was empty. Button was missing.

"Button!" Kyle called out.

"Kyle, check upstairs," Grace said. "I'll search down here."

Kyle hesitated, but only for a moment.

Grace found her bedroom door suspiciously ajar. Grace swung it open wide and marched inside. "Button?" The light was on in her walk-in closet. A look inside revealed Button, dressed in her clothing, sitting cross-legged in a heap of shoes and stockings and hats, babbling to Kitty, who was presently curled up on a heap of lingerie.

She stared up at the pair, her round face aglow. "Hey, Gwace. You get that ice cream?"

Chapter Ten

"Come out of that closet right now!" Grace commanded with the crook of her finger. Button meekly obeyed, lifting the hem of Grace's dress, slogging along in Grace's pumps. It occurred to a dazed Grace that the shoes and dress were a frightful clash of color, a dire fashion emergency.

Dickie rushed into the bedroom. "Hey!" he shouted, "kid!"

With a squeak of dismay Button ducked behind Grace.

"She's wearing my pearls!"

Grace felt Button's arms curl around her calves, saw the child's head pop through between her knees. Sure enough Grace's birthday necklace was dangling from Button's neck. "I thought they were my pearls, Dickie."

"They are, but—but—look!"

Button peered at him with huge eyes. "It's a yucky monster!"

"I am not!" he sputtered. "You are the one making trouble, messing with someone else's property."

When Grace didn't respond, his voice rose to a squeak. "Are you going to just stand there like a zombie?"

For the moment, yes. In fact, she felt a lot like Dickie looked, stricken, annoyed. But she didn't intend to act like Dickie. His outburst seemed overdone, an embarrassment.

Freaking out would solve nothing. And it gave her a small lift to realize that Button trusted her enough to protect her.

"Button is only a child," she said at last. "We have to show patience."

"But to allow her access to your possessions, the run of your house. Why, *I* don't even get to come in here!"

Kyle braked in the doorway just in time to catch Dickie's lament. He inhaled the scent of perfume, disgustingly happy to learn that Dickie hadn't made himself at home in here either. He shouldn't let it matter, as it was none of his business. But controlling his emotions for Grace was getting tougher and tougher.

"The pearls are fine, Dickie," Grace hastened to assure.

Dickie stomped his wing tip. "But they are not a toy!"

"True enough." Grace turned around and lifted the necklace over Button's head.

"Tell me you'll keep them in a much safer spot from now on," Dickie demanded.

Grace turned to her ornately carved bureau to find her jewelry box open and overflowing. "Thought I was doing enough…"

"It won't be a problem again," Kyle assured humbly.

Grace noticed his arrival for the first time. "I thought you explained her limits to her, Kyle."

"I did."

"You said play nice, Daddy," Button said. "I do play nice."

"In the kitchen and living room, Button."

"She come in my room."

Dickie made a disgusted sound. "No cooking could be worth this—"

"That's not your judgment call," Kyle cut in.

"Any fool can see—"

"You're any fool all right, Trainor!"

"Hey, guys, I pay the electric bill here!" Grace spouted,

surprising both of them. "As I see it, I am the only one who belongs!" Propelled by a head of steam, she stalked across the room and roped the pearls around Dickie's neck. "There you are, Dickie. In total charge of your pearls. Now I'd like you to leave."

"But Grace!" Dickie sputtered. "I don't want the pearls back. I don't want to go."

"Sorry, but you came uninvited—and have outstayed your welcome!" Grasping Dickie's narrow shoulders she gave him a shove in the direction of the door.

"No boys allowed in here!" Button called from a safe distance. "'Cept my daddy!"

Secretly elated, Kyle cleared the doorway for the other man, trying not to look too smug as Dickie passed by.

Grace's voice soon broke through his glee, however. "The same goes for you, Kyle. Out."

"How far out?"

"Please take Button and go back to the kitchen."

"What about our lunch?" he asked helplessly. "Together."

She gestured to her closet. "I can't possibly eat until I sort out this mess."

Kyle beckoned to his daughter, then reluctantly followed Dickie down the hallway. Dickie crossed the kitchen, pushed at the storm door, pausing to meet his opponent's gaze. "McRaney, I am sorry about shouting at the kid."

"Sure." Kyle tried to disguise his surprise over the apology.

"Not used to them you see. And the pearls are valuable."

"Not a problem. But if you're going back to work, someone at the firm's bound to notice the pearls clash with your tie." He winked. "Might want to sacrifice one or the other."

Grace, meanwhile, had dropped to the edge of her bed.

With elbows resting on her knees, she covered her face with her hands. If someone would have told her in advance that Kyle's return would increase the action in her bedroom, a whole different kind of scenario would have sprung to mind.

Suddenly she felt some light pressure on her back. Kyle? She peeked out between her fingers to find Button standing beside her, the pink chiffon scarf still swathed frothily under her chin, her floral sundress pooled at her feet.

"Don't cry, honey," she crooned.

Grace set her hands on her knees. "I'm not crying, just calming down."

"Want to stand in the corner for time-out?"

"No thanks."

"Nothing got broke."

Grace could imagine Kyle trying to soothe the child in a similar manner. Her mouth twitched upward at the idea. Staring hard at Button, she said, "You should have asked me before playing in here."

"Daddy says to share. It's good."

Grace smiled. "Yes, that's right, sharing is a good thing. It means sharing the work, too. You can help me clean up."

Button's mouth fell into an *O*. "I go stand in the corner," she bartered.

"No, Button. Go tell Daddy you're helping me, then come right back!"

Grace entered her kitchen a half an hour later to find Kyle cleaning a cupboard beside her sink. "I'm ready for lunch."

He stopped humming under his breath. "Where's Button?"

"Dozing on my bed, watching cartoons."

"How'd she do with the cleanup?"

"Fine. Had a high time matching my shoes, returning them to the cubbyholes."

"How girls like their games."

"We certainly do." She leaned against the counter, close to a cupboard he'd emptied.

"I'm sorry she tore up the place."

"Maybe now that she's had to pick up after herself, she'll think twice before doing it again."

"She won't stop being inquisitive, though. She thinks you're a pretty exciting character."

"She does, eh?"

"Finds you very intriguing."

"And that makes you smile?"

"Yes. But I was also replaying the image of Dickie walking out of here with a hitch in his getalong and a swing of his necklace. And that squeaky voice..." he trailed off with an eye roll.

"He only squeaks when he's very angry."

"Oh, that makes all the difference."

"He is doing well with his law firm."

"Yeah? Then why would he want to invest in the bistro?"

"He told you about that, then?"

"Yes. Why didn't you?"

"It just seemed too trivial to bring up. In fact, Michael and I told him a flat-out no. But he can be a pest about things. I should've known he'd contact you personally."

"He's cocky and self-centered—a good argument for human pest control."

"Oh, Kyle." She gave his solid arm a punch. "Did I ever have a date you approved of?"

"Let me review the parade of strays." Kyle stared out the window between the slots of her yellow mini blinds. "There was the skinny boy, Josh Kramer, who wrote you notes in code—so the communists couldn't read them. The foreign exchange student from England, a Niles Grainger, who claimed he was eighty-second in line for the throne and expected a shot at it. And let's not forget the intense poet, Bruce Milestone, who rhymed his every other verse with dearest and affection."

"Well, when you describe them that way, you make me out to be a—

"Big-hearted softy trying to save the world." He grew serious. "All I mean is, not a one was ever good enough for you."

Still, he remembered their names, as if they mattered. She drummed her manicured nails on the countertop, hoping to control her voice. "Who would be good enough for me, Kyle. What kind of man…"

A loaded question for a man presently feeling incredibly at home under her roof, still smarting from a face-off with another suitor. He cleared his throat uncomfortably. "A nice stable guy, I guess. Friendly, hardworking. Hopefully, you'll know him when you see him."

"Will he know me by sight?"

"He will, unless he's a complete idiot!"

"Let's hope he's only a half-wit at worst," she drolled.

"Maybe that didn't come out right," he said awkwardly.

"Oh, I don't know. It's the thought that counts. And I have a pretty good idea what you're thinking." She stood on tiptoe and kissed his lips, a gentle, friendly graze.

Kyle wasn't feeling especially gentle under the circumstances, though. Tight with longing, he clamped one hand behind her head and the other at her waist, seizing her flush against him. He deepened the kiss to crushing intensity, slipping his tongue between her lips.

Grace made small sounds, savoring the taste and texture of his tongue as it grazed the sensitive recess of her mouth. This was the fantasy come to life, Kyle kissing her like a feverish lover, his hands roving her curves possessively. Dizzily she looped her arms around his neck, pressing her body deeper into him.

His breathing was labored as he tore his mouth free to kiss her temples, her jaw, nibble hotly at her ear.

She tipped her face upward, her eyes sheened with desire. "What do you think of my taste in men now?"

He quirked a world-weary smile. Though indescribably flattered, his first impulse was to push her off with a flat denial. But who would he be kidding? Surely not Grace! Even if he conned himself into believing they were a mismatch, he couldn't bear to leave her at the mercy of the world's Dickies. If not Dickie Trainor, another stray would be along soon. One of these days she'd settle. And he would always wonder if he should've taken a chance himself.

Still, in all fairness he felt obligated to warn her off. "With all my troubles, Gracie," he murmured, "I'm not the most exciting character."

She pressed her finger into the dent in his chin. "Someone's underestimating his kisses big-time."

He captured her finger and held it still. "Please be serious. Battling Amelia's old prejudices, Jerome Anderson's claims—all the while raising Button and trying to reopen the bistro, leaves me little personal space."

Her confidence didn't waver. "I can help you if you let me."

"Your help with the redecorating is one thing, but to expect anyone else to take on these deeply personal burdens would be terribly unfair. Besides, I've grown used to handling things myself. I've had months of practice."

"Our lives are already intertwined," she pointed out. "I see nothing wrong with taking our relationship a step further."

His eyes flicked with a hopeful furtiveness, like a boy deciding whether to misbehave with the neighborhood beauty.

"I won't force my body on you before you're ready," she assured.

"You won't?"

"I'm only trying to say the right thing here," she stumbled.

"Yes, and I'm making it tougher." He fingered the auburn curls on her forehead. "Okay, princess. Give my woes your best shot. But I have to warn you up front, I haven't changed my mind about discussing Jerome Anderson's claim to the bistro with Amelia."

"Oh, c'mon, Kyle—"

"I almost did so last night, but it seems she is already doubting my capabilities as a restaurateur. That threw a bucket of ice water on any immediate plans to hash over the theft and missing sales agreement."

"Then let's attack this from Jerome Anderson's angle. Have you reconsidered tracking down the names of the people in the bistro at the time of the theft? Questioning them about what they remember that day might turn up something we can use. I know it's a long shot, but that sales agreement still might be tucked away someplace where you least expect."

"Agreed. After losing my nerve to speak to Amelia, I fell back on the witness list. As a matter of fact, I called the downtown station this morning, hoping to get a look at the original police report. Hit a brick wall, though. The sergeant I spoke to wrote me off as some crazy pest."

She brightened in the face of his gloom. "Lucky you, latching on to some princess power just in time."

His brows arched in hope. "You have a connection down there?"

"A super one. Chief Windom Milestone himself, the poet Bruce's father. Michael and I used to go on ski trips with his family."

"What a break, knowing those great Milestones."

She regarded him dourly. "Bruce has done very well. He's presently a policeman in Maryland."

"A rhyming cop?" he asked dubiously.

"Sure." She raised her hands over her head and clapped them. "Beware, beware, put your hands in the air. Freeze baby freeze, down on your knees."

"Gee, I'd hate to be trapped on a stakeout with the two of you."

She put a hand on her hip. "You want to harass this princess or do you want her to do some power phoning?"

"Phone," he said solemnly. "While you make the call, I'll just go and check on Button."

Kyle backtracked to Grace's bedroom. There he discovered Button perched atop Grace's pastel satin coverlet and pillows, watching the wide-screen television with a blithe expression.

The term Miniature Power Princess crossed his mind.

"Daddy!" Joyfully she held out her arms to Kyle.

Kyle felt a little awkward crossing the forbidden threshold again, but did so anyway. He even sat down gingerly on the edge of the mattress and ruffled Button's glossy black hair.

"Having fun, honey?"

"I don't move an inch for that girl," Button announced proudly.

Kyle sat transfixed to the huge screen featuring the *Brady Bunch* in digital stereo. He bet if he leaned back against the headboard, like so, he'd feel like he was in a luxury theater. Settling his back, he couldn't resist stretching out his legs. Ah, this was living. He could just imagine watching a football game on this giant screen, like the Super Bowl.

Button patted his thigh. "I want a room just like this, Daddy."

He sighed contentedly. "Someday, maybe, if we fall into some loot."

"Someday, snoopy Kyle McRaney," a familiar voice from the doorway announced, "something dangerous is going to happen to you in this bedroom!"

The very idea made him smile. Wide. "Have any luck with the chief?"

"He's free tomorrow around two. Can you make it?"

"Sure."

"We'll go together." Grace came closer with a gasp. "You actually have your shoes on my satin!" She yanked him to his feet. "And look at the dents you left."

As she leaned down to smooth the coverlet, he crooned sexily in her ear. "Those dents are nothin'. Honey."

Button beamed at Grace. "That's right, honey. Dere nothin'."

Chapter Eleven

"Grace! It's so nice to see you." Chief Windom Milestone approached Grace and Kyle in the police station's busy lobby Thursday afternoon, warmly extending his hand.

"Thanks for giving us some of your time." She turned to Kyle and introduced him to the chief.

Kyle surveyed the tall, solidly built man in a pale blue shirt and dark trousers, with slate gray hair and penetrating brown eyes, gratified to see nothing but mild curiosity in his face. If the chief had any preconceived judgments concerning the robbery file Grace asked him to pull, he concealed them well.

"Come on through to my office," Milestone said, leading them down a narrow hallway. He paused at a door bearing his name. Ushering them inside, he closed the door and gestured to two wooden chairs fronting the desk. "Take a seat." He rounded the desk and sat in a larger, more comfortable chair.

"How is your design business faring, Grace?" he asked genially.

"Going very well, Windom. How is Bruce doing?"

"Just promoted to detective."

"Wonderful!"

"He's also got a sideline," the chief reported proudly. "Self-published a book of his poems and is selling it over the Internet. Remember how he was always rhyming things?''

''Of course.''

Grace glanced at Kyle, not surprised to catch him biting his lip against a grin. *The man who rhymed every other line with dearest*, he had to be thinking.

''How are sales?'' Kyle asked politely.

''Not bad. Even though Bruce resides in Maryland, I've seen lots of copies here around the station. I suppose that's due to some curiosity about the chief's son, but the poems are very good. Many of them are bound to be inspired by Grace,'' he confided to Kyle. ''He had it bad for her, still speaks of her fondly.''

''Completely understandable,'' Kyle said solemnly. Too understandable. His territorial feelings were catching fire at a disturbing rate. Not a good sign for a man who considered himself a self-contained operation.

The small talk finished, a silence fell over the office.

There amidst the clutter on his desktop sat the file tagged Amelia's Bistro.

The chief's chair creaked as he leaned forward and opened the folder. ''I had a look at this report. I wasn't involved in the investigation, but I do remember the incident, being friendly with Andy and Amelia Anderson. Quite frankly, I am puzzled as to what you hope to accomplish here, seven years later.''

''I'm sure you recognize my name as prime suspect,'' Kyle said stiffly.

The chief regarded him with mild irritation. ''You were cleared. I admit there are extensive notes supplied by Amelia herself, speculating your motive, negative things about your background, your poor family life, your father's gambling debts, both parents' abandonment. And she cited revenge on your part, as she'd just fired you that night because you were supposedly inadequate. Only you know how much of this is accurate.''

"She stuck to the facts for the most part. It's all true about my background. But the only reason she fired me was because I was in love with her granddaughter. And stealing from her as some kind of kiss-off never occurred to me.''

"Most likely she was upset about your romance with Libby and spread it on way too thick,'' the chief agreed. "But in the end, no hard evidence could be found against you or anyone else.''

"I am innocent,'' Kyle insisted.

The chief gave him a penetrating look. "Why not let it be?''

"We can't, Windom,'' Grace intervened. She went on to explain Kyle's stake in the bistro, the challenge made by Jerome Anderson.

The chief flipped through the pages of the report. "Oh, yes. I see a sales agreement among the items missing. The very fact that it's listed here might be helpful if this ends up in court.''

"The agreement itself would shut down Jerome best,'' Grace said.

The chief gave her a knowing smile. "You hope to play private eye, don't you? Track down that agreement?''

"Sort of.''

The chief shook his head. "I still shudder over all the stunts you pulled during our family ski trips out west. On the slopes, you were a daredevil, off the slopes you were the life of the parties. Always causing static.''

She brightened in gratitude. "You never did tell my folks.''

"And admit a cop couldn't keep you in check? It was my pride at stake more than anything.''

Grace offered her most beguiling smile. "Windom, we

would just like a peek at the list of potential witnesses. It's bound to be short, the robbery being on a weeknight, shortly before closing…''

''Then what?''

''We don't intend to grill anyone,'' Kyle assured. ''Simply ask them if they remember anything strange.''

''As the officer did seven years ago—to no avail.''

''Oh, c'mon, Windom, someone in that place raided the safe. Maybe after all this time, he or she feels some remorse, would cough up that agreement no questions asked—if it became known it was needed.''

Kyle leaned forward anxiously. ''As far as I know, most of the people there that night were friends of mine in one capacity or another. I might get lucky.''

''No matter how polite, you can't go confronting people for that kind of information.'' The chief tipped back in his chair, rubbing his squared chin. ''Still…''

''You have a suggestion?'' Grace asked eagerly.

''Off the record, I can see a flyer being useful. You could print one up seeking information about the theft, namely any documents found in the safe among the other valuables.''

''And send it to the witnesses!'' Kyle said with pleasure.

''Offer a reward!'' Grace chimed in.

''Still, I must warn you not to get too hopeful. The paper probably meant nothing to the thief and was disposed of. The theft was likely carried out for the easily redeemable contents.'' He glanced down at the file. ''Such as the cash, rings, coin collection.''

Kyle nodded. ''That hit the Andersons more personally than the public knows. The three grand was meant for a vacation and home remodeling. The rings were heirlooms, Libby's parents' wedding rings. And the coins were Andy's pride and joy, Kennedy half dollars set in a folder autographed by JFK himself.''

"Surely all lost forever," the chief said bluntly.

"But you will show us the list, Windom?" Grace urged.

"I don't feel right going that far." He rose from his chair, towering over them. "Still, I have a matter to attend to down the hall," he said with a significant look to the folder. "You can make yourselves at home for a few minutes, can't you?"

The moment he eased out the door, Kyle lunged for the file and found the list of names, complete with addresses and phone numbers. Grace took hold of the page. "I'll just run this through the fax machine over here in the corner and make a copy."

By the time Windom returned, the couple was admiring a plaque on the wall. He handed Grace a book. "Here is a volume of Bruce's poems for you, Grace," he said. "It belongs to a dispatcher, but I'll replace hers tomorrow."

"Why, thank you, Windom." She stood on tiptoe and kissed his cheek. "Thanks for everything."

He was pleased behind his gruff demeanor. "Just be careful—and discreet!"

She nodded. "The next time your wife needs a posh evening gown, it will be on me."

"Kimberly would love a Grace North original. She has several events on the calendar." He reached out and shook Kyle's hand once again. "Nice to meet you, son. Good luck."

"Thanks."

As the couple started down the hall, he called after them. "And do visit Bruce's Web site. It's listed in the book. He'd love to hear from you."

They paused on the sidewalk in front of the station amidst the downtown pedestrians. Kyle shoved his hands into the pockets of his chinos, staring at the bright blue sky. "You aren't going to do it, are you Grace?"

"Do what?"

"Touch Bruce Milestone's Web site."

He appeared genuinely concerned behind the jovial question. Not a bad sign, Grace thought smugly. "Don't worry, I'd have to get pretty serious about a guy before I'd touch his site like that."

"So, you planning to keep the book?" he asked casually.

"Oh, yes." Grace laughed, stuffing it in her tote. "I'm looking forward to reading it. Probably are some poems in here I'll remember."

"All in all, I think that went very well with the chief. But you owe that woman a dress now."

"I will enjoy making it," she assured. "Kimberly was always very nice to me."

"Do you have time for a drink?" he asked hesitantly. "If you're not too busy."

"Not at all. There's a small luncheonette a few shops down. Let's go there."

The luncheonette was the casual, seat-yourself type. The midafternoon crowd was thin, mostly uniformed police officers.

Kyle looked around as they sat down in a booth. "Here's a place no one would dare rob."

"Probably not," Grace agreed. "You wouldn't get a foot out the door without being cuffed."

When the waitress came, Kyle ordered two soft drinks.

Grace sighed fondly. "You remembered."

Kyle felt a stirring in his belly. The way Grace looked at him sometimes, her gem green eyes full of the most intense longing he'd ever encountered, it made him feel as though they were already very familiar lovers, intimate in every way. He wasn't good at expressing things, but he wanted to give her the general idea of how he felt. "You do something to me, Gracie," he said softly.

She hunched forward. "Like what?"

Her eagerness flustered him. "I don't know.... You give

me ideas. Why, I think I could read a whole book of poems to you, if I had one.''

She laughed, leaning back as their sodas arrived. "You're just curious about those poems because you think you might learn something about me you don't know.''

His blue eyes gleamed. "Doubt my old heart can take any more static.''

"Well, for now, let's concentrate on the list.'' Grace pulled it from her tote and spread it sideways on the table so they could scan it together. "Ouch! Heather's husband Nate Basset was there that night. And Michael.''

"There are a lot of names on here I haven't heard in a long while. Friends and co-workers.'' He raked his hair. "Hope we don't upset anyone unnecessarily.''

"We're doing what we have to do.''

"The next step will be to have the flyer put together and mailed. You have any computer skills?''

"No, Michael does my business's left brain function. I intend to tap him—or rather his secretary—for the job.''

"If you like, I can mention it to him. I'm on my way over there soon. He and I are meeting the floor installer over at the bistro.''

"I'll go with you,'' she decided. "We should take the time to sketch out exactly what we want to say.''

North Enterprises was located in the IDS Tower on Marquette. They took the elevator to the twelfth floor, Grace automatically wheeling to the right, pushing open a glass door bearing the family name in a golden scroll.

Even though Grace had no official company title, her status among employees ranked high as the boss's vibrant, boisterous daughter. She kept moving through the sitting area, calling people by name.

Michael's secretary, Sue Meiers, was watering a plant on a window ledge as they opened the door to his outer office. She was a pleasant, middle-aged woman who favored flowing jersey skirts and loose sweaters—today it was a pleated lavender bottom and stretchy white top. She clicked well with Michael, Grace thought, because she shared his passion for organization.

"Why, hello Grace!" Sue set her watering can down on the ledge. "Is your brother expecting you?"

"No, Sue. Is he in?"

"Yes, but he's on the telephone."

"We'll wait."

Sue smiled. "I'll jot him a note and take it in."

Grace and Kyle were admitted to the inner office moments later. They found a formally dressed Michael busily hammering away at this computer keyboard's number pad. He was wearing a headset, speaking to someone on the telephone. "Sure. I'll have some hard numbers for you by four. No, think nothing of it." Pushing the disconnect button, he peeled off the headset. Swiveling forward in his chair, he greeted his visitors. "Hey, this is a surprise. You here together."

Grace gave him a sweet smile. Michael still seemed blind to the idea that Kyle could take Grace seriously on any level.

"You still on for Mort the floor man?" Kyle asked.

"Sure, partner." Michael slapped Grace's hand as she dipped into his M&M's candy bowl. "So, Gracie, you just tagging along?"

Grace related Windom's suggestion of a flyer.

Michael looked suitably impressed. "I suppose you want me to get that flyer designed and printed," he wagered.

"Along with address labels."

"Oh, Gracie…"

"What, big-shot investor?"

Michael's eyes twinkled. "You've actually come up with a feasible plan."

Delighted, Grace nested a hip on the edge of his desk

and picked up a yellow legal pad. "Okay, let's sketch out what the flyer should say. Wanted, information on Amelia's bistro robbery." She began to jot on the paper. "Five hundred dollar reward leading to recovery of lost document—"

"Five hundred?" Kyle echoed.

"I'm treating," Grace retorted.

Michael frowned at his ever impulsive sister and overruled her. "We can tally that into bistro expenses."

Grace realized that she was trying too hard once again for the fragile macho pair and concentrated hard on the flyer. "Suppose we should guarantee no strings, no questions."

"That seems fair enough," Kyle agreed. "Though I hate the idea of any reward going to the thief who caused me this misery."

"Maybe it'll just go to a tattler," Michael said practically.

"So what form of contact do you want?" Grace asked.

"Let's use the bistro office phone," Kyle decided. "I have an answering machine set up in there." He rattled off the number.

They spent ten minutes more blocking out the message. Michael took the pad from Grace and peeled off the page. "Right. I'll go see if Sue can put this together."

"Oh, here are the names." Grace removed the printed witness list from her purse and crossed out unnecessary names including elder Andersons and Libby. Then she updated Nate's new address. She handed over the paper. "The old addresses should be verified right off to save a mix-up."

Michael glanced at the list with a squawk. "Me? I'm on this list?"

"You were at the bistro...." Kyle recalled in a Columbo-like tone.

"Oh, heck, cross yourself off," Grace generously invited.

"Thanks a lot, princess," he drolled. "Hey, what about Nate Basset? Shall I cross him off? He wasn't part of the machinery—too young."

"He stays."

"The fact that he stole your best friend away hardly makes him a con."

"Cute." Grace smiled thinly. "Nate is connected to Jerome Anderson. He knew all the scoop about Jerome's claim and was salivating over the idea of getting his mitts on the bistro for resale."

"Damn." Michael was properly shut down.

"Hope Sue won't mind this extra job," Kyle ventured.

"I already intend to give her a bonus for her dedication, so I'm sure she'll comply. But don't expect results today," he cautioned. "She is very busy." With that he left the room.

Grace rose from the edge of the desk and oozed into Kyle's arms. "I need a hug."

He gave her one, and a deep, circuit-blowing kiss.

A side door near a bookcase abruptly flew open in the midst of their passion. Victor North stood in the doorway.

"Father!" Grace broke free of Kyle.

"Well. Kyle." Victor heaved a startled breath. "I'd welcome you back to town on behalf of the Norths, but Grace seems to be taking care of that."

"Hello, Mr. North."

Victor advanced stoically. "Your bistro project sounds intriguing."

"Yes. I'm so happy that Michael wants to be a part of it."

"I've been told that I have to expect my children to enter ventures without my input. Seems you've been tempting them both."

"Oh, Father!" Grace reddened.

"Just heard you were on board, came in here to say

hello. Stop in for dinner sometime." With that he turned on his heel and left.

"Father doesn't know how brusque he sounds," Grace apologized.

Kyle said nothing. Of course Victor knew. Kyle had plenty of experience with that look, thanks to Amelia Anderson.

GRACE WAS UP IN HER second floor studio that evening unfolding a blue velvet jacket for Cinderella's miniature Prince Charming on her worktable when her telephone rang. The Caller ID signaled the North household.

"Hello, Dad," she greeted without hesitation.

"How'd you know which North was calling?"

"Just knew."

"Are you busy?"

"Working on a costume for the community center play."

"Be sure you keep good records of all that charity work, dear."

"I do, Dad."

Her father sounded unusually hesitant. "I was surprised by what I saw today. You and Kyle…"

"Kissing? You have a right to your surprise," she said politely, "just as I have a right to choose my own dates."

"You're actually dating?"

"Not officially. Not yet. As it is, he's here so much already, there's been little chance."

"Oh, yes, the damn cooking job."

"But you wanted me to have the meals," she couldn't help taunting.

"But who'd have ever thought…what about Dickie?"

"May as well give you fair warning, I will never be serious about Dickie. I can see a friendship in our future, but nothing else."

"But Grace, Mother and I got an entirely different impression, at first anyway...."

"Maybe that is partly my fault," she admitted. "I went through a brief phase where I thought I could love someone like him, partly for your sake."

"Then what the hell happened?"

"Kyle came home, Dad," she replied in soft counterpoint. "I've always been attracted to him, even as a teenager."

"I don't even want to hear this."

"The idea of pleasing you and Mom does have its attraction, but things are so natural between me and Kyle. I have to work so hard at my relationship with Dickie. It's like the romantic energy is forced."

"As if solid relationships are built on such whimsy."

Grace inhaled, seeking inner strength. Explaining passion to a practical man like Victor seemed impossible. "Call it a connection then. Hard as I tried, Dad, I've never felt I was totally connecting with Dickie."

"Nonsense. You kids grew up together—our families blended!"

"Our families collided politely. Dickie never mixed much with us, Dad. He was awkward and guarded."

"He's really polished up his act now, though. Good job at that law office, trying so hard to be noticed. He's not difficult to talk to as you say. He and I can really talk."

"About what, Dad?"

"Finances, cars. We've come to know each other very well indeed."

"Unfortunately, I will be the one who has to take the vow."

"What will happen to Dickie?" Victor demanded.

"Don't be silly. As you say yourself, he has a whole life of his own, an upcoming attorney, all the manners and connections his heart can hold."

"But he's intimated that you complete him."

"Dad, have you already forgotten the pops concert the other night? There he was, jolly as you please, with another woman on his arm."

"It turned out to be his secretary, Miss Evers. A minor thing. Like Michael taking Sue to an event. Dickie even ended up taking you home."

"Admit it, Dad, for a minute there at the concert, when you saw him with Haley, you feared you might not know Dickie as well as you thought. I could read it on your face."

"True, but the error was mine. He didn't deserve my distrust."

They dueled for a few minutes more. Quite accustomed to such battles, Grace took it in stride. And it felt good to get the air cleared a bit. As she went back to her worktable and arranged tissue pattern pieces on the rectangle of velvet, the memory of Haley Evers lingered. She still wondered if the secretary had another issue on her mind, apart from her sister's Harlequin costume. All Grace could think of was that Haley was in love with Dickie and wondered if Grace was her competition. Poor girl. Maybe she could make the chance to reassure her that the field was wide-open.

Chapter Twelve

Grace found she couldn't wait for Button to arrive on Friday morning. Despite her misgivings over their rocky friendship, Grace had good news for the child and anticipated her delight like a child herself.

"My kids are coming!" Button squealed after arriving at Grace's house, clapping her hands to her round cheeks.

"Yes," Grace confirmed. "They need their next costume fitting. Between the three of them, I will probably work a few hours. So you, Button, will have someone to play with all morning."

Button bypassed Grace to give Kyle a fierce hug around the waist. "Daddy, the kids."

Kyle chuckled. "That is wonderful, honey. And I think it's pretty nice of Grace to include you."

She stared up at him with a puzzled look. "What's that?"

"I mean, it's nice of her to let you play with her kids," Kyle said. He turned Button around slowly. "Tell Grace so."

"Thank you, Gwace, for having those kids."

Grace laughed and tugged at her pigtail. "You are very welcome." Button dashed over to the front window and stood on tiptoe to peer out. Kitty appeared and Button picked her up, babbling the news to her.

"So what's on your agenda?" Grace turned to ask Kyle with a playful tweak to his chin.

"Well, I intend to whip up a mushroom herb quiche for you. And maybe an angel food cake because you're so downright angelic." In a burst of delight Kyle snagged Grace in his arms and kissed the tip of her nose.

"Mmm…a saintly reward."

"Thanks for making our day, Gracie."

She scanned Kyle with twinkling eyes. "You like those kids, too?"

"My happiness very often hinges on Button's," he whispered. "It's a Daddy thing."

"You wear it well, Daddy."

He sized her up carefully. "I suspect I'm not the only one under the Button spell. When she asked you about the kids the other day, you seemed in no hurry to have them back."

"Maybe I jacked up the project with her in mind," Grace conceded softly, her fingers skimming his throat. "Her invasion of my closet, facing Dickie over the pearls, couldn't have been easy. Besides, Mitzi's anxious too. The costumes do have to be done fairly soon and I had some free hours to work last night."

"You are the greatest." Slanting a peek at Button to assure she was distracted, Kyle dipped his head to steal a kiss from Grace.

MITZI AND THE KIDS weren't at Grace's for fifteen minutes before there was a makeshift restaurant centered around the studio's sofa. Kristin and Rachel and Kitty frolicked with Button while Tony stood dutifully before Grace, allowing her to adjust pins in the basted velvet jacket he wore.

"Hey, everybody." Kyle's appearance in the doorway startled everyone to silence. "How are things going?"

Grace rotated on her knees to face him. "Moving slower

than expected. So, was I right to let you pick up that last phone call? When I saw the flooring outfit's name on the ID, figured it was yours.''

''Mort wants me downtown and make sure they delivered the correct parquet tiles. So if you don't mind, Button and I will take off an hour early today. The food is ready—''

''No, Daddy, no!'' Button jumped free of her restaurant. ''We play nice.''

''Of course you do,'' Mitzi bellowed from her perch in the studio's broadest chair.

Button hugged Kristin and pulled her onto the sofa. ''I'm playing waitress. At the rest-rant.''

Kristin smiled at Kyle. ''Can't she stay here with us? We'll watch her.''

Kyle locked eyes with Grace. He thought he noted a flicker of uncertainty, but it was impossible to tell. Especially when she smiled broadly.

''Button's welcome, if she doesn't mind being in my care.''

It was Kyle's turn to pause in uncertainty. ''So, honey, do you really want to stay?''

''Pwease, Daddy?''

Kyle threw his hands up in mock despair. ''Okay. See you later.''

When Kyle called in later, Grace answered above a joyous din.

''Sounds like a circus!'' Kyle said.

''It is. We've just finished your quiche—which Mitzi wants you to know was delicious—and are back up in the studio sewing and playing rest-rant. How are things going with you?''

There was a pause on the line. ''Not well. They delivered the wrong flooring. Even worse, the parquet tile we chose is out of stock. Mike and I have to dash down to a warehouse and pick another one—if we want them to start immediately.''

''Go ahead,'' Grace invited, shifting on her sewing bench to watch Button imitate Kristin pirouette across the room. ''Button's fine. Having a great time.''

''You won't be able to reach me for a while.''

''We'll manage.''

''Okay, if you're sure.''

''Positive. Bye.'' Grace hung up and beckoned Rachel closer to her machine. ''Let's slip your dress on one more time before we call it a day.''

By the time the troupe was ready to leave, Button was sound asleep in Mitzi's lap on the sofa.

''She's darling, isn't she?'' Mitzi mouthed to Grace. She shifted the sleeping child from her lap to the cushions, and rose to her feet.

After Mitzi left, Grace wandered to the sofa, admiring the beautiful child, her cherub face relaxed in slumber, thumb stuffed in her mouth. She could only imagine the wonder of caring for such a child, being the recipient of such a fierce and devoted love. Perhaps one day, she too would be loved that way.

Button eventually roused from her nap. Sitting up on the sofa, she rubbed her eyes.

''Hello there, sleepy,'' Grace said cheerfully from her sewing machine.

Clearly disoriented, she looked around the spacious workroom. ''Where's those kids?''

''They had to go home—''

''Huh?''

''Sorry, Button.''

''Daddy!''

Button's scream tore through Grace's eardrums. She turned off her machine and nervously rose to her feet. Easing out of her work smock, she laid it over the machine. "Daddy isn't back yet, honey."

"He downstairs," Button declared stubbornly.

Grace moved closer but not close enough to spook her. "No, I'm taking care of you right now."

Button suddenly scampered off the sofa and barrelled out of the room. Grace galloped after her, frightened to watch Button pound down the staircase at blinding speed, Kitty on her heels.

"Daddy!" In a whiny cry she trotted into the kitchen. "You hiding, Daddy? Hiding in heaven?"

Grace desperately trailed after the child as she checked every room on the town home's main level. Button ended up back in the living room, her hands clutching her tummy. "Daddy, oh my Daddy."

"Daddy will be back real soon," Grace assured.

"Want him now!"

"How about me?" Grace asked lamely.

"Don't want you!"

Grace should've seen the next frame of action coming. Button dashing back to *her* closet with *her* Kitty, slamming the door soundly shut, pushing in the button lock with a sound click. That ridiculous lock on the closet, Grace fumed. Her mother's idea, in case Grace had to one day bar herself from an intruder. She hoped to have the sense to run to a room with an escape window for Pete's sake!

She rapped lightly on the door. "Button, come out of there. Now."

"No."

"At least turn on the light."

"No."

To Grace's relief, the light did flick on beneath the door. She jiggled the knob.

"Go 'way."

Grace paced on her plush bedroom closet, her heart beating frantically. What to do? Minutes dragged like hours. She rapped on the door again. "What are you doing in there?"

"Crying," Button sobbed.

"Please don't."

"Want my daddy."

What had she done wrong? Grace wondered. She was trying to hard to make Button happy.

Maybe she wasn't cut out to be a caregiver, except to a sleeping child. Tears crowded the corner of her own eyes as she moved to the phone on the nightstand to punch in the bistro's number. Naturally the machine popped on. It would've been a miracle to find Kyle back so soon. Realizing she would have to solve this matter long before Kyle could reach them, she hung up, leaving no message.

She returned to the closet. "Button—"

"Get my daddy!"

"I can't. Come out, Button, or I will have to call your grandma."

Button did not reply.

In a rush of frustration and fear, Grace went back to the nightstand and looked up Amelia's number in her address book. Her hand shook as she dialed and listened to the rings on the other end, grateful when she finally heard Amelia Anderson's voice. "Mrs. Anderson? This is Grace. Grace North. I hate to disturb you, but I have a small crisis here...."

Grace recalled the Andersons' favoring big sedans for transportation, so therefore she expected to see one every time she glanced out the living room window. Unexpectedly, however, Amelia arrived in a taxi.

The moments to follow would forever live in Grace's memory bank. With aplomb that did not fit the taxi driver's gala print shirt and baggy shorts, he made an unprecedented move of alighting from the driver's door, rounding the car, and opening the back door against the boulevard.

Curbside service? The last time Grace had taken a taxi home from dental surgery, the driver had hit the brakes long enough to collect his fare and give her time for a tuck and roll to the grass! Apparently this was a kind and patient man…who was helping an elderly lady with a cane onto the sidewalk.

Elderly? Was this the same woman who'd climbed a rooftop to rescue a ball? Ejected rowdy college students from the bar? Run four taps of beer at once without wasting a drop?

The reality was undeniable. Amelia Anderson had grown ancient in the past decade. A thin, hunched shell of her former robust self. Grace felt shame, shock as Amelia hobbled up the walk with the aid of the driver, the hot summer breeze dashing beneath her loose fitting cotton dress to reveal her bony legs in support stockings.

Grace summoned a superhero and got Grandma Moses instead!

She paced her foyer waiting for Amelia to make it up the stairs. Upon hearing the bell she opened the door wide, trying to keep her expression placid. "Hello, Amelia."

"You're as white as ghost, young lady! Is my little Button the cause?"

"Yes," Grace stuttered. "About my calling, I didn't mean to…" Amelia's clear hard eyes stopped her from voicing her thoughts on frailty. "Well, I hated to disturb you."

"If Kyle gave you the impression that I am incapable of caring for that child, he is telling tales. Tall ones!"

"No, no," Grace assured quite honestly. "I've always considered you one of the strongest women I know. Kyle's said nothing." As seemed his very bad habit. Why hadn't he told her Amelia was so frail now?

She led Amelia through the foyer toward the living room, timing her steps to the slow click of Amelia's cane on the tiles. They paused in the living room, Amelia taking everything in with what Grace thought might be a measure of approval.

"All right, Grace. I am at your service." Amelia smiled rather wistfully. "Though I must caution you, Button doesn't respond very well to me, either. She's good enough in relaxed situations, but when things tense up, only her father will do."

"Well, she won't listen to a thing I say."

Amelia shrugged her rolled shoulders. "Where is she then?"

Grace fluttered her hands in a nervous motion. "In my closet."

"Your closet!"

Grace recalled that the closets in Amelia's home were miniscule. "Yes. Don't worry, though, it's bigger than…big," she finished awkwardly.

She didn't relish allowing the old woman into her plush quarters but seeing no other choice she led the way. Grace directed her to the closet door and pointed.

"Button?" Amelia proclaimed reedily. "It's Grandma. Come out—"

Before she could finish her sentence the door was swinging open and Button was charging for Amelia. Obviously she had some sensitivity training with the woman's frail condition, for she very gently hugged her, crying softly into her dress.

Amelia laid a shaky hand upon her black head. "You gave us quite a scare, Button, behaving this way."

Grace noted that although Amelia's voice held a slight reprimand, she was glowing over this mastership. The child preferred her, at least to someone.

"It's all right now. Grandma's here."

"Daddy," Button hiccupped. "Woke up. He gone."

"You know Daddy's busy sometimes." Amelia tsked, dabbing Button's wet cheeks with a hanky. "Grace was kind enough to watch you."

"You stayin', Grammy?"

"I wouldn't budge without you, if that's what you mean."

Grace noted that Amelia's lined face showed signs of fatigue, suggesting she would rather not budge under any circumstances for the time being. "Shall we sit in the living room for a while?" Grace suggested awkwardly. "I can make tea."

"That would be lovely." Amelia agreed. "Come along Button. But leave the kitten please."

Button gazed at Grace. "Pet dander," she explained simply, as though the past hour of dramatic exchange had never happened.

By the time Grace whisked into the living room with a tray holding her grandmother's teapot and cups, Amelia was seated stoically on the sofa and Button was twirling round the room, back to normal save for her red owlish eyes.

"Can I get you anything, Button?"

"Want to play shoes," she said with a defiant lift to her tiny chin.

Grace gasped, gripping the ends of the tray. "After everything, you want to go back into my closet?"

"I won't cry. Pwomise."

"I'm not sure that's the point, Button," Amelia interceded. "Perhaps Grace would rather you not play with her things."

Grace would definitely prefer she not play with her things! Still, now that Button had plowed through even her lingerie, the trauma was lessened. "Go ahead," she invited. "But be gentle and don't lock the door again."

"Course I don't." With a breath of exasperation, Button trotted off.

Amelia looked around. "All very lovely, Grace, your home, your possessions."

Grace set the tray on the coffee table fronting the sofa. "Lemon? Cream? Actually, it's just milk," she confessed.

"A dash of lemon will do nicely."

Grace set Amelia's cup and saucer on the table before her. Serving herself, she settled back in a nearby chair. "I am so sorry about this alarm. I didn't know what to do."

Amelia looked brighter and more relaxed. "Most children are disoriented after a nap," she explained, "a fact you wouldn't be expected to know, dear. In Button's case, it's worse than average. Apparently there were times during the months after Libby's death that Kyle was forced to bring in sitters for Button while he worked. She would awaken and discover a stranger caring for her." Amelia sipped her tea. "Very disturbing, no doubt. It's been difficult for Kyle to rebuild that sense of trust between Button and other females. To Button, our gender arouses instant suspicion."

"Kyle hasn't told me a lot," Grace admitted, her disappointment evident. "Knowing even that much would've been helpful."

"He is a man of few words," Amelia said. "Prefers to take care of things himself. Still, he's bound to be blue, deeply hurt over losing Libby. It must be terribly difficult to speak of it, even after a year. After all, they were married for many years. People grow close. Andy and I certainly did."

Grace didn't like to think of Kyle with Libby. Perhaps as he didn't like to think of her with past dates, the strays as he called them. Whether he knew it or not, his attitude oozed with jealousy.

She pointedly changed the subject. "Kyle tells me you're keeping busy."

Amelia sipped her tea approvingly. "A widow's best chance of survival. After Andy died I couldn't bear to run the bistro without him. Instead I stepped up my social life, began to attend more club meetings, make new friends. Of course, having Button in my life is my biggest distraction by far. Parenting has unique rewards. Why, Button is like a dose of youth serum to me."

Amelia sighed. "Though her case is such sad déjà vu. Libby came to me in much the same way, having no mama, needing so much reassurance." She gazed off dreamily at a print of Loring Park. "I believe Libby was angry at times simply because she'd been robbed of her parents at such an early age. Such a brilliant, remarkable girl. She and I needed more time together, to explore, to enjoy."

Amelia was to some surprise a dreamer on the subject of Libby, Grace decided, speaking as though they'd been thick all along, when everyone at the bistro knew they fought constantly and had broken ties so completely. But people frequently made saints of dead loved ones, didn't they?

Was Kyle doing the same? Would it hurt her chances of building something with him?

Noting Amelia's cup was empty, Grace gave her a refill.

Amelia nodded appreciatively. "It's so nice that Kyle and Michael have renewed their friendship. I always thought Michael was a fine boy. Even thought maybe he and Libby might click. But that didn't happen," she said wistfully. "Amazing that he is still single. Such a pity. In any case, he will be a marvelous asset to the bistro."

The front doorbell rang. Grace set down her teacup and saucer. "Excuse me for a moment."

She opened the door with some surprise. "Dickie!"

The lawyer looked especially handsome today, his blond

hair gleaming in the sun, his three-piece suit a neat dove gray. "May I come in?"

Grace blocked his way apologetically. "I must warn you, I do have company. Amelia Anderson."

His smile froze. "Just came to return your pearls." His hand snaked out and he looped them around her neck.

"Thanks." She was breathless, feeling she'd offended him. "On second thought, why not join us?"

Dickie's shine faded. "She may know all about my run-in with the kid."

"She's older now. Won't be winning any knuckle-cracking contests or booting out undesirables."

He smarted openly. "I was never an undesirable at the bistro."

How could he be so sensitive? "C'mon, take a chance."

He impulsively leaned over and kissed her cheek. "Later."

Grace returned to the living room and her chair, facing an expectant Amelia. "That was Dickie, a friend."

Amelia adjusted her glasses, peering over at Grace's chest. "Lovely pearls."

"A birthday gift." Amelia's expression didn't change. Apparently the pearl incident had not been reported to her. "It's such a small world sometimes. As it happens, Dickie would like to invest in the bistro, too."

"Any number of people would, I dare say," Amelia suggested proudly, settling back on the cushions. "Great opportunity. I thought of selling to strangers after Andy passed, but something stopped me. I just closed up." She met Grace's eyes, as if to share a special confidence. "Perhaps it was Andy sending me a divine message, knowing about Button before I did.

"Discovering her existence gave me renewed interest in saving the place. It is after all the child's birthright. I know Andy is looking down upon me proudly, eager to see new life in that old place. If I didn't need money for living expenses, I'd have given it to Kyle outright. But as it is, I do need the boost. Figure any leftovers can go into Button's name."

Confronted with Amelia's burst of warmth, Grace was tempted to speak to her about Jerome, get her current take on the theft. But dare she risk going against Kyle's wishes? He did have reason for doubt. Amelia's account of him in the police report had been fairly brutal, and she wasn't singing his praises even now. Whether accidentally or by design, she said nicer things about Michael.

As impulsive as she was, even Grace knew when she might be holding an emotional grenade.

Amelia made motions to leave soon thereafter, summoning Button, who promptly obeyed. Button looked none the worse for wear, though she needed help getting her tennis shoes back on. Grace offered to help.

"I will try and call Kyle," Amelia announced, reaching for the telephone at her elbow. She dialed the number, then listened. "This is Amelia," she said formally, presumably speaking to his machine. "I am presently at Grace's house as Button needed me. Obviously, you are not there to give us a ride home, so we will make our own way. Meet you at home. Goodbye." She hung up. "If you have a telephone directory handy, I would like to call a taxi."

"Unnecessary," Grace said, attempting to catch Button's flying left foot and aim it into the shoe. "I'll gladly drive you home if we can get by without a car seat."

Amelia glowed. "Button weighs over forty pounds, which puts her over the weight limit. We would deeply appreciate a ride, wouldn't we Button?"

Button nodded. "I 'preciate going home."

Button's interpretation caused Amelia to frown. "You are such a generous young lady, Grace," she went on in damage control. "That Cinderella book you gave Button is much appreciated too. We look at it nearly every night. Don't we, Button?''

"Yes, Grammy," Button agreed, smiling shyly as she allowed Grace to catch hold of her right foot.

Grace held that tiny foot tight for a minute. She discovered she very much liked this sort of praise. In fact, if she weren't careful, the feeling could become habit forming.

GRACE HAD NO SOONER assisted Amelia into the house on Ashford Lane when Kyle's Jeep swung into the driveway. She met him on the driveway.

"Just missed Amelia's message," he said breathlessly. "What went on, anyway?"

Grace felt a rush of irritation. "Oh, Kyle, why didn't you warn me that Button might wake up all upset?"

The query threw him. "She took a nap at your house?"

"Yes!"

"She okay now?"

"Yes!" she hissed. "But she locked herself in my closet and I had to call Amelia to the rescue—who I assumed was still strong as a bull and probably as tough—"

"Can't believe Button dropped off in all that commotion."

"Is that all you have to say?"

"What do you want?" he demanded helplessly.

"Kyle, I was smacked with too many surprises today. It made the hassle much worse."

He rubbed his hands together thoughtfully. "For starters, calling Amelia wasn't such a bad idea. She may not be the threat you remember, but she is fairly sturdy and adores catering to Button. In fact, I would guess that she was thrilled to be needed in a crisis. As for Button, she causes hassles in one form or another every day. You probably made strides with her today, not cracking under her pressure."

Grace folded her arms in a huff, feeling competently blocked.

"Be proud. You improvised and worked things out."

"Then why do I feel so incompetent?"

"Now if you had been the one to lock herself in the closet, I'd be worried."

"Kyle, I'm trying to make a big point. If you confided in me more in general, I would've handled this whole situation better."

Just the point he was frantically trying to sidestep. He wasn't prepared to tell her things. No matter how much he cared. Which was proving to be a lot.

Hoping to comfort her without words, he reached out to stroke her throat. A scowl gathered over his dark brows as his fingers touched the all too familiar string of pearls. "So Dickie's back in the picture."

His knuckles skimmed the tender skin of her collarbone, causing her to shiver. "You didn't expect him to fall off the face of the earth, did you?"

"A guy can hope."

"He stopped by while Amelia and I were having tea. Didn't come in though. Didn't want to confront Amelia."

"Why not?"

"Basically, he seemed worried that Button spilled the beans about their clash, that Amelia might be lying in wait for him."

He nodded sagely. "A wise precaution whatever his fear. I believe she could have taken him, given the cane advantage."

Grace bit back a grin. "You probably won't like this either, but Dickie's appearance triggered some talk between Amelia and me. I mentioned to her that Dickie wanted to invest in the bistro and she got to talking about how happy she is about the reopening. I was tempted to tell her about Jerome's talk with you and our flyer—"

He gripped her arms. "You didn't though. Did you?"

"No. I felt a twinge of discomfort in speaking up."

A sigh of relief escaped him.

"Still, a part of me wishes I had just spilled my guts," she confessed.

He was horrified. "Grace, this is my judgment call to make. I want you to accept that there are areas of my life I'm not ready to share with anyone. I've grown accustomed to operating alone and insist upon moving at my own pace. Okay?"

"Not really."

His eyes softened over her soulful expression. Cupping her chin he kissed her forehead, her lips. "Please try and understand. It's nothing personal."

Grace let it go. But Kyle was only kidding himself. Everything between a man and woman who kissed the way they did was personal. And somehow she would prove it to him.

"BUTTON IS FINISHED WITH her bath."

Kyle looked up from his magazine as Amelia entered the living room that evening. "Already?"

Amelia leaned on her cane. "You know this conversation is inevitable."

Kyle looked helpless. "What do I say to her? Button, you shouldn't have a fit every time I vanish?"

Amelia pursed lips. "Let her do the talking. Then respond."

He eased his large body out of the medium-size chair. "Guess I can't screw up too much, just responding."

"Hi, Daddy," Button said brightly as Kyle hovered in her doorway. "I want a big TV in my room. Okay?"

"Someday, honey," he replied. "After I get a big TV in my room." With a sigh he sat down on the futon.

"Read to me?"

He rubbed his temples. "In a little bit. Let's talk about your day first."

Button scampered closer, nightie hem flying. Hanging her body over his thigh, she swung in the air like a monkey, hair and arms dangling. "I cry for that girl."

Kyle was taken aback by her matter-of-fact report. "Why did you do that, Button? Why?"

"I wake up. No Daddy. I get scared."

How open and concise she was! If only grownups could hang on to the knack. Kyle rubbed her back, speaking gently but firmly. "Button, there was no need for you to be upset. You weren't alone or with a stranger."

"But I always want you."

"That's very nice to hear, but we can't always be together. I am busy, I have places to go, things to do."

"I don't like baby-sitters!"

"You never did. But Grace is different. She wanted you to stay at her house because she is your friend. And you pay her back by bursting into tears at the sight of her." He peeled her off his leg and sat her upright in his lap. Her disheveled hair landed in a dark flat mop on her head, her eyes focused with intelligence.

"Don't be mad, Daddy."

"I'm not mad."

"Gwace mad?"

"I don't think she was ever mad, just scared, like you."

"Why?"

"Because some older people don't know how to handle small children, especially a crying child."

She extended her lower lip. "Poor Gwace. My poor friend."

Kyle smiled in relief, as Button laid claim to Grace. "She'll be fine. What I'm trying to tell you, Button, is that you need more friends, especially girls with whom you can share, well, girl stuff. Grace is good for that."

"Okay, Daddy. I play nice with Gwace next time."

"Fine." He set her little bare feet on the floor. "Time for our story."

Button moved to her nightstand for the book. "Wonder what she's doing now?"

"Grace? I can't even imagine."

Button nodded confidently. "She playing shoes. I would."

Kyle shrugged. Was it too much to hope that, like Button, after a hard Friday, Grace did prefer to sulk in the safety of her closet?

Chapter Thirteen

Grace wasn't particularly surprised to spot Michael on her back doorstep Sunday morning. He'd called earlier to scope out her plans for the day, and seemed delighted to learn she intended to laze around the town house.

"Since when don't you barge right in?" she called out.

"My hands are full, had to ring your bell with my nose."

She scooted across the room and pushed open the screen door, delighted to find him carrying a pastry box and a brown envelope. "A geek bearing gifts."

Michael eased inside with a good-humored smile, placing his offerings on the table.

She opened the pastry first, ogling the array of frosted delicacies. "Mmm. Can't remember the last time I had a napoleon."

Michael walked over to the coffeemaker and poured himself a mug of coffee. "The flyers are in the envelope. The leftovers anyway. Sue mailed one to everyone on the list yesterday."

Grace slipped a yellow flyer out of the envelope, scanning it approvingly. "I'll have to call and thank her."

"She'll be gone for a few days. I'm treating her and the family to a short trip up north at the Bluefin Bay Resort."

Grace was openly pleased. "Excellent choice."

"Her husband is a big fisherman and Lake Superior is

the place for it.'' Michael rooted round in her refrigerator, delighted to find some milk for his brew. ''It's so nice to find staples here now. Kyle's the greatest, isn't he?''

She shrugged. ''Gee, there are some ladyfingers tucked beneath the twists. Talk about flaky perfection.''

''So, have you spoken to him recently?''

She sank her teeth into a ladyfinger and savored the taste.

''I mean Kyle, you know.''

''Well, today is Sunday, and he was here on Friday.''

''Not since then?''

''No.'' She glanced at him in suspicion. ''What are you trying to tell me, Michael?''

''Well, for starters, I'm ready to admit that I was wrong about your chances with Kyle. There must be a spark between you—one that he knows about this time, I mean.''

''What a sensitive observation. What finally made you pull the paper sack off your head?''

''No choice. Kyle's made his interest very obvious, was full of questions during our floor excursion.''

''Like what?'' she asked eagerly.

''Oh, everything an interested man touches on, your goals, your job, your relationships. Plainly, he was trying to figure out what you admire most in a man, size up any competition.''

''Well, he's pretty nosy for someone who is tighter with his secrets than the CIA.''

Michael leaned over Kitty's basket to give her fur a ruffle. ''Glad you noticed he's changed some.''

''Of course he has! We all have.''

''But in his case, with that solitary man bit, it's harder to read the changes.''

She refilled her mug, then leaned against the counter. ''Given time, I am confident that I can break through those barriers.''

''Of course you would be. A North never gives up.''

"Your support would be helpful," she ventured. "As the folks wrote the book on stubborn and still have eyes for Dickie."

"I'll do my best."

"Even go against Dad?"

"Yes."

Grace sipped her coffee in silence, suddenly alert to the sound of running water. "Hey, are you running my sprinkler out back?"

"No. I can explain though."

Not liking his guilty look, Grace charged to the back door, swung it open and stepped out for a look. To her amazement, there was a kiddie pool about five feet in circumference in the middle of her small backyard near her arrangement of lawn furniture. Her garden hose lay in the pool, filling it with water at a dribbling pace. She stepped back inside with a baffled look.

"The man at the store said if you fill it slowly, in the sunshine, the water heats up faster."

Her confusion deepened.

"It's the kind of pool you always wanted, remember? When we were kids and you were so afraid of the folks' Olympic-size one."

"That was twenty years ago, when I was just a toddler. As much as I appreciate the thought, it's a slight I've dealt with."

Michael brightened. "Ah, but speaking of toddlers..."

Grace leveled a finger at him, a new light dawning. "Oh, ho! So this whole deal, the treats, the fast work on the flyers, the humbling admission that Kyle actually might find me attractive, has an ulterior pint-size motive."

"Add cleverness to your assets—"

"Oh, shut up. This is all about Button. Somehow."

Michael expelled a breath, pouring out the bottom line. "The wallpaper for the bistro arrived. We'd like to get it up today if we can. I'd hoped you could watch Button. The pool idea seemed like a nice distraction, something you could do together.''

Panic filled her eyes. "Michael North! If only you knew what happened here on Friday.''

"I do know. Met up with Amelia at the bistro yesterday and she spilled the entire fiasco to me. She was only complimentary to you, though. Thinks you're great, for a pampered rich girl.''

"That's the sweetest backhanded compliment I've had in ages. So why can't she baby-sit Button?''

"Some kind of committee meeting at church. Please,'' he begged. "I've already performed half a miracle rounding up a half-dozen guys from the old crowd to pitch in and help us. Your cooperation would make it a total miracle.''

"You guys are a couple of operators.''

"Only me,'' Michael promptly assured. "Kyle was totally against asking you.''

"What!'' She did an about-face and bristled over the rejection. "Like I can't handle it! That's what he thinks!''

"He just doesn't want to impose.''

"Yeah, right.''

"You'll have to make up your mind where you stand here, you're either the brave helper or the huffy incompetent.'' He glanced at his watch. "Can you hurry it up? He's sort of on his way over. Told him to meet me here.''

True to Michael's prediction, Kyle arrived soon thereafter with Button. There was a nervous anticipation in the air as they shared coffee and pastries. Michael teased Button to distraction, feeding her pieces of doughnut, pretending Kitty was a huge tiger on the prowl for her.

Grace and Kyle edged around one another rather uncomfortably.

"Would you like to see how the flyer turned out?'' Grace finally asked, gesturing to the table.

"Yeah." He sauntered closer as she opened the envelope. He examined the sheet with care. "Michael said they went out yesterday. Wouldn't be surprised if we get some action by tomorrow."

"If nothing comes of it, maybe you can distribute these things at your grand opening."

"Which should be soon. The floor's going in tomorrow. And we're wallpapering today...."

Grace could tell by his tone that he wondered what Michael told her about their plans, her potential part in it. She tried to decline the baby-sitting job, but found herself tongue-tied.

Kyle picked up the conversation again. "I can't decide if Jerome's silence at this point is good or bad. You'd think he'd be back in touch by now."

"Jerome wants you to open with gusto, that's when he'll be back to propose a buyout figure." The ice between them began to melt as Grace bolstered him. "Hopefully by then we'll have some answers. Maybe you can even nail him in court for something—like extortion."

"I just want him gone," Kyle said quietly. "Want to put my energies into positive projects, like Button."

Button. Grace touched his muscled arm, this time determined to form a proper rejection. "Kyle, it's nothing personal, but I can't imagine Button wanting to stay with me. Alone. Just the two of us."

"Daddy, look!" Button cried.

Kyle turned to find the toddler in Michael's arms, standing at the back door. "What, honey?"

"Dere's a swimmer pool outside!"

Michael gasped at the child wriggling against his chest, then kissed her cheek. "Oh, gosh, you're right! Let's take a closer look."

The four of them trailed out to the backyard. Noting the

pool was nearly full, Grace moved to the house and turned off the spigot.

Michael set Button on the grass and reached down to flick her with water. Grace's heart melted as Button squealed with delight and ran circles around the pool. Hard to believe a hard shell of plastic filled with plain old city water could dazzle so. "Would you like to stay here and swim with me?" she asked shyly.

"What?" Button asked softly, staring up at Grace.

Kyle flashed Grace a heart-stopping smile of gratitude. "C'mere, honey." He dropped to his knee and Button ran to him. The conversation was meant to be intimate but echoed through the yard. "You can stay here if you like, play in the water."

"You, too, Daddy?"

"Not right now. Mike and I have to go to the bistro and glue paper to the walls."

"I do that, too. You say so."

"But this would be more fun for you."

"Grammy come over?"

"No, just you and Grace."

Button gazed longingly at the pool, then hesitantly at Grace.

"We'll have fun," Grace encouraged.

Moments passed as Button thought. "Okay. I stay."

Joyful, Kyle gave Button a squeeze and whispered in her ear. "Remember what you were going to say to Grace today?"

She turned to Grace, finger hooked to her lip. "Don't be scared of me, honey."

Kyle gulped in shock. "Not that, Button!"

Button turned back in innocent confusion. "What, Daddy?"

"Closet," he coached.

"Oh. Sorry I runned in your closet and cried."

"We'll forget all about it." Grace angled a dour look at Kyle. "So I'm supposed to be scared, uh?"

Kyle shrugged sheepishly.

Michael tweaked Button's cheek. "Just think, we'll be working and you girls will be splashing around like a fish."

"Oops, just thought of something," Grace intervened. "I bet Button doesn't have a swimsuit."

Her small round face fell. "Never got one since I was a born baby."

"Wear your little dress in there," Michael said.

"It's brand new," Kyle objected, "from Amelia. But you could go in your underwear, Button," he suggested.

She clapped a hand to her mouth. "Oh, Daddy," she squealed in disbelief. "I don't wet pants."

Kyle's expression fell. "I give up."

"Hang on," Michael protested, "this seems a minor catch. Grace can fix it. Sure, Grace can take Button to the store and buy her one."

Button hid behind Kyle as Grace balked. "Me?"

"You are a pro shopper," Michael urged. "And we really have to get downtown. The guys will be waiting."

"I suppose I could do that," she relented.

"I'll go lock up my house," Michael announced.

Kyle paused before Button. "So you'll be set. You can play store with Grace first. Like you play rest-rant and shoes. Then go for a nice swim."

"I might even buy you some candy," Grace tempted.

"Keep costs down, won't you princess?" Kyle directed. "I'm not made of money."

"Target okay, Rockefeller?"

"A family favorite." He moved closer to Grace, fiddling with his key ring. "Here is my extra key to Amelia's front door. If for any reason things get funky for Button, you can take her over there."

Now that Grace was pumped she hated to see Kyle express even vague doubts. Her tone was mildly sarcastic. "We'll try and control the funk."

With a wink he retreated across the lawn.

"I COME HERE BEFORE," Button announced as Grace reached into the back seat and unbuckled her seat belt. "With Daddy."

Grace set her on the blacktop. "It's very important that you stick right by me, like you must do for Daddy." Without a word, Button slipped her hand in Grace's.

Grace would've breezed right past the bank of red carts if Button hadn't laid her hands on one. "Daddy gives me a ride. Real fast."

Grace helped her climb into the back. "Just the same, we'll go slow."

"Why?"

"We don't want to knock anyone down. And we don't want to miss seeing anything."

They wheeled around, Button scanning the departments, her finger extended like a dazzled tour guide. She spoke in a babble. "What's that big doll lady? Mann-what? Look at the books. Got candy corns for Kitty."

The cart was holding a variety of goodies by the time they reached the toddler department. Grace rummaged through the swimsuits, narrowing it down to a half dozen for Button's inspection. She felt it very important that Button have a say in what she wore.

Button gave a purple striped suit and a red one an immediate thumbs-down. Ultimately, the yellow and white one with a ruffled skirt proved a favorite. They stood before a mirror and Grace held the tiny nylon suit in front of Button. "I like this one best, too." Grace then reached into a nearby bin of hats. "Here's a cute straw number." She set it atop the child's dark head. "Like it?"

"Cute," she mimicked. Button pointed to a bin of plastic sandals. "Look, flippy flops."

"Oh, yes, we must have flippy flops. And sunglasses." Grace pointed to a rack. "Here are some yellow ones, shaped like daisies! Gee, Button, you're coordinated!"

"Get some, too. Be like me."

Grace donned a pair of the plastic daisy frames. "I'll do that."

They loaded these purchases into the cart and Button decided she wanted to walk from then on. Grace felt like quite a dupe when they were soon passing the toy department.

"Here's those toys!" Button scooted ahead.

"Wait for me," Grace called in alarm. To her relief, Button meekly obeyed. Grace was sure a couple of mothers glanced at her sharply, but she was new to this kind of responsibility. Keeping track of Kyle's precious daughter seemed an awesome responsibility in her mind. Better alarmed than separated.

Grace couldn't help taking an interest in the vast array of toys. "Look here, Button, here are some beach things. An inflatable ball, floating ducks, a bucket and shovel. Let's get them for the pool."

"Okay!" Button helped her deposit them in the cart.

Grace followed Button into an aisle of girlish items, where some tiny plastic shopping carts caught the child's eye. "Look, a kiddie cart. To play store."

Grace noted that the price was miniscule. "Let's buy it."

"Here's play food, Gwace." She held up a package of miniature boxes and molded plastic fruit.

"Take that along, too. Then I think we better get out of here before we buy out the place."

With a small detour through the Arby's restaurant drive-through lane, they returned to the town house. They unloaded their purchases, ate a quick lunch of beef sandwiches and root beer, and changed into their swimwear. Button gasped at the sight of the woman's miniscule bikini. "I see your belly button!"

"So you do."

"It's bigger than mine."

Grace laughed as Button dipped an exploratory finger into her navel. "Now stand still so I can rub this sunscreen on you." Button couldn't seem to stop squirming, but Grace did the best she could to cover all her exposed skin. "That'll do it. Let's go out and test that water."

Armed with their beach toys they stepped into the pool. Button released an involuntary shiver. Grace was sure the child wasn't cold, merely nervous with the new experience. She sat down in the center of the pool herself, relaxing. "Ah, this feels good."

Button slowly dipped her bottom down into Grace's lap. "Feels good."

Grace pushed the floating rubber ducks around them in a circle. "Look at these guys swim."

"Two are girls."

"Which ones?"

Button giggled. "Guess."

They lolled around in the water for a long while, playing with the bucket and shovel and ducks.

Grace didn't even spot their visitor until she was casting a shadow over the water. "Mom!" Grace slid lower by accident, jostling Button as she righted herself.

"What are you doing?"

"Playing with my good friend, Button. Kyle's daughter," she added.

Button shielded her eyes, staring up at the long shadow. One look at the regal woman in the neat lilac pleated shorts and blouse and she shrank against Grace.

"Oh, yes, Betsy. I spoke to you on the telephone," Ingrid said cheerfully. "About Cinderella."

"Mom, what brings you here?" Grace asked, trying to avoid upsetting Button.

Ingrid appeared startled by the question, though she rarely dropped by unannounced and even more rarely without a motive. "I was golfing at the club and thought I'd swing by and say hello, that's all." She leaned closer. "You're a shy one, aren't you?" she said to Button.

"Mom," Grace murmured, "Button is uneasy with you."

"Ridiculous."

"Remember, you were a little curt with her on the telephone."

"That was nothing."

"She is only three."

Ingrid was taken aback. "Truly, I didn't mean anything, Betsy."

"My mom is always nice to my friends," Grace said meaningfully. "And now that she knows you're my friend, she'll be very nice to you."

"Well, I..." Ingrid huffed a bit.

"Take a chair," Grace invited, gesturing to her umbrella-covered table a few feet away. "Have some root beer. That glass without a straw in the cover is an extra."

"Arby's restaurant?"

"It's good," Button piped up.

Ingrid sat down under the shade of the umbrella, forgetting to check the cushioned deck chair for specks of dirt, as was her habit. She peeled the cover off the spare drink and sipped. Stiffly looking around the yard, she complimented Grace on her blooming azaleas. Every time Button giggled, Ingrid stared hard at the pool, then at the sky.

For all her airs, Grace was sure her mother was intrigued, perhaps even envious of her newfound kinship with Button. Rolling around in a wading pool with toddler Grace would've been unthinkable twenty years ago. Ingrid had standards to maintain, even for the benefit of the household staff.

How sad to miss such fun. Until this moment, Grace didn't know exactly the depth of loss involved. Never once in all the years had she ever seen Ingrid's dignity shaken.

In other words, she'd never had a small finger resting in the curve of her belly button.

Feeling cheated, Grace couldn't resist having a little fun with Ingrid now. "Mother, would you do me a favor?"

"What is it?"

"Please toss me that beach ball on the table. Oh, inflate it first, would you?"

Ingrid picked up the clump of plastic and hesitated.

"There's a hard plastic stem you blow into—"

"I know! I've seen it done." Determined to conquer, Ingrid blew. And blew. Grace and Button watched her in fascination as her face pinkened beneath her tan. Finally the ball was inflated to bouncy rainbow proportion. With force she batted it into the water. Button stood up and caught it.

"Good one!" Grace applauded. She noted her mother was mistaking the compliment for her but didn't bother to correct her. Ingrid looked just too pleased with herself.

"Do you know where Michael is today?" Ingrid asked after taking some fortifying breaths.

"He and a few of the old crowd are wallpapering the bistro."

"Really! Wish I'd known."

"Why, Mother?"

"Because I'm certain Dickie would've liked to have been included."

Grace wrinkled her nose. "He was never really part of that crowd."

"Sadly, no. But it shouldn't be too late."

"He certainly is determined—with all of us."

"Mainly because of his interest in you, of course."

Grace sensed that Button was trying to understand the conversation, and might even come to realize Dickie was the owner of the pearls, the man who confronted her. Explaining any outburst to Ingrid would be torture.

"You need anything, Button?" she asked in misdirection.

"I need to go potty."

Grace grinned. The ultimate excuse to get out of any jam. "All right. Let's go inside for a while."

Grace attended to Button's needs. She returned to the kitchen to find Ingrid helping herself to some aspirin.

"Headache?"

"A mild one."

Grace drew her a glass of water. "Those beach balls can be murder."

"Very funny. We played the long course today and Faye Brinkman was a royal pain, criticizing everyone." She washed down her pills and looked around. "Where is she?"

"Taking a TV break on my bed."

"In a wet suit?"

"She's bundled in two beach towels. And I'm not changing her clothes yet because we're going back out."

"All right, all right, you've got it well in hand." Ingrid set her glass in the sink with a pensive sigh. "Must say I'm surprised by this friendship, though. You've never shown any interest in children outside your actor clients."

"She's an extension of Kyle, which of course, sparked my interest in the first place. But Button stands alone in charm and warmth. Didn't realize how rewarding such a relationship could be." Grace wasn't about to confess how new her alliance with Button was, how much emotional strain it took to get this far. Ingrid always homed in on weakness.

Ingrid wandered over to the table to rearrange some freshly cut flowers Grace had in a vase. They both noted the brown envelope spilling with flyers at the same time. Grace meant to stash those away from any prying eyes. Picking up one of the bright sheets of paper, Ingrid demanded an explanation.

"It's a long story, but Kyle intends to solve the theft of Andy Anderson's safe."

"And you intend to help."

Grace lifted her chin defiantly. "Yes."

Surprisingly, Ingrid chuckled. "Over and over again, you are attracted to men in distress!"

"Most men are in distress," Grace shot back.

"Guess that's Dickie's main problem, isn't it? He isn't in dire need of your support. He's a success story, comfortable in his life."

"That's right, Mother," she drolled, "Dickie is just too perfect for me. I need a tortured man on the fringe, like poor Kyle."

Grace's sarcasm rolled right off her mother. "I believe I overdid the charitable lectures when you were young. Taught you to give of yourself and you've gone haywire."

Grace sized up Ingrid shrewdly. "Even you don't think he's guilty, do you?"

Ingrid paused, looking trapped. "No, neither your father nor I ever believed Kyle had done wrong. Despite his family troubles and lack of fashion sense, we always found him well mannered and reasonably intelligent. Oh, go ahead and fix him up as you have the rest!" she invited on impulse. "You have my blessing."

"Why?" Grace asked suspiciously.

"Because once you help Kyle, the thrill will be gone. The pattern's always the same, you eventually tire of your fixer-uppers and move on."

"Bet it won't happen this time."

"Care to make a wager?" Ingrid asked.

"What terms?"

"If I win, I want you to date two men of my choosing, and Dickie—if he'll still have you."

Grace smiled confidently. "If I win, I want you to give Kyle and Button a royal welcome into our circle."

Ingrid's confident mask cracked. "Treat them like part of the family?"

"No, better that," Grace retorted. "Like one of Dad's top clients."

Ingrid blanched slightly under her makeup. "Very well. It's a deal."

Chapter Fourteen

When Grace didn't answer her front doorbell later that afternoon, Kyle trotted around the side of the town house to the backyard.

What he discovered there blew his mind. Grace and Button poolside under a shade tree, stretched out on lounges! Both were dressed in swimwear, their eyes covered with children's daisy sunglasses.

The girls at play. Relaxed with each other, still in one piece.

The worrying he'd done was all for nothing. Grace had handled it.

Grace promptly sensed company and sat up. She smiled at Kyle, standing there in cutoffs and a T-shirt, baseball cap in hand. "Daddy's home."

Kyle's pulse tripped over the sultry greeting, his eyes scanned her curved tanned body, set on enticing display in a postage-stamp bikini. Like her red beaded dress, the bikini got his libido ticking, giving him crazy ideas.

"A few hours and you've managed to transform my child into a princess in training," he jokingly complained.

"We had a lot of fun," Grace admitted.

Kyle scanned the yard, noting the new toys, including the shopping cart full of fake groceries. Button had begged him for the very same thing their last trip to Target. He'd said no, concerned she might wheel the cart into the unsteady Amelia as she navigated around on her cane.

"I didn't spend much, really," Grace said defensively, measuring his frown. "Never had so much fun dollar for dollar."

Kyle lifted his arms. "Don't know why I bothered to return at all."

Grace bit her lip. "Button's fallen asleep, so as it happens, I am very glad you're back. It's better if you're the first person she sees."

"Good point." He stripped off his T-shirt, tossed it on a chair at the table, then wandered over to the pool to stretch out on the lawn. Covering his eyes with the brim of his baseball cap he rumbled in content. "Ah, feels good to rest."

"Finish the papering?"

"Yup. Most of the old college crowd showed up, so it went fast. A lot of those guys have had their own homes for years, so they're real experienced with papering. Libby and I, we always rented, never did much decorating."

Grace detected a trace of wistfulness in his tone, as though he felt he'd been cheated. How she wanted to comfort him on every conceivable front, climb inside him and lay his troubles to rest. Determined to at least be noticed, she rose off the lounge chair and sauntered over to a patch of lawn between him and the pool. Sitting down noiselessly, she dipped her fingers into the water and flicked his chest.

To her frustration, he made no response. His face remained placid under the brim of his cap, his body still. Feeling slighted, especially with all her assets on display, she began to set rubber ducks on his chest, lining them up in a weaving pattern, perhaps accidentally grazing his nipples with her nails.

He lay still for so long, she was unprepared when he

struck. His huge hand locked around her wrist and pulled her down over him. Bare hot skin connected with a seductive smack. With a soft cry she peeled off his baseball cap. His eyes were burning slits.

She'd never looked lovelier, he decided, those silly daisy specs perched in the center of her nose, her mouth ajar in surprise.

"You messin' with me, lady?"

"I'd sure like to." Grace dipped her mouth to his for some gentle play. Her daisy sunglasses flipped off onto his forehead. He reached up and tossed them aside, then slid his hand into her auburn curls to press her even closer.

Grace shuddered against the length of his solid plane of muscle. If Kyle was another of her fixer-uppers as Ingrid claimed, he had the best foundation she'd ever climbed upon! In fact the foundation was actually rising beneath her, right around the middle.

So Kyle did desire her in the most basic way. It seemed an ideal time to let him know how much she'd welcome such intimacy.

Breaking free of his mouth, she propped her forearms on his chest, centering gemstone green eyes upon his hazy blue ones. "How I wish we were on some deserted island right now," she murmured, "rolling round on the sand."

He clamped a hand low to her half-exposed cheek of flesh. "I'd settle for a free pass to that bedroom of yours, rolling around on that big mattress."

"You might just make it, if you quit complaining about my stuff."

"That's all it will take?" he teased. Sobering he said, "Guess our timing is lousy here, considering Button. It's mostly your fault, too."

"Why me?"

"You shouldn't have jumped me this way out in broad

daylight. I may have to report you to the baby-sitters' union or something.''

''Why, you big—'' As his chest began to shake she realized he was joking. Soon he was roaring with laughter. Grace could think of no retaliation but to squeeze his nose and twist.

''Ouch!''

''Hey, Daddy?'' Button piped up. ''What you doing?''

Glancing over Grace, Kyle spied his daughter, sitting upright on the lounge in her new ruffled swimsuit, watching them through her daisy glasses. With a swift movement he hoisted Grace over the edge of the pool and together they rolled in with a splash. ''We're swimming, Button! Come on in.''

With a whoop of glee, Button scampered over to the pool and flung herself at the adults.

After their splash party, Kyle and Grace pulled lounge chairs into the sunshine to dry off, with Button nearby playing supermarket with her new accessories. When Grace took him up on his offer to make dinner off the clock, she hadn't noticed the package of hot dogs in the back of her freezer, nor the box of macaroni and cheese concealed in a cupboard. Button's favorite foods, on hand just in case. Grace wasn't thrilled by the menu, but she couldn't resist wanting to please Button, who had been so well-behaved all day.

After depositing the dirty dishes in the sink after their meal, Kyle swung a leg over one of the kitchen chairs, sinking down. Grace appeared in the living room doorway.

''Button wants you to know, Daddy, that she is watching the big TV, but is ready to go home.''

''Did she accept why she has to leave the toys here?''

''I think she realizes how fragile Amelia's balance is. She seems to treat her quite gingerly—from what I've seen.''

Kyle regarded Grace with a sigh. "I'm ready to face it, you are officially hooked."

"Hooked on what?"

"Button. You can't stop jumping through her hoops. Buying her stuff, defending her. You even ate a hot dog for her."

"They're not half-bad, broiled that way." She sauntered over to his chair, biting his neck. "Seems there's nothing you can't heat up."

He dipped his hand inside her gaping terry beach jacket, grazing her rib cage, the bottom edge of her breast. "I've been thinking, how would you like to go down to the bistro tonight and check out the improvements?"

She raised a skeptical brow. "Think I might enjoy that?"

"Might play a few tunes on the old jukebox. Have a dance like we used to."

"You actually remember dancing with me?"

"Sure." His hand glided to her hip. "There wasn't as much of a shelf to set my hand on. But you smelled real good."

She placed a hand on her heart. "With a line like that, no girl would have a chance."

GRACE AND KYLE DECIDED to meet at the bistro after ten o'clock. That way Kyle could go home, spend a little time with Amelia, and make sure Button was down for the night.

Even with all his duties however, he was waiting in his Jeep in the modest parking lot when Grace pulled her BMW convertible up alongside him and cut the engine and lights.

"Hey," Grace said, climbing out of her car to join him.

"Hey, yourself."

They stared at one another for a long moment. Grace was dressed in a strapless coral sundress and matching sandals, Kyle in crisp chinos and pale blue oxford shirt. A quiet anticipation hummed between them. He held out his arm and they strolled up to the delivery entrance arm in arm, their voices drifting off on the warm night air.

Kyle unlocked the steel door and ushered her inside. The storage room they'd entered was dim, but to their amazement, the main room up front was ablaze with light. Kyle placed a finger on his lips to keep her quiet and motioned for her to stay put.

Having none of it, Grace was right on his heels as he crept forward.

"You!" they cried out in unison.

Michael North whirled around in surprise. "Nice trick! You scared the hell out of me!"

"Why are you here at his hour?" Kyle asked. "You've put in your time."

"Just cleaning up remnants. Especially didn't want these rolls of paper and buckets of paste to get tossed out. We can get a refund on them."

Kyle grinned. "That is good news."

"So why are you back?" Michael asked pointedly.

"I wanted to see your handiwork," Grace was swift to explain.

Michael didn't look completely convinced as he surveyed the showered and primped couple but beckoned Grace over to one of the walls. "You picked a nice paper, sis. The eggshell color, the tough finish. It adds light without going too far."

Folding her arms, she roamed around the room, willing her brother to take off. She was here to perform the mating dance with Kyle, reawaken the old thrill of swaying in his arms, feel his hands on her new shelf. Any brother, no matter how useful, would make a crowd.

Kyle felt it his duty to help Michael load the returns into his car out on the street. Grace sauntered into the small kitchen to find it very neat, with stainless appliances buffed to a shine. A connecting door led to Andy's office.

She had never been in this office as a teenager. It was rather small, held a wooden desk, a sofa, and a couple of extra chairs. Wondering where the safe was located, she began to peek under wall hangings. An ocean print behind the desk proved to be on hinges. Giving it a tug, she pulled it open to expose the door to the safe. Absently, she twirled the dial of the lock.

"Hey, you're a natural," Kyle said.

Grace whirled to find him at another doorway, the one leading to the dining room. "Just checking out the scene of the crime. Michael gone?"

"Yes, with a very quizzical outlook on our motives."

"I believe he's getting the idea that we're, well, getting cozy. It's just tough for him to make the adjustment."

"He never was big on change. C'mon, have a drink with me."

Grace followed him out front. He'd been working with the dimmer switch, for the room was now turned down to a golden glow, basking the wood and brass in a sheen. On the bar sat two champagne glasses and two bottles of beer.

"Sorry I don't have anything fancier. The bar's not stocked yet, I brought this beer in for the workers."

"Beer is fine."

He uncapped a bottle and split the contents between the flutes.

Grace took her flute and wandered over to the small dance floor holding the jukebox. "Ah, the same old songs."

Kyle came up beside her, touching her bare shoulder. "Some of them date back to the sixties. The Andersons liked that music."

Grace sipped her beer and set her glass on the top of the box. "You have any change to run this thing?"

"Don't need any. I rigged it earlier on to play for the workers."

Grace punched some buttons. As an old George Michael tune swelled to life, Kyle set down his glass and gathered her in his arms. Slowly, they began to sway to the music.

"You know, if you think about it, it could have been me," she said, alight with mischief.

"Huh?"

"I could be the thief."

"Yeah, right." He spun her around on the floor.

"I could've slipped in and out of the office easily—through the kitchen, then the service door."

"Oh, c'mon."

"Don't give up so easily. I like the idea of consuming your thoughts late at night, being a threat to your very psyche."

"Sorry, there's no way I'd buy it. You simply had no motive, already having everything a girl could want."

She laid her head upon his chest. "Not quite everything."

What did she mean? He guided her around slowly, burying his face in her soft fragrant curls. Grace had all the trimmings an executive family had to offer. Even romance seemed no problem, always a parade of strays hanging around her house, begging to be noticed.

"You are a threat to my very soul, if that makes you feel any better," he consoled, "niggling into mine and Button's hearts. What was supposed to be a simple job for you has become a way of life."

"Seems like a decent beginning."

"You know what I appreciate about you most, Gracie?"

She sighed blissfully. "Can't imagine."

"That you haven't pushed me hard, tried to hammer out terms between us. Given my situation I'd have found it impossible to live up to them."

This narrow and unrealistic speech given by any other man probably would've compelled her to storm off in a huff—after pouring a beer over his head! Grace was indeed in the habit of expecting more, attacking men and other causes with direct gusto. Just the same, here she was, walking on eggshells with Kyle out of sheer instinct. As difficult as Grace found any kind of patience, it seemed to be paying off here.

They danced on and on, slowly, languidly, a slow fever rising between their bodies.

Then Grace reached up to kiss his jaw, and the world stood still. As if set afire, Kyle clamped his hands on her bare shoulders and dipped his mouth over hers. Grace tipped her head back, welcoming his kiss, a kiss full of potent intent. It was finally happening after all these years—Kyle only had eyes for her, wanted to make love to her.

Grace's hands, already circling his waist, skimmed lower to his hips, pushing his pelvis into her belly invitingly. Their kiss deepened with searing intensity. His tongue skimmed the sensitive surfaces of her mouth, drawing her senses to life. Grace allowed herself to completely let go, to savor every move, every taste, every sensation.

Kyle groaned, tearing his mouth from hers. "When I think of you in that bikini... And there isn't much to this dress, either. What is holding it up?"

"Magic," she said coyly.

He chuckled. "What else?"

"Actually, a very long zipper in back keeps it molded to my body." Her eyes flickered green flames. "Now if that zipper were to open..."

Eagerly Kyle's hands fell to her shoulder blades, seeking the zipper tab. Finding it, he gave it a ride down her back. The dress fell to the floor, leaving Grace standing in... absolutely nothing.

"Grace..." Kyle reeled, riveted to the sight of her body in the pale light, in the center of a very public dance floor. Her skin was darkened to a honey color, even in the areas that the bikini had concealed that afternoon. She didn't seem to mind at all that he wanted to look. How completely she was giving herself to him. How much trust she was putting in him. He might not deserve it, but it wouldn't stop him from accepting her offer.

"Dance with me now," she crooned, wrapping her arms around his neck.

This was insane, Kyle knew, fully dressed, dancing with a nude princess. Still, he couldn't wait to hold her close. The jukebox was playing a vintage Gloria Estefan ballad. Holding her tight he glided around the floor, his hands roving the silken skin of her bottom, her breasts.

"I have to get out of my clothes," he confided urgently. "Now."

"Let me get you started." Grace laughed softly, indulgently, unbuttoning his shirt. He would probably never know she'd deliberately tortured him a little, just to give him a taste of the frustration she'd felt for so long, wanting to climb inside him, almost tasting how it would be, only to be denied. She'd waited years, he about a minute for every year. It was the best sweet revenge she could manage under the circumstances.

By the time she loosened his belt, he lost patience. Hoisting her over his shoulder he took her into the office and laid her on the sofa. Grace watched with pleasure as he finished undressing himself. She gave a soft gasp as he pulled off his briefs to reveal himself completely aroused.

Crowding her on the tight divan, he whispered hotly in her ear, "Now, where were we..."

Grace was entranced as Kyle began to make thorough love to her, far surpassing her hottest daydream ever. Nuzzling her breasts, he took each one into his mouth, bringing her nipples to achy erection with a drag of his teeth. A large roughened hand dragged over her belly, caressing her nest of curls. Plunging two long fingers between her intimate lips he created a friction, causing her to writhe and buck against him. "You had to be ready for me well ahead of time," he growled in wonder as she reached her peak.

If only he knew how ready. For how long.

Unable to contain himself any longer, Kyle drove his rigid flesh inside her, once, twice, languishing in her searing moist heat. She rose up to him eagerly, wrapping her legs tight around his waist, riding his every motion with rolling hips.

Feeling tense, irresistible pressure, Kyle reached for his pants, patted down the pockets and claimed a foil condom packet.

"I'll do that," Grace offered. Taking the packet she opened it with her teeth. Kyle was spellbound as this pampered, put-together princess excitedly took hold of the rubber ring and unrolled the condom over his sex.

Kyle saw stars within seconds. He glided into her opening several more times with increasing thrusts and exploded with force.

They lay together for a long while, content with their intimacy.

Grace eventually noted that Kyle was wearing a far-off expression.

"A penny for your thoughts."

"I think I'd like to do that all over again," he admitted.

Grace rolled on top of him. "With some variations…"

THERE WAS A RAP ON Grace's back door on Monday afternoon, right in the middle of her nail session with Chev.

"Come in!" Grace called out from her place at the kitchen table.

Heather and Nate Basset entered. The tall slim blondes

were dressed in opposing styles. Heather was casual in shorts and sleeveless blouse; Nate, in a crisp beige suit, looked as though he'd popped out of his real estate office.

"Hello, Chev!" Heather said brightly to the small dark Frenchmen at work on Grace's fingernails.

Chev bobbed his dark, slicked head. "Ah, the bride."

"Is this the man who did your nails for our wedding?" Nate asked.

"I am the artist," Chev corrected genially. Holding Grace's left hand, he went back to spreading acrylic over her index finger. "Pleased to meet you, Mr. Basset."

"Same here. You did a stand-up job, Chev."

"This is a surprise," Grace said lamely, despite the fact that Nate was clutching their yellow flyer in his hand.

"Nate is on his lunch hour and we thought we'd come over to clear up any misunderstanding. Is Kyle here?"

"Yes. Just went down the basement to turn up the thermostat on my water heater. The water just isn't hot enough. Kyle!" she called in the direction of the staircase.

There was a thump on the stairs. Kyle and Button appeared. Button marched over to Grace and climbed up into her lap. Planting her pudgy hands on the table, she said, "My turn, Mr. Chevy?"

The normally uptight Frenchman smiled. "Not yet, wee one."

Button twisted half around. "Why you call me, Gwace."

"I really called your Dad."

Button wiggled her fanny deeper into Grace's lap, as if staking out her territory. Then she gazed up at an amused Heather. "It's gonna be my turn."

Heather's eyes widened. "Hey, I'm only visiting."

Grace didn't want Button to linger to eavesdrop and appealed to Chev. "Dab a little polish on her nails now, will you?"

"Very well. Pink?"

Button leaned forward to peer into his chest of supplies. "Black."

Chev lifted his chin. "I refuse. You are a baby."

"How about magenta?" Grace stared at Chev. "Just do it."

He swiftly dotted Button's nails. "There, now blow on them."

Everyone chuckled as she puffed on her hands. Beneath the cordial surface, however, Grace could feel a rising tension. She pulled Button off her lap. "You can go watch TV, but sit on the floor and lay your hands on your legs. It'll take a while for them to dry."

"When?"

"Sit for one cartoon and we'll see."

"We must also wait for your acrylic to dry before we proceed with your color, Grace," Chev said, standing up. "I will slip out for a smoke."

That left the foursome alone in the kitchen. Heather sat down beside Grace and spread the flyer on the table. "Now, what is this all about? I mean, Nate has nothing to do with it!"

"He was questioned by the police back then, Heather," Grace said. "He was there that night."

Nate stiffened. "That much is true. I was there for a fraternity prank. As a freshman, I was coerced into a night of petty stealing. Had to prove myself to the upperclassmen by swiping something from a list of grills and bars downtown—you know, ashtrays, glasses with logos. Frankly, I was too young and dumb to know anything about loot in a safe."

"We're trying to cover the whole field is all," Kyle said smoothly. "Nate was on the witness list, so he got a flyer." He did slide Grace a wary glance, however. *Nate was there to steal?*

The Bassets got the gist of their exchange.

"I am not connected to any of it!" Nate insisted.

"But you said differently on our tennis date last week," Grace argued. "You have been in contact with Jerome Anderson, who you know full well is trying to muscle in on the bistro deal."

"I was just mouthing off a little. It would be a big sale for any real estate agent if it went through." Nate paused. "Say, you don't think I stole the sales agreement along with the other stuff! That I kept it all these years, then recently went into cahoots with Jerome Anderson, do you?"

Well put, Grace thought. But the fear in Heather's eyes made her crumble a little. She loved her like a sister and couldn't afford to be rash. "The flyer wasn't as personal as you think," she said kindly. "We've sent it to everyone on the premises the night of the theft. If that doesn't work, we're just going to hand them out to the public—to the whole wide world!"

Openly relieved, Heather rose to stand beside her distraught husband. "We made too much out of this, sweetie. They only want to know if you saw anything you might not have told the police."

Nate hung his head. "There is something. Look, I was too frightened to tell the police that I nearly went into Andy's office that night. I lingered round the door for a while, tempted to swipe something real impressive—"

Heather gasped. "You didn't tell me that!"

"See anything?" Kyle cut in.

"Well, I saw one of the waitresses go in there."

"Which one?"

"I don't know any names. Only remember she was young, dark hair, had on a bistro T-shirt. She did glare at me as if resenting my presence."

"Wow," Grace murmured. "That might be something."

Nate inhaled. ''There was also a guy in the vicinity. If memory serves me, Kyle, it was you.''

Kyle's jaw tightened and he leaned against the counter. Maybe he deserved some of his own medicine. Lots of the employees, himself included, buzzed in and out of that office.

''As far as Jerome Anderson goes,'' Nate went on, ''it's a coincidence that we spoke about the bistro property. But don't worry, no deal—honest or bogus—is worth upsetting this personal situation. Grace and Heather have been pals for years and I won't jeopardize that for anything. And I apologize for blowing my horn too loudly at the club, Grace, misleading you. Jerome made only the most surface inquiries, trying to get a ballpark figure of what the bistro is worth. He wasn't hiring us to do anything.''

Grace glanced at Kyle. He half smiled, as if willing to give him the benefit of a doubt.

''Thanks for letting us know,'' Kyle said, shaking Nate's hand.

''Good luck with your hunt.''

Chapter Fifteen

Kyle received a telephone call at Grace's home later that afternoon, just as he was ladling French onion soup into single serve containers. Grace had answered and tried to make sense of the man's panicky message.

"It's the floor guy down at the bistro. He says the place is overrun with people—"

Kyle grabbed the cordless instrument from her. "Mort? Yeah, it's me. What's the matter? Okay, okay, I'll be right down." He hung up, turning to Grace at the kitchen table, dressed for a business call, sorting through her half-loaded tote bag. "Apparently some of the bistro's former employees are looking for me."

"Over the flyer, no doubt." Grace frowned indecisively. "Maybe I should cancel my appointment at the community center."

"No, don't. Button wants to see that Cinderella rehearsal so badly."

"See those kids," Button chimed in.

"You girls head for the center and I will run down to the bistro."

"But we were all going—"

"Grace, go do your thing. I'll do mine."

She shook her head. How badly she wanted to combine their things!

Mort was waiting for Kyle inside the bistro's service door in the kitchen. "This is nuts, Kyle," he vented. Huffing in disgust, he hoisted his belt over his sagging belly.

Kyle smiled tentatively at the floor installer, a short broad man who could probably stop a train in a pinch. "Hope they haven't interfered too much with your work."

"Luckily I had the front door bolted. When they plowed through the service door into the kitchen, I managed to funnel them into the office." He pointed a thick finger at Kyle. "Don't let none of 'em out in the dining area. That parquet is fragile stuff. Ain't sposed to walk on it for a day."

Kyle saluted him and forged into the office. Voices rose at the sight of him. Someone closed the door with a slam. "Hello, everyone." He scanned the sea of faces, spotting waitresses, waiters, a cook and a bartender. "Iris, Joan, Phil, Dominic, been a long time."

Iris, who had been sitting on the desk, slid to her feet. A large-boned woman with a forty-four-inch bustline and brassy gold hair, she still commanded the same presence she had as head waitress here a decade ago. "Well, boy, we crooks just couldn't resist your invitation for a reunion."

"Excuse me?"

She raised a yellow flyer in the air. "How dare you accuse us of that robbery?"

"I didn't! I'm not!"

"What's this all about then? We all want to know, don't we?" Cheers rose in the cramped room, then fell away to complete silence.

"I especially want to know," a frigid lone voice asserted.

The crowd parted then, to reveal Amelia herself, seated behind the desk in Andy's old chair.

Kyle reddened, raking his hand through his jet hair. "Amelia."

"Do tell. What on earth are you trying to accomplish? Furthermore, how could you keep this from me, living in my own home?"

"I didn't want to trouble you yet, Amelia," he said.

Iris crowded his space. "Had she known, she would've stopped you from calling us crooks, I can tell you."

He choked on her strong perfume. "I didn't mean to accuse any of you. I'd just hoped you'd be able to give me some answers."

"That's rich, as we've always assumed *you* were the guilty party."

"Well, I'm not," he said hotly. "I happen to need something that was taken from that safe though. I'm doing my best to recover it."

"Recover it from one of us!" Dominic complained. "All the years I cooked for Andy, he never accused me of any wrongdoing."

"Well, lucky you," Kyle smarted. "For your information, you'll be helping Amelia if you cooperate." He met her eyes, speaking more gently. "I hoped to clear it up before involving her, but that idea's shot."

Voices rose again. Iris eventually overrode them. "We talked amongst ourselves before you arrived. There's some of us who could use the five hundred buck reward, but we don't know anything helpful. We dealt straight with the cops at the time. Our recollections were best back then."

Kyle held his hands up to the rowdy crowd in surrender. "Okay, okay. I'm sorry if I insulted any of your delicate systems." A ripple of laughter rose, causing him to smile. "I'd appreciate it if you'd just have faith that I am trying to do the right thing here. And if I do manage to get this venture off the ground as planned, I'll gladly give any of you employment—if you'd like."

The group dispersed shortly thereafter, Kyle funneling them out the service door for Mort's sake. With heavy feet he returned to Amelia. Her greeting was curt.

"What in blazes is going on?"

He nervously rubbed his stiff neck. "They shouldn't have bothered you. I specifically put the bistro's number—"

"Hush up and start talking," she chortled, pounding the desk.

Kyle outlined everything that had happened since Jerome threatened him.

"You should have come to me immediately, that very day."

"But back in Chicago, you said you didn't want to dredge up the past."

She bobbed her gray head. "Seems you took me too literally."

"But you knew about Jerome yourself, didn't you? He contacted you first about this very problem."

"He did not! That sniveling coward doesn't have the guts to lie to my face. No, I only heard from an attorney, shortly after you returned, in fact. A Mr. Richmond, I believe. Said his firm was representing Jerome in a possible dispute over bistro ownership. If I didn't have the sales agreement between Andy and Frank we'd better make room for Jerome in the business."

"What did you do?"

"I called his bluff and showed him the door."

"Because you figured I had the agreement," Kyle suggested.

"Well, yes," she admitted begrudgingly.

"So there you are, Amelia. The idea that you still thought me guilty hurt. I didn't want to hash it out all over again, see that same old disappointment in your eyes."

"Look, I meant it when I said I wanted to put our past

behind us. Figured if you stole from us, it was because your parents left you desperate, broke. You know, if you hadn't been romancing Libby, I probably would've given you a lot more aid. But Andy and I couldn't see straight back then about you romancing Libby. You were a good worker, but from such a troubled family. Seemed unlikely you could make a good husband.''

''Is it any mystery why I have trouble confiding in people? Trusting them?''

''No, it isn't. But believe me, I am far from disappointed in the man you've become.''

''No offense, but your confidence hasn't been overwhelming.''

''I've grown accustomed to living alone, so learning to make compromises under my roof is an adjustment in progress.'' Glancing up at his expectant look she added, ''I'm not much for sugary speeches, but if you need to hear it, I am proud of the way you handled Libby's death and Button's needs. Very proud indeed.''

''Thank you, Amelia,'' he said grandly.

Amelia rose from her chair. Using the desk for support she stepped up to hug him. ''And what have you to say to me?''

''That you are the best,'' he enthused. ''Still gutsy, determined and selflessly dedicated to family.'' Kyle held her bony frame in his arms, aware of her trembling beneath her shirtwaist dress. For all her tough talk, this whole thing was taking its toll on her.

''I don't know what we'll do about Jerome,'' she admitted, ''but it is good to have all this out in the open between us. Very good indeed.''

Grace proved further support to Kyle when they met up at the community center an hour later. They were seated in the darkened theater, watching Button sitting on stage left not far from the Cinderella players, in the midst of doing a very informal costume rehearsal. "I am glad you and Amelia made some progress," she whispered.

"At least the flyers accomplished some good. Figure they're a dead end now unless a customer on the mailing list calls. So far, not one has."

"We can hand them out at the grand opening."

"True, but I wanted to settle this before we got rolling. The idea of Jerome showing up to share the glory burns me."

Grace turned her attention to the wicked stepmother scolding Cinderella on stage. The stepmother's skirt needed to be raised an inch if she was going to pace around that way. She jotted down a note on her tablet. "Jerome sure is a creep, hiding behind some attorney to attack his own widowed aunt."

Kyle silently punched his fist into his hand in the dark theater. "The term creep doesn't begin to express my opinion."

Grace covered his fist with her hand. "Take it easy."

"Why should I?"

"Because, I want to invite you to a sleepover tonight and don't want the moment spoiled."

"You're inviting me to the Land of Oz? Really?"

"Don't looked so shocked, McRaney."

"But you were so determined to keep that part of you a secret."

Her green eyes twinkled. "After last night, hotshot, I don't imagine I have a single secret left."

That night, as they lay entwined together, spent from lovemaking, Grace's thoughts turned to the bistro. "Kyle, why don't we go and see Jerome's lawyer, see if we can appeal to his ethics."

"If he has any."

"He might not know how low-down this situation is, that the agreement is even mentioned in the robbery report."

"It's possible. Don't know the firm though. Amelia couldn't recall the name."

"She remembers nothing?"

"Well, she thought his name was Mr. Richmond. Yeah, that's it." Kyle gave her temple a gentle tap when she didn't respond. "You there, Gracie?"

It took her a moment to rally. "You have any free time tomorrow?"

"About what time?"

"I have some sewing to do…. How about early afternoon?"

"Should be all right."

"We'll need Amelia to watch Button for a couple hours."

"Okay. But what's up?"

"Nothing yet. I want to play out my hunch first, be fair about it. Though I don't think someone has been giving me the same courtesy."

KYLE MET GRACE DOWNTOWN the following afternoon in front of the Plato building. She led him through the lobby to the bank of elevators. "What are we doing?"

"Visiting Dickie."

"But why?"

The elevator doors opened. Grasping his hand Grace tugged Kyle into the crowded car and pushed the button marked twenty.

"Why Dickie?" he persisted quietly. "You think he can help us track down Jerome's lawyer because he knows other lawyers?"

"We'll see." Grace lifted her shoulders beneath her tailored navy jacket, the image of cool unbending power. Kyle could feel the steely North force emanating from her. He felt underdressed, underclassed and totally confused.

Grace burst out of the car as the elevator doors opened

at floor twenty, marching off to the corridor on the left. She slowed up at a door marked Frazer and Dupont Associates.

Kyle glanced at the roll call of names on a framed plaque. "Oh, God."

They entered the suite, Grace appealing to the receptionist. "I would like to see Haley Evers, Mr. Trainor's secretary." She gave her name and the receptionist picked up the telephone to check. "Go right on through. Do you know the way?"

"Yes, thanks." Grace touched Kyle's arm. "Let me lead on this one."

"I'll try. But you may be sorry you didn't tie me to a chair out here."

Haley Evers was seated behind her desk, pecking at her computer keyboard. She stopped work at the sight of Grace and Kyle. "If you're here to see Dickie, he's still at lunch."

"I'd like to begin with you, Haley."

She nervously tossed her long brown hair over a shoulder. "Oh?"

Grace sat down in the chair opposite the secretary's desk. Kyle remained standing, ill at ease. "First of all, let's touch back on the night we met at the Ordway."

"Right, when I wanted to compliment you on the Harlequin outfit—"

"Never mind about your sister's costume," Grace cut in. "Were you or were you not on a date with Dickie that night?"

Haley slumped. "Yes."

"You should've said so. I wouldn't have minded."

Haley glanced up at Kyle's tall, dark, imposing figure, swooning a little. "Guess not. But I was under orders. Dickie told me to keep my mouth shut, that he would handle you."

"*Handle* me?"

"Yes. I am so sorry, Grace. It all happened so fast. He

spotted you and your parents and freaked. Boy, can your dad deliver a glare. Anyway, he planned some quick action to brush me off. I know my sister thinks the world of you, so I decided I'd try and clue you in—at least a little.''

"Then Dickie joined our conversation and you chickened out."

"Yes. Dickie backed up his position with me the very next day, I keep away from you or lose my job."

"What exactly were you going to tell me that night?"

"My job..."

"I'll get you a better job at North Enterprises if need be," Grace promised. "One without any kind of sexual harassment unless you enjoy dating Dickie."

"He's impossible! Pompous." She trailed off in disgust. "But can you really do that, get me a better job?"

"Certainly. Have to be some benefits for having a mogul for a father."

"A change would be nice."

"As a bonus, I'll give you a picture of Dickie at age eight, a slimy little drip in a snorkel. You can post copies everywhere before you leave." She leaned over the desk. "Now what were you going to tell me that night?"

Haley took a breath. "That Dickie seemed to be dating you under false pretenses—for business reasons. I don't know all the details, but I do know he promised one of the partners that he could get close to you and your brother if need be."

Dickie entered the office then, looking relaxed and sophisticated in a gray summer suit. "Grace, what a surprise."

"Mr. Pock," she greeted meanly.

He was set off balance. "That isn't very nice."

"No, it isn't. Perhaps we should get formal, *Richmond* Trainor."

He gave a startled laugh. "I don't understand what's going on."

She jumped to her feet. "Can it, Dickie, the jig is up."

Dickie glared down at Haley, who was fidgeting behind her computer.

"Don't even bother with her," Grace scolded. "This is between you and me and a little old lady named Amelia."

Kyle sidled closer, a dangerous glint in his eye. "Don't forget me."

"We can't seem to," Dickie said, smarting a little. "You are becoming quite a nuisance." He paced a bit, shaking his blond head. "So the old girl finally remembered me coming to see her on Jerome's behalf then? Gambled she wouldn't, she couldn't find her specs and kept calling me Mr. Richmond."

"She did lead us here indirectly," Grace confirmed. "Once I heard the name Richmond, I got to putting pieces together. Remembered the way you knew Kyle was back before I did, and mentioned it the night of my birthday party, the way Jerome showed up unexpectedly at the bistro while we were stripping wallpaper. The latter seemed especially unlikely as few people knew we'd be there.

"Then there was the day you came to return my pearls and discovered Amelia was inside. You looked downright mortified. You hid behind the excuse that you had dueled with Button, that Amelia might be holding it against you. But that seemed strange behavior for a smooth operator. I'd have expected you to stay, to try and charm your way out of it."

Dickie sniffed. "Yes, there I was, doing a good deed by returning the pearls and you had a trap waiting inside for me."

Grace's final question was bound to be ego crusher for herself, but she saw no choice but to proceed. "The timing seems unbalanced, but you were dating me under false pretenses all the time, weren't you? Using me to get information for Jerome Anderson, yes?"

The faint lines around Dickie's eyes tightened. "Yes."

Grace stomped her sensible pump into the plush carpet. "Oh, Dickie! How did all this get started?"

"Quite by accident." Dickie took on a philosophical pose. "I was sitting in on a consultation with Jerome Anderson one day. He'd come to explore his rights to his father's share in the bistro. Had gotten wind—through gossipy relatives here in the Twin Cities—that Amelia planned to sell out to Kyle, encourage him to reopen. According to Jerome's information, things were rolling fast, Kyle was already back in town and Michael was in on the deal, providing a pile of that North green.

"Pure luck that I knew of the bistro through you and Michael, that I'd actually gone there several times while in college. You should've been here when I announced I had an in! Partners clicked their heels. When I offered to donate my services as a spy—to date you—I was the golden boy in line for a promotion. I worked fast, wriggling into that leukemia fund-raiser dinner through your father. He actually thought he was hooking me, when all the time it was vice versa! The timing was all so smooth. You nor your father even had a clue that Kyle was back yet, that he and Michael had plans. By the time you found out on your birthday, our relationship was already in gear."

"Didn't anyone in this firm care that Jerome's father might very well have sold his rights away years ago? That the sales agreement could be lost?"

Dickie regarded her piteously. "We deal in legalities here, Grace. Naturally I downplayed that possibility to the partners, but even so, if we could make a case for half ownership, we were going to do it."

"What about Nate Basset?" Grace thought to ask. "Is he another stroke of luck?"

"No, I steered Jerome to him to get a ballpark estimate on the bistro. In the event that any of you got suspicious about Jerome's pipeline of information, I hoped suspicion would rest upon Nate first. Why, he even bragged about the Jerome contact in the bar at the country club. How cooperative. Must say it's been fun manipulating you Norths, who for years considered me a homely jerk."

"You are no longer homely," Grace conceded.

He took her sarcasm with humor. "Don't make any mistake, Grace, I do think you're sexy. All those times I tried to get you in the sack, I really hoped to make it."

Kyle made an instinctive move toward the other man, which Grace quickly squelched with a body block. "We need him alive. For now."

For a second, there was a flash of fear in Dickie's eyes. "I'd like you two to leave now."

"Not until you tell me exactly what Jerome intends to do," Kyle demanded.

"I shouldn't—"

"Give it a try," Grace insisted, again blocking Kyle.

Dickie rubbed his hands together, openly intimidated. "Jerome's still studying the angles, can't make up his mind whether to buy you out, sell off his own half, or find an outside buyer altogether. It was up to me to close in, decide if you were capable of handling the place, making Jerome a decent profit."

"No wonder you wanted me to use Kyle as a chef," Grace said in sudden realization. "It gave you more exposure to him."

Dickie shrugged. "That was a bonus. Kyle under your roof, handling his business out in the open, making delicious food. Told Jerome, that man can cook."

"Also explains why you tried to invest in the bistro. That would've given you access to all the records."

Dickie nodded. "In other circumstances, I sincerely

would've liked to invest. But I'd never be good enough for Michael, no sirree."

"You went to so much trouble, Dickie, I'm stunned."

"Hey, that place is worth a lot of money, certainly a lot more than Amelia is asking Kyle and Michael for. And Jerome is a rich man already. The firm wanted very badly to please him."

Grace clenched her fists, fuming. "You haven't changed at all, Dickie."

"If that's the worst you have to say—"

"It's quite simply the worst there is." Gratified that the slam hit the child deep inside him, she gave Kyle's arm a tug and they left.

"Wish I'd seen through him sooner," Grace lamented as they strolled the streets of downtown Minneapolis amidst the shoppers and professionals.

"Not sure it would've done much good," Kyle consoled.

As they paused on a curb for a red light, she gazed at him to find him smiling a little. "What are you looking so smug about?"

"I have one less hassle."

"Which is?"

"Dickie Trainor is out of the race."

"Oh." She blushed. "Unbeknownst to me, he was never in it."

The light turned green and they crossed the street. Kyle led her over to a bench under a tree near the public library. Sitting her down he took her hands in his.

"You shouldn't feel embarrassed by Dickie's trick. He was a fool not to recognize your value—which is far higher than any client or promotion." He squeezed her hands tighter. "You know I care deeply for you, Grace. It's been difficult for me, wanting you for myself, but wondering if you'd be better off with a man in your own league." He shook his head. "As far as I'm concerned, his exit was spectacular. Even your parents won't be able to buff up the shine on him after the stunt he's pulled.''

Grace laughed. ''That is true. Though I feel kind of sorry for them and Dickie's folks. Our families have a history.''

''I'm sure they can work it out,'' Kyle assured.

''The sad part about all our efforts, is that we still are no closer to finding that agreement.''

''The grand reopening is still a week away,'' Kyle said. ''But I have my doubts we'll have any luck before then— if ever.''

''Jerome won't be giving up just because we've busted Dickie.''

''We won't be giving up either. Mike already has an attorney briefed and ready, so when Jerome attacks next, we'll be prepared.''

Grace smiled. ''Can't wait for that grand opening. Should be extravagant.''

''I intend to invite all the guys who've helped me, treat them to a first class evening.''

''What about the girl who's helped?''

His blue eyes smoldered. ''I intend to spoil you rotten that night. The works. You will be my very own princess.''

Grace felt a quiver of excitement as he brushed his lips against hers. Aware that some students loaded with library books were watching them from another bench, she got a hold of herself.

''So you have clothing picked out yet?''

''Nope. I'm no good with my wardrobe. Always depended upon Libby for that.''

''Well, we can remedy the situation right now. There are some very nice stores downtown. Let's go find you a sharp suit.''

Chapter Sixteen

When Kyle and Button showed up at her house Wednesday morning, Grace led them directly up to her work studio. "I've been up for a couple of hours on a rush job," she explained. "Let me show you what I'm working on."

Button was extremely interested to see what her job entailed. She slid the knapsack off her shoulders and scooted up the stairs right behind Grace. Kyle was preoccupied and followed at a slower pace.

There was a faint acrylic odor in the air, despite the fact that she had the windows open and a fan rotating. A wheeled garment rack stood apart from her worktables. The rack's single rod held a row of large white T-shirts painted with abstract designs.

Kyle inspected the shirts, swaying slightly in the breeze of the fan. "These are...strange."

Grace laughed. "They're for an interpretive dance group. That isn't what I wanted to show you though." She moved over to the end of the rod and whisked a smaller shirt off the end. "While I had my paints out, I whipped up a shirt for your daughter. Careful," she warned as Kyle reached for it. "It's still a bit damp."

Grasping the hook of the hanger he turned the shirt around. Then burst into laughter. Painted front and center was a huge red dot. Beneath the dot was written Panic Button.

Button tugged at his pocket. "What's that, Daddy?"

"This says panic button, honey."

"Why's that funny?"

He tapped her nose. "Because sometimes, you are a panic."

"That's good?"

"It's fine with me."

Button clapped her hands together. "I want to put it on."

"Not today. I have to let it dry and then I'll wash it for you." To Grace's surprise, Button took the delay rather well. It was Kyle who wore a faint scowl. "Is something the matter, Kyle?"

Button hugged his middle. "You want a panic shirt, Daddy?"

"No, I'm just a bit pressed for time. The building inspector is meeting me at the bistro for one last check and I have a shipment of glassware arriving." He held up his hands. "But don't worry, I intend to cook you something first. Shouldn't take long."

"Oh, go along and do your thing," she invited. "I have plenty to eat."

Kyle sighed in relief. "Okay, thanks. So, Button, let's go down and grab your knapsack."

"No, Daddy. I don't want to go."

"But Grandma has an appointment this morning and we've imposed on Grace enough."

"Let's pose on Gwace."

Grace thought he might find the innocent innuendo sexy and fun, but Kyle's mouth only tightened. "Daddy doesn't have much spare patience today."

Button stomped her foot. "I don't either."

Grace intervened. "I don't mind Button's company." But strictly for the child's benefit she added, "I have to sew beads and sequins on all these shirts. I could do that downstairs, though," she said, already turning off her fan, "while you play nice with your toys."

"That shouldn't be hard," Kyle groused, "considering how many toys you have over here." But he was obviously grateful and gave Grace a quick hug. "You're worth a million. I'll keep in touch."

"We go to Arby's!" Button rejoiced.

"You like Arby's better than Daddy's cooking?" Kyle asked.

"'Course I do, Daddy."

Kyle moaned and left.

For the next two hours Grace sat in a rocker in her living room hand-sewing notions on the shirts. Button played house with Kitty for a while, then trotted off.

Grace looked up from her needlework as Button entered with her shopping cart. "You going to the grocery store?"

Button exhaled. "No, I just come home. See all the groceries?" She gestured to the cart loaded with the toy items.

"Now what are you going to do?"

"Go to a jewel store."

"To buy something out of my jewelry box?" Grace asked suspiciously.

Button's cheeks bunched as she nodded. "Don't worry, I pay you, honey." She dashed over to her knapsack and brought out a small plastic purse. "I got this full of money."

"Okay, what kind of jewelry do you want?"

"I want pearls pwease. From that yucky man."

"You're in luck. The yucky man did bring those pearls back." Grace pressed a purple bead to the shirt and sewed it in place. "You may wear them for a little while if you want. They're right on top of my dresser."

Button giggled. "I got them." She reached inside her T-shirt and pulled out the necklace.

Grace balked, still struggling with the child's intuitiveness. "Oh, Button, you should always ask me first."

"I gonna pay." She pounded the coffee table near Grace's knees. "I pay here."

"Fine." Grace clicked her tongue, her eyes falling back to her sewing. She was startled however, when real coins did clatter onto the table, a dozen shiny coins, in mint condition.

Grace stared at the coins for a good long time. Kennedy half dollars. Exactly the kind stolen from Andy Anderson's safe ten years ago.

She felt her pulse trip wildly. "Button, where did you get this money?"

"My room." She came over and edged onto Grace's lap, fingering her auburn hair.

Grace flung aside the shirt she was working on. "Does your Daddy know about it?"

"I don't tell Daddy."

"What about Grandma?"

"They are my money. From my mommy!"

From Libby? Grace didn't know what to think. As was her nature, she fell into action. She reached for the cordless phone and punched in Kyle's number at the bistro. To her frustration, the machine tripped on. "Kyle, it's Grace. Something's happened. Button's gone through Libby's belongings and found some things we've been searching for. I'm taking Button home for a closer look. Meet me there when you can. Bye." Quickly she shoved her feet into sandals, gathered up her purse and handed Button her knapsack.

Button was puzzled by her alarm. "Why you tell Daddy that?"

"I want to go over to your house," she said with forced cheeriness, double-checking her key ring for the spare house key Kyle lent her on Sunday.

"What about Arby's?"

"Maybe afterward, we'll go to Arby's."

"Pwomise?"

"Oh, Button, let's just go." Grace urged her out the back door.

The key Kyle gave Grace fit the front door of the old Cape Cod home. She tripped the lock, pushed open the door. "Anybody home? Amelia?"

"Amelia?" Button parroted, trotting into the kitchen.

"Looks like nobody's home," Grace decided. "Now Button, show me where you found those coins."

"Why?"

She paused thoughtfully. "Because we can play bank."

"What's bank?"

"Stores have food and clothes, banks have money," Grace reasoned.

"Okay!" Button dashed off in the direction of the bedrooms. Grace followed to find her tearing into her closet. When she attempted to drag out a box, Grace intervened. "Let me help."

Grace tugged the box to the center of the room and fell to her knees, thinking of her tour in here with Heather. If memory served her, Button had said these boxes were Libby's. Did Libby of all people hold the key to the theft?

"Mommy's stuff." Button blissfully dug through the box. "I found the coins in here." She tugged loose an old yellow star-burst pajama bag.

Grace sat cross-legged, taking the bulky bag in her lap. "I haven't seen a pajama bag like this in a long while." Not in ten plus years anyway. The JC Penney store had run a special on them back in the late eighties. Grace had had a similar one long ago and recalled it had a few secret compartments inside.

Button sat down and used her small fingers to unzip the bag. Grace gasped as she began to pull out the contents, an empty collector's folder which had presumably held the half dollars and loose hundred dollar bills!

Button kept working, pushing aside the pearls still hanging around her neck as they got in her way. "I use this kind of money next time," she said, raining the air with hundreds.

Grace's memory clicked back to the list of stolen items on the Anderson robbery police report: Kennedy half dollars, three grand in cash, some rings and the sales agreement.

The answer to all their troubles—that simple little agreement—might very well be stashed in this battered old bag!

"Let me have a hand in there," she suggested as calmly as she could manage. With Button's permission Grace dipped deeper, fishing through the bills, ultimately hitting upon a compartment that held rings. To the touch they felt like a pair wedding bands and two with stones. She kept them in place.

All these years, this childish pillow held the Anderson's stolen loot.

Oh, Libby, why did you do it?

And where was that agreement? She checked every compartment and checked again. Nothing. She dropped the bag and glanced down at the coin album. Offhandedly she flipped it open. There sat a folded sheet of paper.

Grace unfolded the paper and joyfully read its contents. *This was it!* Several minutes passed before she realized someone was standing in the doorway. "Kyle. You got my message." Grace excitedly rose to her feet. "You'll never believe what's happened."

Plainly, he didn't need a road map to figure out the scene. But his feelings at that moment were unreadable. "Grace, come out here. Bring that pillow and its contents."

Button faced him off, hands on hips. "It's mine, Daddy!"

"You can have it back. I just need to speak to Grace alone. So stay in here for a little bit."

Grace picked up everything they'd discovered. Once she had cleared the threshold, he closed the door firmly. "Come into the kitchen."

They sat together at the table. Kyle emptied the pajama bag, unfolded the agreement and scanned it.

Grace couldn't conceal her excitement. "Must be hard to believe of Libby, huh?"

Kyle stonily sorted through the rings, stacked the hundreds and tried to keep control. Unwanted tears rimmed his eyes, however.

Grace welled with sympathy as she watched him suffer. "Didn't you ever go through her stuff, even after she—"

"No! Just stuffed it in boxes for someday." He rubbed his face.

"At least Jerome is no longer a threat." She searched his face for some hint of gratitude. "Tell me, is there anything else I can do?"

He leveled a shaky finger in her face. "You've done more than enough!"

His thunder made her heart jump. "I did wrong?"

"Let's review. You've crossed a deeply personal boundary without a care to your welcome. You've piqued Button's curiosity over something she cannot understand—"

"She was already curious."

"Your excited reaction won't go unnoticed, I guarantee. I'll have to do some fast talking to satisfy her."

"A simple explanation will be enough. She's only three."

"Worst of all, you've risked being caught by Amelia. I know she won't be popping in, but you didn't."

"She'll have to be told eventually," Grace reasoned. "I would've done it as gently as possible."

"Your audacity is unreal, Grace! How can you possibly

tell a woman in a gentle way that her cherished grand-daughter completely burned her before running off?''

This stumped her. A feeling Grace didn't particularly like. She sank in her chair. "I don't know. I didn't think that part through. I only saw results.''

"If you had stayed home until you reached me, instead of charging right in, rifling through personal property—''

"You make me sound awful!'' she cried.

"Given the chance,'' he continued sternly, "I would've told you to sit tight, give me time to consider the angles. Sometimes people need time to consider the harsh reality of a situation before they respond.''

Grace stiffened with dignity. "Reached any conclusions yet?''

"Yes. Amelia couldn't possibly handle this development and I won't be telling her. Because of you, I'll have to make sure Button doesn't tell her much either.''

"You're attempting a cover-up?''

As she shook her head in amazement he said, "What would I achieve by hurting an old woman beyond repair? In fact, exposing Libby's sin to anyone would serve no one.''

Grace stared over at the refrigerator, featuring Button's crayon artwork. "That seems wrong.''

"Maybe that's because you've barely begun to live, never been faced with the murky issues that go with ma-turity. You've never been married—why, you've never been truly traumatized over anything.''

Grace gasped in affront. "You can't be sure.''

"You are still young—''

"At twenty-four? Women have endured plenty by twenty-four.''

"Some women, maybe. But not you, Grace. You've been sheltered, pampered.'' He hit his forehead. "I told myself over and over that it doesn't matter, you being so sincere.

You have so many other wonderful qualities. But it seems I misjudged our chances.''

Her throat tightened. ''What are you saying?''

He stared her down, fueled with fury and regret. ''You have a lot more growing up to do, Grace. And quite frankly, a man in my position can't afford to let you blunder around his family.''

She popped up out of her chair, chin set defiantly. ''Oh, I see. Now that your problem's been solved in an undesirable way, you are back to the lone wolf bit again. Fine. But you were content with my help along the way, you damn well enjoyed me—in about every conceivable way.'' With that off her chest, she stormed out.

''HEY, GRACIE!''

Grace wandered into her kitchen that evening as her brother eased through the back door. ''Hello, Michael.''

He scanned her disheveled appearance, from her tousled curls to her owl-like red eyes, to her sagging terry bathrobe. ''You look shot.''

She pointed to him. ''You are the sharp sibling. Just like the folks always said—that Michael, he's got a keen mind.''

Distress flashed in his eyes. ''What's happened?''

She marched across the room in a huff. ''I've given up talking about things. It's better to just clam up and take the hard knocks. Act like a complete self-contained jerk.''

''I won't pressure you into a conversation,'' Michael assured, holding up cotton shorts. ''I've stopped by because I have a button emergency here.''

Her lower lip quivering, she snatched the shorts away.

''Think you've got a button that will pass for the original?''

There was only one Button as far as she was concerned. The sweet baby Button she'd come to adore and begun to fantasize mothering one day. Faced with her loss all over again in vivid completeness, she burst into tears.

Michael eased her into a chair and listened to everything. "Gee, that agreement is found and he didn't even call me. Must be in terrible shape."

"What about me!"

He reached over and massaged her shoulder. "You're right. I'm sorry."

She blew hard into a tissue. "How dare he be so mean? I was only trying to help."

"Grace, most of what you told me was nearly verbatim, wasn't it?"

"Yes."

Michael paused, weighing his words. "Did it occur to you that Kyle wasn't just scolding you for putting Amelia's feelings at risk, but his feelings as well?" He smiled faintly as she leaned into the table. "I mean, the blunt clinical way you reported what Libby had done had to be rough on him. They were married almost a whole decade. Lots of emotion must have been invested. Then to have you blurt out that she'd pulled such a cruel robbery, let him take the blame for it. It's amazing Kyle was able to function at all."

"No, I can't say I thought of that." She sniffed proudly, but the insight rattled her.

"Makes sense though, doesn't it?"

"Yes." She covered her mouth. "No wonder he was so upset."

"It isn't too late to maybe give him a call, rehash things."

"After the send-off he gave me, I'd say it is." Her temper flared again. "Why, he called me impulsive, audacious!"

"In the heat of anger." He touched her damp cheek.

"Well, anyone who would go crawling back into that

mess over there on Ashford Lane would have to be all those things and more.''

"Those very same traits can be used for good, too,'' Michael encouraged, "in the form of an apology.''

"Maybe. Eventually.''

"KYLE, YOU'RE HOME!''

"Just got in.'' He smiled at Amelia, hovering in the living room doorway. Leaning hard on her cane, she looked especially tired tonight.

"I was putting Button down to sleep.''

"It's a good sign that she'll let you.''

"Oh, we grow closer by the day.'' She treaded into the living room and sat in her recliner. Reaching out to the end table she clicked on the lamp and took up her magnified spectacles.

"Don't pick up your knitting. Yet,'' he said abruptly, leaning her way. "I have something to show you.''

Amelia studied the plain brown envelope he set in her lap. It had his name scrawled across the front. With shaky fingers she extracted the agreement. "Good Lord, son, where did this come from?''

He met her eyes earnestly, speaking with a crystal-clear conscience. "I'm not sure. Found it on the desk at the bistro. With all the workmen moving in and out, anyone could've left it.''

Her eyes glimmered behind her spectacles. "It's a miracle.''

He smiled broadly. "No doubt about it.''

"I imagine those flyers helped after all,'' she surmised. "Maybe even one of the employees who stood there protesting had it all the while.''

"Hard to say.''

"Maybe once they spoke to us—and you offered them employment in the new place—one of 'em cracked.''

"All good people in any case, Amelia."

"Oh, yes. Worth forgiving a past indiscretion."

"Spoken like a true pioneer, focused on the present and the future."

For the first time since his return, Amelia laughed, broadly, fully, until her bosom shook and tears fell down her cheeks. "I suppose you've contacted Jerome."

He stiffened in mock affront. "Not at all."

"Why ever not?"

"Because, that honor belongs to you."

"Thank you. I would like that honor." She slipped the agreement back in the envelope and set it on the table. When Kyle made a motion to rise, she stopped him. "Hang on a minute."

He froze in tense anticipation.

"Button tells me she found some money amongst Libby's belongings."

Not sure how much Button knew to tell her, Kyle measured out his prepared explanation carefully. "As far as I can figure, Libby was saving up for my birthday gift as she always did. That pajama bag was a favorite cache of hers."

"Oh, yes, the star-burst pillow thing. She loved to hide things in there."

He tried to leave again, only to hear her grunt.

"Button also told me you are mad at Grace."

Kyle exhaled and sat down again, relating his practiced spiel. "There was a skirmish. Grace had agreed to sit with Button at her place, then overstepped by bringing her back here. The sight of them going through Libby's things was shocking to me. So nervy of Grace."

"I imagine Button instigated most of it."

He twined his fingers. "I don't care! Grace was in charge."

Amelia had picked up her knitting and was already clicking away. She kept her eyes to her work as she spoke.

"Naturally, you'd be upset. But all in all, I figure you were bothered for reasons apart from Grace. You are grieving still, so much that you put off going through those boxes. Having those things exposed jogged loose emotions you've been keeping in check. Grace happened to be there, so you blamed her most." She met his gaze over the tops of her specs. "I believe if you'd discovered Button rummaging around on her own, you would've been just as upset, but would've tried hard to cut her some slack." Her expression was as tender as he'd ever seen. "Make any sense?"

"I'll sleep on it." He rose then before she could go on and kissed her good-night on the cheek. "Enjoy that agreement."

Chapter Seventeen

Grace was a bundle of nerves by Friday. She awoke early both dreading and anticipating Kyle's next move. He was due for work. Would he come?

He didn't show up, leaving Grace ready to explode in anger. How could he stay away? Michael had paid him, said he was stuck.

But deep inside she knew. He was still hurting badly over her mishandling of his affairs. But she was hurting too! Didn't that count for anything?

For the first time in her life, Grace realized she would have to make the first move or perhaps forever lose out on her dream. She could do it. After all, this was for *Kyle*, the man she'd loved nearly half her life! So much of her life was invested in the chemistry between them, her faith that they were meant for each other.

She decided a cold house call was best, to just arrive on the doorstep and let Kyle react as nature intended. But she did have a backup excuse if he ended up snapping in her face. Whoever opened the door would find her surrounded by a shopping cart full of groceries, a sack full of leftover Target sweets, and a T-shirt bearing a panic button.

In short, a princess bearing gifts.

It was Amelia who ended up greeting the princess at the

door. Grace seized a breath behind a frozen smile, wondering what Kyle did and did not tell her.

"Hello, Amelia. Is Kyle home?"

"No, he's off getting a haircut, running errands. So much to do, with the grand opening tomorrow night. Do come in, anyway," Amelia invited. Leaning on her cane she grabbed the sack of treats. Grace followed with the brimming cart and T-shirt.

"The suit you helped Kyle pick out is splendid," Amelia complimented, pausing in the living room. "A lot like Regis Philbin wears on that millionaire show. Button!" Amelia called out. "Grace is here!"

Button appeared instantly, dressed in a cute orange top and white shorts, black hair adorned with twin barrettes. "Gwace!" She clamped on to Grace's middle.

The child's faith, her welcome made Grace's eyes mist. "Look, sweetie, I brought your panic button shirt."

At the sight of the T-shirt, Button quickly peeled off her orange top. "I wear it now."

Getting the okay from Amelia, Grace tugged it over Button's head.

Then Button spied her shopping cart with a squeal. "You bring all I need." She scooted up to take possession of it by the handle, her expression sobering. "Don't worry, Grammy, I won't smash you."

Amelia's gray brows jumped. "Why, thank you very much."

The adults watched Button scoot back to her room with her treasures. "Button wanted a cart so badly," Amelia confided. "But Kyle was so concerned that she was going to mow me down with it."

Grace clapped her cheeks. "I forgot that."

"No matter. We just heard the child say she would be careful and she will. Please sit down." When Grace hesitated, she added, "I have something to tell you."

With that threat, Grace sank like a stone into a chair. Amelia sat in her recliner alongside. "Don't give me that stoic look. It's Kyle who's scrapped with you, not me. I've already taken him to task on it, too. To put it mildly, he's being much too sensitive about the whole works. He over-reacted to his discovery and I told him so. How I've come to enjoy our candid talks! Gets the blood pumping."

Grace smiled faintly. What did Amelia mean exactly? Had Kyle a change of heart, told her everything? A week ago—heck two days ago—Grace might have impulsively jumped to this very conclusion, lavished in the idea that he'd taken her advice in the end. But not now. Never again would she assume facts not in evidence. There was some truth in Kyle's rude lecture, she did get into jams by being impulsive, confident she had all the answers.

The restraint paid off as Amelia spoke up. "I mean, what's the harm in Button exploring Libby's belongings? They are meant for her. And Button wasn't the least bit upset by it. As far as the money in the pajama bag is concerned, Button wasn't about to spend it at her age, and can't be as much as Button believes. Kyle doesn't even have to save it for her if he doesn't want to, as Libby most likely was saving it up for his birthday gift." Amelia made a dismissive hand flutter. "Kyle's attempt to blame you for Button's curiosity is preposterous. It's his own grief he must face. The grief in seeing my angel's belongings on display."

Clearly, Kyle hadn't told Amelia about Libby's trans-gression. Instead he made up some sugary story about only the cash. Faced with Amelia's peaceful acceptance, Grace was certain it was for the better good. Love shone in the old woman's eyes every time she mentioned her late grand-daughter. She needed to keep on believing Libby was an angel. Such faith would harm no one.

"But enough sentiment," Amelia declared. "That isn't

even what I wanted to tell you. Believe it or not, the sales agreement has turned up!''

"No kidding!" Grace forced surprise into her manner.

"Someone dropped it off at the bistro yesterday. It has to be thanks to your flyer, Grace. I do so appreciate your helping Kyle so much."

"Glad to do it."

"I figure we'll never know who it was." She tapped her chin. "Though you'd think they'd have wanted the cash reward."

"Maybe someone was simply trying to do a good deed," Grace suggested. "It happens."

Amelia shrugged, delighted in any case.

"Have you contacted Jerome Anderson yet?"

"Not yet. I've been savoring the event first."

Grace laughed. "I don't blame you."

Amelia clasped her hands gleefully. "But I see no time like the present. If you can stay for a while, I'll call him now. My guess is he'll give us a show."

"I am free," she said with some doubt.

"Oh, come now. It'll be fun to watch him crumble, won't it?"

Grace smiled impishly. "Sounds like great fun."

The doorbell rang about an hour later. Grace responded. She approached the screen door to find Dickie and Jerome standing side by side on the stoop, mismatched bookends, young and old, blond and gray respectively. Both did share a look of complete disorientation, however.

"Grace!" Dickie squawked, reaching one of his higher notes. "So that *is* your car in the driveway."

"We'd like to see Amelia," Jerome said formally.

"Show them in!" Amelia lilted.

The men followed Grace into the modest room, where Amelia sat regally. "Please *don't* have a seat," she taunted brightly.

"What's this all about, Aunt Amelia?" Jerome snapped, dodging the fidgety Dickie.

"Grace, please go collect the brown envelope atop my bureau."

The room was electric when Grace returned, the men shifting uneasily from one leg to another. They exchanged a wary glance as Amelia instructed Grace to show them the agreement.

Amelia didn't say as much, but Grace kept a tight hold on the paper as she unfolded it for perusal.

"Let me see that," Dickie snapped.

"You are seeing it," she snapped in return, pinching it harder.

Jerome's ultimate growl convinced the ladies that he knew it was authentic.

"Where did this come from?" Dickie couldn't help asking.

"None of your damn business," Amelia said briskly.

"Well, Dickie, what next?" Jerome asked worriedly.

The smaller man shrugged elegantly. "I'm afraid the war's over."

"It's over all right."

All heads turned to Kyle in the kitchen archway dressed in tight jeans and T-shirt that enhanced his muscles, with a fresh haircut that sharpened his grim features. As he strode in, Jerome edged his way to the front door.

"That's right, Jerome, get the hell out. And take your whipped pup along."

Dickie grew rigid, fingering his tie. "I will meet you at the car, Jerome. Please, wait for me there." Jerome didn't delay his departure. Dickie, however, turned boldly to Grace. "I've wanted to speak to you."

She handed the agreement to Amelia. "About what?"

"I was wondering…" he trailed off for her ears only. "Can we possibly start over, from scratch?"

"Start what over?" she demanded. "Our dating was a pretense! You used me as a stepping stone to get to these people!"

He pressed fingers to his temples. "I only did what I had to do for business reasons. Look, Mother is furious over our breakup. Like Ingrid, she thought we were making a real match. They had dreams of marriage, the works."

"Confess what you've done, that you weren't planning anything of the kind!"

"Oh, she knows. Both sets of parents know. Thanks to Michael." He gritted his teeth. "Are you going to make me crawl? All right. I did play the carefree big shot while we were dating, smug to be in the driver's seat with your family, knowing I had an ulterior motive. I didn't realize how you'd gotten to me until you were gone. I reevaluated what we had and it seems worth saving. We already have common backgrounds. As for our children, they're bound to be superior in every conceivable way."

The room fell quiet with what could only be described as a proposal.

Kyle was dead certain his heart stopped beating. Richmond Trainor was a class-A jerk, but he had the guts to express his desires. Something Grace would appreciate at least on principle.

Had he completely blown his chances with her over that stupid box of stuff? Damn, maybe he was destined to be a class A bungler all his life.

Grace's reaction came moments later, in a burst of uproarious laughter. "Save the speeches for the courtroom, Dickie."

"You doubt my sincerity?"

"In your own way, you probably do mean this strange proposal of yours. In fact, you are very much a young version of my own mogul father. Can't begin to count the stunts he pulled in the name of business, expecting to be forgiven in the name of business. It's no wonder he'd like you in the family.''

"So I have a chance?"

"Only with Father." Grace clucked in regret.

"But we could have a life!"

"My parents have shown me firsthand exactly what it would be like. You may very well end up in a similar situation, Dickie, but I intend to hold out for true passion.''

"Perhaps a cooling off—''

"Time's up, dapper Dick!'' With a growl Kyle collared the other man and showed him the door.

"What do you think you're doing, McRaney?"

"Clearing the way for my own apology." Opening the door, he shoved the smaller man onto the stoop. In a low tone he added, "I figure I'll take the best of yours and add to it.''

"What the hell could a caveman like you add to it?"

Kyle grinned. "Passion. Bye-bye." He slammed the door shut.

"Well, that was mighty satisfying, Kyle." He turned to find Amelia hobbling over on her cane.

"Can't beat a bit of cheap fun.''

She peered out the door. "Good, they're gone.''

"So?"

"So, you're taking Grace for a walk.''

"Oh, Amelia," Grace was quick to protest from a safe distance away.

"But you came over here to speak to Kyle, didn't you?" Grace blushed. "I might have.''

"And you, Kyle, didn't we decide you owed Grace an apology?''

"Well, not—''

"Hush up. I waited all day yesterday to hear you'd delivered it. Nothing happened! This sweet girl had to come over here with gifts for Button, looking for you.''

Perhaps hearing her own name brought Button on the run, pushing her shopping cart, dressed in her new T-shirt. "Look out, Daddy! I'm rollin'!"

"Slow down with that thing!" Kyle ordered. "Button shouldn't—"

"You are overruled," Amelia said. "The cart stays."

He took survey of his amused females with exasperation. "Far as I'm concerned, you all should come with a panic button on your shirts." Grabbing Grace by the elbow, he ushered her outside.

Starting down the tree-lined sidewalk, they both began to speak at once. "You go first," Grace insisted. "I'm determined not to be so impulsive."

Kyle took a breath. "Grace, I overreacted the other day. I still maintain you made a mistake, but I went too far in driving you off. Like Dickie, I didn't realize how you'd gotten to me until you were gone."

"As for my part, it's plain that you handled Amelia right," Grace conceded. "I can be too idealistic, blurting out the truth without consideration. That might come from watching my parents do too much phony damage control socially, but it is no excuse. There is middle ground between the poles of thought. Your white lies were necessary for Amelia's well-being. And whatever Libby's intentions at the time, I'm sure from her perch in heaven, she is grateful for your discretion."

They strolled along in the sunshine, both shoring their defenses. "I'm also sorry that I wasn't more sensitive with you the other day," she continued. "It wasn't just Amelia's feelings on the line, it was yours, too. Must've been an awful moment for you to endure, seeing what Libby had done. The way she allowed you to take the blame."

"Yes, it was terrible. Especially having to hear it from you. I felt like your hero, only to have my privacy and dignity stripped away."

"Michael helped me see that angle." As they paused at the lane's dead end, she grasped his arm. "Oh, Kyle. I only wanted to make your life better, easier, to share your trouble. But can you see that I've also been under trauma, trying to please you and cope with Button? My world has been turned upside down! I was liable to make some mistakes."

He deflated. "I know I've been too closed up with you. It's because my marriage with Libby was complex, left me confused and wary and downright guilty."

"How? Please tell me."

"I'll try." Looping Grace's arm in his, he guided her across the street and back along the opposite sidewalk. "At your age, I was an idealist too. Libby presented herself as a victim of aging overprotective guardians, a mysterious prisoner in a gilded cage. I bought the whole shebang. Figured I'd be the hero to rescue her, give her the freedom to be her own woman. After my rough childhood, I desperately wanted to be loved by someone, belong to someone. Marriage seemed the perfect remedy."

"Understandable."

"We were so young, though. Both of us had chips on our shoulders over the past. Nothing improved by pooling our troubles. Neither of us had the skills to work out disagreements. We kept blaming our environment, kept moving around the Chicago area looking for a comfort zone. I considered divorce, thought we'd both benefit. And then Button came along. Changed my whole outlook on everything. I was a hero for an innocent child, had reason to be the best man I could be. Suddenly, keeping our family together seemed crucial. Even Libby was giving happiness a try."

"Why didn't you come back here then?"

"I pushed for it time and again. And when I heard Andy died, I tried one last time. Shockingly, she resisted. Of course now that I know she pulled off the robbery, I realize she probably thought the rift too deep to fix.''

"Why did she pull that heist, Kyle?"

"I believe she did it because she wanted to assure our clean getaway. I was dragging my feet, preferring to prove I was nothing like my father, worthy of their granddaughter. Libby only wanted out, though, to escape.''

"So she staged the theft to…''

"To condemn me for good in the Andersons' eyes.'' Kyle choked out the facts with effort. "Amelia had just fired me. Libby knew they'd blame me. With my reputation destroyed, I'd be more inclined to do what she wanted, to leave.''

"Guess Nate Basset gave you a clue when he said he saw a dark-haired waitress in the office.''

"Even with all my knowledge, I never considered Libby!''

"Have to give Amelia credit,'' Grace said. "She is certainly trying to mend her family. Even supporting us.''

"Yeah, if only Libby had given her a second chance…. But she didn't. It's over.''

They paused on the sidewalk across from Amelia's house as Grace gave him a hug. "Don't you feel better, getting things out in the open?''

"I guess. But it's tough work.''

She patted his chest. "Well, I am going to share something with you.''

He brightened. "You are?''

"Yes, tomorrow at the grand opening.''

"Why not now?''

"Because I need to build up my courage first.''

"So I'm not the only one then.''

"No, darling. If I have my way, you'll never be the only one in any circumstance, ever again.''

Kyle kissed her tenderly. "Care for one more loop down the street?"

"Why?"

"Because all the old duffers are hidden behind bushes and windows watching you walk. The day you and Heather breezed over was a big deal around here. I promised if ever I had the chance, I'd make their day again."

Grace took the news with humor. "Well, Daddy, guess one more round-trip can't hurt."

SHE WORE THE RED BEADED dress to the bistro's grand opening.

Kyle was standing near the bar the following night as Grace and Button entered Amelia's Bistro with its namesake. He had been on site nearly since dawn and had hired a limo to bring his girls in style.

They'd outclassed anything he'd ever imagined. Amelia and Button were every bit as striking as Grace in their new outfits—the elder woman was in a smart black sheath, and the toddler in lacy white.

Anxious to make contact with the trio, he moved through the crowded, dimly lit room.

Grace watched his progress as he wended his way forward, cutting a handsome figure in his charcoal suit with burgundy shirt and tie, dodging guests and clapping backs.

He was home, she realized. At peace with himself at last.

"Hey, someone's been shopping," he greeted, scooping up Button, kissing Amelia's cheek.

Amelia's aged face beamed a decade younger. "It's all Grace's doing, of course. Ushered me to Dayton's Oval Room this morning, where they treated us like royalty!"

Button, riding along Kyle's torso, touched his freshly shaven face. "I'm from Dayton's too, Daddy."

The adults chuckled. Kyle and Grace locked eyes. They

shared a knowledge, a secure confidence that this was meant to be.

"Well, well, it's the whole gang," a familiar voice boomed close by. It was Michael, wearing a neat tux and a broad smile. He hugged Amelia. "What do you think of your old place now?"

"Splendid," Amelia lilted, looking around. "The fresh wallpaper, new flooring and refurbished wood are improvements. I see more familiar faces than expected, too. And oh my, you did hire back some of the old help."

"Hired all the ones who showed up," Kyle assured with a wink. "Enjoy yourself, Amelia. Must still be your place, as your name's on the door."

"It's the family's place," she corrected.

Ingrid and Victor came up then to shake hands with Kyle.

"Nice work, Kyle," Victor complimented. "I respect you for sticking to your guns."

"Dad, you'll have to start a firm tab here," Michael suggested.

"Why?" Amelia chortled, "when his own son is an investor?"

As the issue lit a discussion, Grace spoke to Ingrid. "So, Mom, about our bet. You now have proof that Kyle is saved. And I'm not a bit bored with him. Seems high time you give up your matchmaking."

Ingrid smiled wistfully over her martini glass. "Both your father and I plead no contest. Kyle's proven a winner who will, I daresay, never bore you. He's hardworking, full of integrity." She took a gulp of martini. "Even I am ready to admit Dickie is hopeless—which is tough as I adore his parents so. Naturally your father is furious with him, as well. Imagine, that twerp—Mr. Pock using our daughter as some kind of stepping stone!"

Grace's heart warmed over her mother's sincere indignation.

"If you will all excuse me," Kyle announced, "I'd like to dance with my lady now."

Button hugged him closer. "Okay, Daddy."

He nuzzled her face. "You come later, baby. I'd like to dance with Grace first."

"C'mon, Button," Michael intervened, peeling the child from her father. "I need someone to dance with."

Button joyfully looped her arms around Michael's neck. "Don't you got a girl, Uncle Mike?"

"No!" the crowd said in unison, with different levels of disappointment.

Kyle gathered Grace in his arms and swept her off to the small dance floor. They swayed with the slow music, leaning against each other.

"Hey, I can't help but notice there's some new tunes playing tonight—on a new jukebox!" she remarked.

"I don't want this place to become a retro joint playing old forty-fives," Kyle explained. "We're beyond that phase."

"Where is that old jukebox?"

"In the office. Don't worry, I intend to keep it for my own personal use. Just hope to marry someone willing to decorate around it."

She rested her head against his chest. "Hon, I'd probably marry you just for the jukebox."

"Would you?"

"What?"

"Marry me?"

She gazed up at him matter-of-factly. "Of course."

"Be Button's mother, Amelia's stand-in granddaughter?"

"Bonuses to the long-range plan," she confided. "You see, I never intended to marry anyone else."

He was stunned. "What do you mean?"

"Remember the secret I promised to share with you?"

"Remember?" He gave her a sharp twirl round. "I've been aching to hear."

"Well…"

His dark brows gathered. "C'mon, Gracie."

"Oh, Kyle, I have adored you since the day we met," she confessed in a rush. "So much so, that I actually thought you were intending to elope with *me* that night so long ago."

"Seriously?"

"Every dream a seventeen-year-old girl has is very serious. I was so jealous of Libby, of any girl who looked twice at you."

He kissed the top of her head. "Must say I've gotten my own dose of envy lately, fretting over Dickie and the poetry man."

"Dickie's toast. And I could burn Bruce's book if you like."

"No way! I want a look at that book."

"Why?"

"A quiet man like me can use some wooing tips."

She laughed. "You're free to look at it tonight if you like. You'll find it on my nightstand."

"That sounds like an invitation."

"There's a surprise under my pillow too."

"Kitty?"

She shook her head with a flutter of lashes. "A nightshirt, with a big girl's panic button on it."

"You can count me in." He squeezed her closer, smiling crookedly. "You can read the poems while I push the button."

Grace gazed up at him with starry eyes. "You're already turning into quite the sweet-talker."

"I love you, Grace North."

"And I love you, Kyle. Always have."

And with that they continued to dance into forever.

USA Today bestselling author

STELLA CAMERON

and popular American Romance author

MURIEL JENSEN

come together in a special
Harlequin 2-in-1 collection.

Look for

Shadows and *Daddy in Demand*

On sale June 2001

HARLEQUIN®
Makes any time special®

Double your pleasure—
with this collection containing two full-length

Harlequin Romance®

novels

New York Times bestselling author

DEBBIE MACOMBER

delivers

RAINY DAY KISSES

While Susannah Simmons struggles up the corporate
ladder, her neighbor Nate Townsend stays home baking
cookies and flying kites. She resents the way he questions
her values—and the way he messes up her five-year plan
when she falls in love with him!

PLUS

THE BRIDE PRICE

a brand-new novel by reader favorite

DAY LECLAIRE

On sale July 2001

HARLEQUIN®

Makes any time special ®

Visit us at www.eHarlequin.com

PHROM

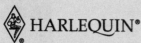

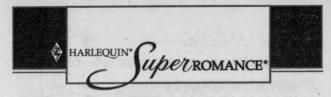

*Harlequin truly does
make any time special. . . .
This year we are celebrating
weddings in style!*

A Walk Down the Aisle

WEDDING CELEBRATION

To help us celebrate, we want you to tell us how wearing the Harlequin wedding gown will make your wedding day special. As the grand prize, Harlequin will offer one lucky bride the chance to **"Walk Down the Aisle" in the Harlequin wedding gown!**

There's more...

For her honeymoon, she and her groom will spend five nights at the **Hyatt Regency Maui.** As part of this five-night honeymoon at the hotel renowned for its romantic attractions, the couple will enjoy a candlelit dinner for two in Swan Court, a sunset sail on the hotel's catamaran, and duet spa treatments.

A HYATT RESORT AND SPA

Maui • Molokai • Lanai

To enter, please write, in, 250 words or less, how wearing the Harlequin wedding gown will make your wedding day special. The entry will be judged based on its emotionally compelling nature, its originality and creativity, and its sincerity. This contest is open to Canadian and U.S. residents only and to those who are 18 years of age and older. There is no purchase necessary to enter. Void where prohibited. See further contest rules attached. Please send your entry to:

Walk Down the Aisle Contest

In Canada	In U.S.A.
P.O. Box 637	P.O. Box 9076
Fort Erie, Ontario	3010 Walden Ave.
L2A 5X3	Buffalo, NY 14269-9076

You can also enter by visiting www.eHarlequin.com
Win the Harlequin wedding gown and the vacation of a lifetime!
The deadline for entries is October 1, 2001.

HARLEQUIN®
Makes any time special®

PHWDACONT1

HARLEQUIN WALK DOWN THE AISLE TO MAUI CONTEST 1197
OFFICIAL RULES
NO PURCHASE NECESSARY TO ENTER

1. To enter, follow directions published in the offer to which you are responding. Contest begins April 2, 2001, and ends on October 1, 2001. Method of entry may vary. Mailed entries must be postmarked by October 1, 2001, and received by October 8, 2001.

2. Contest entry may be, at times, presented via the Internet, but will be restricted solely to residents of certain geographic areas that are disclosed on the Web site. To enter via the Internet, if permissible, access the Harlequin Web site (www.eHarlequin.com) and follow the directions displayed online. Online entries must be received by 11:59 p.m. E.S.T. on October 1, 2001.

   In lieu of submitting an entry online, enter by mail by hand-printing (or typing) on an 8½" x 11" plain piece of paper, your name, address (including zip code), Contest number/name and in 250 words or fewer, why winning a Harlequin wedding dre would make your wedding day special. Mail via first-class mail to: Harlequin Walk Down the Aisle Contest 1197, (in the U.S P.O. Box 9076, 3010 Walden Avenue, Buffalo, NY 14269-9076, (in Canada) P.O. Box 637, Fort Erie, Ontario L2A 5X3, Canad Limit one entry per person, household address and e-mail address. Online and/or mailed entries received from persons residing in geographic areas in which Internet entry is not permissible will be disqualified.

3. Contests will be judged by a panel of members of the Harlequin editorial, marketing and public relations staff based on the following criteria:
   - Originality and Creativity—50%
   - Emotionally Compelling—25%
   - Sincerity—25%

   In the event of a tie, duplicate prizes will be awarded. Decisions of the judges are final.

4. All entries become the property of Torstar Corp. and will not be returned. No responsibility is assumed for lost, late, illegible incomplete, inaccurate, nondelivered or misdirected mail or misdirected e-mail, for technical, hardware or software failures o any kind, lost or unavailable network connections, or failed, incomplete, garbled or delayed computer transmission or any human error which may occur in the receipt or processing of the entries in this Contest.

5. Contest open only to residents of the U.S. (except Puerto Rico) and Canada, who are 18 years of age or older, and is void wherever prohibited by law; all applicable laws and regulations apply. Any litigation within the Province of Quebec respecting the conduct or organization of a publicity contest may be submitted to the Régie des alcools, des courses et des jeux for a ruling. Any litigation respecting the awarding of a prize may be submitted to the Régie des alcools, des courses et des jeux o for the purpose of helping the parties reach a settlement. Employees and immediate family members of Torstar Corp. and D. L. Blair, Inc., their affiliates, subsidiaries and all other agencies, entities and persons connected with the use, marketing or conduct of this Contest are not eligible to enter. Taxes on prizes are the sole responsibility of winners. Acceptance of any pri. offered constitutes permission to use winner's name, photograph or other likeness for the purposes of advertising, trade and promotion on behalf of Torstar Corp., its affiliates and subsidiaries without further compensation to the winner, unless prohibited by law.

6. Winners will be determined no later than November 15, 2001, and will be notified by mail. Winners will be required to sign a return an Affidavit of Eligibility form within 15 days after winner notification. Noncompliance within that time period may resu in disqualification and an alternative winner may be selected. Winners of trip must execute a Release of Liability prior to ticket and must possess required travel documents (e.g. passport, photo ID) when applicable. Trip must be completed by Novembe 2002. No substitution of prize permitted by winner. Torstar Corp. and D. L. Blair, Inc., their parents, affiliates, and subsidiaries are not responsible for errors in printing or electronic presentation of Contest, entries and/or game pieces. In the event of printing or other errors which may result in unintended prize values or duplication of prizes, all affected game pieces or entrie shall be null and void. If for any reason the Internet portion of the Contest is not capable of running as planned, including infection by computer virus, bugs, tampering, unauthorized intervention, fraud, technical failures, or any other causes beyond the control of Torstar Corp. which corrupt or affect the administration, secrecy, fairness, integrity or proper conduct of the Contest, Torstar Corp. reserves the right, at its sole discretion, to disqualify any individual who tampers with the entry proces and to cancel, terminate, modify or suspend the Contest or the Internet portion thereof. In the event of a dispute regarding an online entry, the entry will be deemed submitted by the authorized holder of the e-mail account submitted at the time of entry Authorized account holder is defined as the natural person who is assigned to an e-mail address by an Internet access provid online service provider or other organization that is responsible for arranging e-mail address for the domain associated with submitted e-mail address. **Purchase or acceptance of a product offer does not improve your chances of winnin**

7. Prizes: (1) Grand Prize—A Harlequin wedding dress (approximate retail value: $3,500) and a 5-night/6-day honeymoon trip Maui, HI, including round-trip air transportation provided by Maui Visitors Bureau from Los Angeles International Airport (winner is responsible for transportation to and from Los Angeles International Airport) and a Harlequin Romance Package, including hotel accomodations (double occupancy) at the Hyatt Regency Maui Resort and Spa, dinner for (2) two at Swan Court, a sunset sail on Kiele V and a spa treatment for the winner (approximate retail value: $4,000); (5) Five runner-up prize of a $1000 gift certificate to selected retail outlets to be determined by Sponsor (retail value $1000 ea.). Prizes consist of on those items listed as part of the prize. Limit one prize per person. All prizes are valued in U.S. currency.

8. For a list of winners (available after December 17, 2001) send a self-addressed, stamped envelope to: Harlequin Walk Down Aisle Contest 1197 Winners, P.O. Box 4200 Blair, NE 68009-4200 or you may access the www.eHarlequin.com Web site through January 15, 2002.

Contest sponsored by Torstar Corp., P.O. Box 9042, Buffalo, NY 14269-9042, U.S.A.

PHWDACONT2